# ECLIPSYS
# Through the Darka

# Book 1: Haunted Minds

## By: Elana Vital

### Illustrated By:
### Cong Zhou

*"There are no haunted houses. Only haunted minds."*
*– Stenne's Grimoire*

PHANTOM
SEQUENCE
LLC

*For my beta reader, Chris Stout, who taught me how to speak Human. For my precious Skibbs, who with me conquered the Sea of Time. For my mother Sylvia, who brought me to its shores. For Grandpa, who's gentle ear tugs in the Darka gave me comfort and direction in the squall, even when I was too simple minded to understand 13.*

# AUTHOR'S NOTE

## *(Prologue?)*

I'm not a writer. I'm an actor. I don't make word salad, I vomit the stuff. But here we are. This book was written by someone who suffers from an undiagnosed mental illness, with no money and no idea what I'm doing. Don't expect perfection. I'm just doing whatever it takes to create the portal. Everything after that is up to you.

Looking through my eyes is like looking at a window through a window. I have a brain that makes thoughts that sometimes scare me. Swing sets in New York City parks sound like seagulls. Recycling is the five pointed star to the pentagram, and when they get you to go green you bet you're skipping your happy ass out of that hell dance.

The problem is, I hear voices. I'm a broken radio set, picking up the secret number stations of the dead. I was like them once. Forgot everything. I always forget things. Maybe that's why I got so lost. But he was there to help me remember. Now I'm here and alive. The least I can do is return the favor. So I search and search and it is insane hearing the demon voices and the dead voices and the crazy voices down in the dark basement of that other place in all of our heads. But he's down there, in the Darka. That's why I'm writing this book. Not because I'm a writer.

If we all work together, we can find him. Maybe you'll hear the voices, too. And in the din of all of the screaming, we can pick his out above the rest. Like a giant CB radio; we are all one big fat brainwave of the planet. <LOST SIGNAL>

## END NOTE

# PART I: The Tool of God
# Chapter 1

It would be supper time soon. One last bit of work to be done, and then off to the kitchen. It was a quiet evening, to be sure. Not a sound could be heard, save the rustle of hay and the soft coo of the rock doves that built their nests in the stable roof. Kulbit slung his grooming satchel over his shoulder, and opened the last stall for the day.

As far back as he could remember Kulbit had never once had a nightmare. Not in the strictest sense of the word, where one has dreams where one falls into a slumber of dark terrors and uncontrollable happenings that always end with the sleeper sitting up in bed with their hearts in their throat and a scream in their mouth.

That never happened to him. Nor had he ever experienced a frightening sense of things that go bump in the night, even though he often heard things go bump in the stable loft where he slept. But usually that was to be expected when one shares a living space with ponies and horses.

No, Kulbit never had bad dreams. Sometimes his dreams would start with frightening beginnings, mostly involving pirates. That was natural, of course. Pirates were bad men. Thieves, robbers, lechers, the lot of them. He hated them and hated stories about them, and would only read of them if the stories told very vivid details of the pirates being run through by a nobleman's blade, or being burned alive on the breath of a dragon, or having his brains eaten by wild natives. Those stories were not so bad if told delicately and with good writing and elegant prose, of course.

If he did read about pirates, he would find that it would be harder to fall asleep or to use the outhouse behind the stables for a midnight wee. He would light a lantern and go out into the darkness despite the empty shed in the far back being a perfect place for a pirate to hide.

It was a babyish thing to do for a boy of his age, but on these occasions he would whistle loudly, believing superstitiously that this might frighten spooks away. As he would lose his water, in the darkest of the nights he would swear that he heard footsteps in the gravel outside of the waste shack, smell the faint scent of sweat, sea salt and rum.

But as far as dreams were concerned, he was always safe. No whistling loudly and starting wide-eyed at every little sound. In his dreams, he was always able to overcome the secret things that crept in the darkness in the back of his mind. It was a funny trick he learned when he was small, and it was a very simple thing to do. Be awake while still in slumber, and rewrite one's dreams as one might see fit.

If he thought especially hard during the day, and remembered to think of it as he blew out his candle before bed, there was a way of turning the frightening thing of dreams up over upon itself in a wide loop, flipping up and up into the sky until it would begin again, as if anew; a wonderful, wild thing back from whence it began to go wrong.

It was so that whenever a nightmare would come in his dreaming, or even something he found commonplace and boring, he would welcome the adventure of what he called *dream flipping*; a monster to slay, a damsel to rescue and perhaps steal a kiss from. His dreams always ended well, and all that truly matters is the ending, of course. They were his dreams, and he was in complete control. If only real life could be the same. If only he could simply flip his mind and change his world.

Kulbit was just a simple a barn worker who lived in one of the many stable houses of His Royal Majesty King Leonard. He loved his stable, and the ponies and horses he shared it with. He had secretly named each one, and though he was a mute and had never spoken a word since babyhood, in his heart of hearts he called them by name and sang them songs silently through his own mind. He swore as he looked into their large, melancholy eyes that they all heard him through his mind, though no one else ever could.

As Kulbit curried Mr. Gray Horse's dappled pelt, his strange mind rolled blissfully away into a dreamer's world of its own creation. A world of purple mists over rolling green hills. A world where one always had the means of winning at any challenge. A world where he could speak, and there were no such things as pirates.

He was a strange lad. But not simply because he was mute, nor because his skin and hair were such strange colors, and not because his only friends were Mrs. Whickerstaff and her young foal Kippers (of all the horses, these two were his favorite). He was strange in the head. He knew this. For on the occasion of a quiet moment, if he thought hard enough, he could see the strangest things.

He knew one might always think their hardest when one's eyes are shut tight, but one's mind is wide open. But even with his eyes closed, his mind rolling about like a crisp autumn leaf in the wind, he could still see the world around him quite clearly. However, he would not see through his eyes, but through his mind's eye, and a clearer sight had never before been seen.

It is difficult enough to describe in words, but of course, he never had any words to hinder him. He would see things that most would not even know are there. And this was not strange to him. Not a bit.

For example, when the old horse Chester had fallen sick with belly rot. The black steed was far older than any horse had a right to live, and had been laying what Bugger called horse's eggs for some time. Bugger said a clubbing would be merciful, yet one would never dare club the King's horse without written permission. So they watched Chester grow more and more ill, until the last night of his life.

The night the old horse died, Kulbit stood over the great heaving barrel of a chest, sorrow like a heavy cloak upon his shoulders. In his strange mind he had imagined Chester to be something of a grandfather to him. When he was at his saddest, he would climb into Chester's stable and rub noses with the old horse. And he would imagine he heard the horse's voice ringing loud and clear in his head.

*Cheer up, little one. Things will turn up for you yet,* the aged steed would say, nuzzling Kubit's neck.

But the night that Chester fell sick, Kulbit could not hear the old creaking voice in his head that he had come to imagine as the voice of the steed. Chester looked up with his great sad eyes, and in a moment Kulbit saw the beast through his mind's eye. The old horse seemed to smile up at him softly, but in moments poor Chester was dead. Kulbit wept silently.

Bugger had bellowed his oily laugh at Kulbit's tears over the dead animal saying, "Ha! The boy's crying! Living in a dream world that Dainty Cupcake is! Always lost in that funny lookin' head!"

*Always lost in that funny looking head, he says. Dainty Cupcake, he says. Blasted old fool...*Kulbit frowned, throwing the curry comb into the bucket as he reached for the dandy brush.

*Do keep your temper boy,* Mr. Grey Horse snorted softly, his ears tipping back. *It isn't my fault if you're having a nasty afternoon.*

*Beg pardon, sir,* Kulbit thought, patting the horse's long neck.

Old Bugger, the Head Groom, was right. Kulbit had a terrible habit of daydreaming. He also loved to read, and when he wasn't having imaginary conversations with his friends the ponies and horses, or running about doing the dirty work of a stable hand, he sometimes would crawl among the big haystacks in the sun and read adventure books he had bought from the marketplace. He would read and read until the sunlight was gone and his eyes would ache, and spent the night flipping his dreams into wonderful adventures.

A few days prior, Kulbit had fallen asleep and old Bugger found him lying in the hay with a book upon his face. It was not a story book this time, but a book of poems and sonnets entitled *A Hero Thou Art*. Kulbit had bought it from Dr. Mountebank's Traveling Medicine Show and Circus.

Earlier that week he had rushed up to the old wagon with the other children, and watched marionettes dance to the tooting of the street organ and the rolling music of guitars. Kulbit daydreamed and wondered what it would be like to run away with the gypsy folk, free from the cares of town living. The smell of camp fire and incense in your hair and clothes, roaming the endless roads of *LeBois*. A dark-haired woman in purple robes bent over a bright crystal orb, waving her bejeweled fingers and whispering charms and spells for starry eyed lovers.

On the puppet stage, a hydra made up of a patch work of old stockings and long johns sewn together roared and flailed at giggle-some boys and girls. A wild eyed little man dressed in strange nightclothes with black numbers printed across the back leaped from behind the curtain. He wore a metal colander like a helmet on his head and a baking sheet tied across his chest like armor. He twirled his little black mustache and drew a wooden sword from the rope about his waist.

"Fear not, sweet children! I am the great Sir Skgt, and I shall slay yonder Demon Beast!"

The children squealed and laughed as the little man began attacking the hydra, and yanked it clear from the stage. The poor puppeteers remained, baffled and peering over the puppet stage as the man began wrestling the tattered hydra across the ground.

Dr. Mountebank himself, with his gray beard and his brightly colored coat and his tall dark hat and his big silver earring, was singing an old Sheep Herder's ballad that reminded Kulbit of his Da.

While the Doctor peddled his wares, the other children crowded about to buy the miraculous healer, Mount Olympus Elixir; the Nectar of the Gods. It was a delicious fizzy pop that tasted like cherry flavored sassafras. The children had no ailments in need of curing, but the cool, sugary drink was quite refreshing in the summer heat. And at the jingle of so many coin bags, Mountebank was only happy to oblige them. He even handed out free honey sticks to go with every pop.

When it was Kulbit's turn, Mountebank's enormous grin exploded across his face.

"Well, well, well, what have we here?"

Kulbit smiled sheepishly. Once again, he was to draw unwanted attention, when all he wanted was a fizzy drink.

"Oh, that's just Lil' Lilac Lily," one of the boys behind him sneered. "He don't talk. He's dumber than a doorknob." The other children laughed. Kulbit blushed, staring at his dirty work boots.

"Goodness. No need to blush, dear boy. Adding red to the rest of you; what a colorful sight you'd be!" the Doctor guffawed, ruffling Kulbit's fuzzy bright head. He hunkered down on the edge of the stage and tipped Kulbit's chin, gazing into his eyes.

"There falls no shame in leading a strange and colorful life, *cher garcon*. Why, look at our own dear Sir Sgkt. You can see, he is quite mad..."

They watched as the strange little man in nightclothes was still beating the poor puppet of socks in the dust with his wooden sword. The show of the slain hydra had long since ended, but not for the likes of him.

"He knows that he was meant for great things. He has slain the mighty hydra! You are meant for great things *un de ces jours*, despite your misfortune of not being quite as mad as he. But that is all right. Hold your head up high, and know that you are bound for heroic adventures, just as our own Sir Sgkt here."

Kulbit smiled weakly as Sir Sgkt began ripping the mass of rags apart with his teeth.

"Here," said the peddler. "I think I may have something special for a boy like you to go along with your Elixir."

He reached into his breast pocket and brought out the leather book. When Kulbit read the title, he beamed. It looked like a very good book, but it did not have an author listed.

*Thank you so much,* he thought with the voice of his mind.

.

"You're very welcome, *bon amie!*" laughed Dr. Mountebank as he handed Kulbit the book, along with the fizzy pop and a honey stick.

*A Hero Thou Art.* A hero…Kulbit had never thought about what it would be like to be a hero. He read it in a single afternoon, and it lifted his spirits. The book had inspired him. With its pretty gold leafed letters and its musty old-book smell, it led his strange mind to dwell on finer things. That was until that fateful afternoon a few days later, when Bugger caught him napping in the hay. He snatched the book away and cast it into the river, after boxing Kulbit's ears for falling asleep.

"You! A Hero! Ho! Don't you be gettin' lofty ideas in your head, My Little Cake! You're nothing more than a dumb dirty stable boy and you always will be! Now get back to work!"

Kulbit detested the fat, red haired old man and his fat, red haired old laugh. Each day as Kulbit would set about his duties, it seemed Bugger's favorite past time was to give the young boy misery. He would make jest of Kulbit's inability to talk, calling him "Dumb as a pinch!"

But what the boy hated most was when the old stableman jeered at his unfortunate appearance. These words stung, for Kulbit detested his looks. Had he the fortune to be born handsome, he would have given no care. Or he would have settled his mind on looking homely at least, or perhaps even ugly. But as for how he looked now he could find no reason for happiness, and resigned himself to a life of humiliation. Why, anyone could see just at the sight of him how unlucky he was.

You see, as Dr. *Mountebank* had aforementioned, Kulbit had the misfortune to be born *colorful.* To the point of being quite… *darling.* Yes, that was the word that most used to describe him. His skin was light purple. His eyes were green as gooseberries in high summer. His hair was an electric shade of blue that shown pink of hue in the sunlight; fluffy curls in a bright halo about his girlish face. All together when Kulbit looked into the mirror after taking his bath, he thought he looked very much like one of the lovely pastel colored cakes Mrs. Grumsby put out on display in her bakery shop window down by the Post. Sugary and fluffy and bright as a macaron. In the grayness of the overcast Thomish world about him, he stood out like a brightly colored thumb.

This was not at all the face of a mighty hero, one who may bring terror into the hearts of all of his enemies. More the face of a cupcake, which was why old Bugger called him thus. The boys from the village called him Miss Lilac Lily, All Nice and Frilly. One night of summer past a band of them cornered Kulbit in a back alley. They held him and placed a ruffled yellow frock upon him, and pulled his bright hair into two fluffy pigtails with yellow ribbons.

Then they dragged him to the Meeting Post at the town common, and hung him on a hook on the Post by the waistband of his underpants. He spent a most uncomfortable night kicking and dangling silently until morning, still wearing a little girl's ruffled dress, looking and feeling ridiculous. The Watchman found him and took him down. Poor Kulbit couldn't sit on his backside for a day after.

But despite difficult times and his very unfortunate appearance, Kulbit felt he had little reason for discontent. He worked hard and the King's treasurer ensured that all stable hands receive some small wages. He knew things could have been far worse for an orphan such as him, especially one with strange looks and a batty head. And of course there were the dreams.

Perhaps one day, he felt he might be able to prove his mettle and be the unlikely hero. Just as in the many books he had read, and as in his dreams at night. He would flip it all upon itself, and make a happy ending. He would rescue beautiful maidens, slay horrific monsters, and then he would show them all what for. They would all regret that they had once laughed at him.

The kingdom of ThoBromis was a large nation with great cities and smaller towns that the people called "Le Petite Villes". Many of these smaller hamlets and villages were nameless; or if they had names none but they that lived there noted them, for only the wealthiest cities counted for anything in the Thomish kingdom. The first of the three great provinces of Thom was located east on the coast of the Amillo Sea. It was called Srye, a harbor town where the King's naval ships were docked. The second was Ende, which was a vast farmland with rolling hills and grand plantation estates on the far west. And the third a great city, in the middle of the kingdom, served as the capital of ThoBromis.

It was called Post, and this was the place in which the royal palace dwell. It was a long journey between the hamlets to the cities, and the main routes the villagers took to travel to the nearby towns were the North South Road, which lead north and south and the East West Road, which headed east and west. These roads crossed together in the middle of the village commons, and right in the center of this large intersection was the Meeting Post. The tall pillar stood on a large dais, surrounded by opulent pavilions. Here was the heart of Thom, where all royal announcements took place, and the Meeting Post was how the town of Post earned its namesake. All else that was not in Thom was known as *LeBois*. For the Holy Land of ThoBromis had little dealings with heathen foreigners. The Meeting Post was where the Watchmen had found Kulbit dangling that dewy summer morning, his underpants painfully jammed high up between his legs, squashing hard against parts no boy ever wishes to be squashed hard against.

It was here that the townsfolk had been bustling about most at this time, for earlier that month the good king Leonard had died. He was not an old king, no more than fifty winters, and the people of Thom were surprised at his sudden death. He was in perfect health, but one night passed away peacefully in his sleep. They said he must have had a pleasant dream that night, for a soft smile rested upon his whiskered lips. Idle gossips said he looked *relieved.* For one might suppose that the responsibilities of being King would be enough to tax anyone into an early grave.

However, the problem at hand was that the crown must be placed upon the head of another. King Leo had run things quite smoothly over the past thirty years or so. The people were comfortable and well, and life was soft and routine. Each day was just as the one before; safe, predictable and boring. Nothing strange ever occurred in ThoBromis. Unlike the strange tales one might hear from neighboring foreign countries beyond the borders of Thom, in the wilds of the godless *LeBois*. The good people of ThoBromis had not a worry during Leonard's reign. Save for the death of the queen ten years prior. But none spoke of that, of course.

But King Leonard was now also dead, and he had but one son. The Crown Prince, Theodore Ulysses Trydus. He was secretly known among the palace staff as His Royal Wretchedness, for

Prince Theodore was indeed a wretched boy. In all his fourteen years of life as a prince, he had never once heard the word "no".

Mr. Grey Horse gave a soft whinny and nuzzled Kulbit's ear as he packed away his grooming tools. He patted the horse's neck and gazed thoughtfully out of the stable window, as the sky blushed red with the setting sun.

*I'm quite finished sir. I am off to my repast, if you are in no more need of my services,* he said to Mr. Greyhorse with a short bow.

*That will be quite enough, boy. You are dismissed,* said Mr. Greyhorse in his usual superior air (for he was a stern, dignified steed who had once served as a royal charger). *Have a good evening.*

*Thank you, sir. Good evening.* Kulbit quickly washed his face and hands, and hastened to the kitchens of the palace proper.

Though Kulbit had (thankfully enough) never met the prince in person, he heard all sorts of wild tales of this young terror from the ladies who worked the kitchen. Kulbit liked the kitchen ladies because they all liked him. He had supposed the women took a liking to him because of the bright colors of his skin and hair. His appearance had always gotten a better response from lady folk. Women often like pretty colors, and though he had to endure the embarrassment of having them pinch his cheeks and call him their "Pretty Little Man", he didn't mind it so very much. Especially since they typically offered him nice things to eat from the larder.

After a hearty supper of roast pheasant and potato mash, he was enjoying a lovely piece of strawberry pie with whipped cream as he heard Mrs. Templeton telling Miss Nelly about how one of Royal Tutors had resigned. Prince Theodore had set the seat of her skirts afire and chased her about the palace.

"What a perverse little beast he was," said Mrs. Templeton, "running after poor Elsie shouting 'Elsie's got a nice hot little bottom! See her smoking hot little bottom!' The poor girl would have burned to death of she hadn't leaped into the duck pond in the courtyard. Hot bottom indeed! Why, I would give him a hot bottom with a switch if he were any one of my boys."

"What a little brute. Well, Elsie is such a pretty thing. Be certain, she shall find a good husband to care for her and settle down. What a shame to lose such a sweet girl in this musty old palace," said Miss Nelly.

"In the meantime, what is to be done about this Prince? It wasn't as if anyone had given the boy any *guidance*. That old nurse of his only spoils him rotten, and ever since the boy's mother was found dead…" and here Mrs. Templeton lowered her voice to a tone that only Miss Nelly could hear.

Kulbit's heart broke at the news. He adored the pretty, golden-haired Miss Elsie, with her dimpled smile and her funny hiccupping laugh. It was she who had taught him how to read many years ago, and she liked his pretty colors as well. He hadn't minded having a lady as lovely as Miss Elsie ruffle his hair and pinch his cheeks and call him *Darling*. He rather enjoyed it. And now she was gone. Not even strawberry pie with whipped cream could lessen tragedy of it all. Kulbit knew there and then that he never wished to meet this nasty Prince Theodore if he could help it. He may someday be a brave enough hero to slay horrible monsters, but he wasn't so certain about meeting bullies who would someday be the ruler.

But now that the king was dead, everyone dreaded what was to come next. The royal court held many a secret meeting addressing the issue, but there was no avoiding it. Prince Theo was to become the next king.

This had been announced two days after the King's death at the Post. The court had assembled upon the dais at the crossroads, and everyone who was anyone was there, including His Royal Wretchedness.

Kulbit grinned, mouthing the Royal Nickname to himself as the women chattered on. The day the king had died had been a stormy day with a somber chill in the air, but as he would remember it, the announcement was held in weather warm and fair.

The prince had stood in front of the assembly in the orange morning sun, a skinny, pimply boy with a pinched face and beady eyes. He smiled at everyone triumphantly, tossing his limp black hair. At the news of his coronation, there was a very loud collective groan from the townspeople. Even a few of the children who had been excused from class to hear the news began to boo and hiss, their frantic teacher trying to quiet them.

Someone (Kulbit was certain it was one of the boys who had hung him up on the Post) had thrown a tomato at the royal assembly and it landed in front of Prince Theodore, splattering his boots with red goo.

"Who threw that?! Who dares throw tomatoes at the future king?! I shall have him beheaded! I am to be your king! And all of you kids shut up out there! And you people too! I'll have everyone thrown in the dungeon, I will!"

Prince Theodore shouted from the dais in his squeaky voice. He began to stamp his feet and cry in an awkward tantrum, and had to be led off the dais by his nurse. After Prince Theo was gone, the school children all burst out laughing, and even Kulbit had to cover his mouth to hide a snicker. This wimpy whiny-baby was to be the king? The idea was quite funny. If war was ever to come, their Royal Leader would be breaking out in a temper tantrum if the battle hadn't gone as planned. Kulbit supposed he would have to bring his Nurse to every event of state to wipe his chin and change his little bitty nappies. How ridiculous. But Kulbit noticed the grown-up faces around him did not look as though they found this humorous. They looked quite worried. And he realized that having a king such as this was actually not very humorous at all, but quite a frightening thing.

After he finished his pie, he helped Mrs. Templeton put things away ("What a dear pretty little man, you are!" she said, pinching his purple cheeks) and strolled back to the stable houses. He toted buckets of warm water to the privacy of his loft above the stables, and washed the filth from the days' work away while whistling to himself.

That night, belly full, freshly bathed and snug under his blankets, he had a wonderful dream. He dreamed Miss Elsie was a beautiful princess trapped in a high tower; himself a noble warrior fighting to save her. She was being held captive by a horrible dragon that wore a pirate's tricorn hat, its skinny face resembling that of His Royal Wretchedness, Prince Theodore Ulysses Trydus. The thing roared and roared, its reptilian cries a resounding "Arrrrrrrrrrrrrrrgh!"

Kulbit took a sling in hand, and a great red tomato in the other. With a voice loud, powerful and strong, he shouted, "Avast, o treacherous and loathsome Pirate Dragon! I shall see thee to thy doom!"

He swung his sling in a wide loop over his head, and hurled the tomato at the beast. It splattered across its thin face like globs of blood and flesh before there was nothing left to be seen of the beast but a dragon's head of red, pulpy goop. The eye sockets of the dragon caved in on themselves, as well as its nose and mouth, so that very soon it was hard to tell what part of the mess was dragon flesh and what part was smashed tomato.

Princess Elsie then leaped from the window of the high tower, her gossamer gown fluttering about her slender shape as delicate as dragon flies' wings. She landed in his arms as light as a feather. Her lovely eyes sparkled blue in the moonlight, her skin like the smoothest porcelain.

*"Oh, Brave Kulbit...You are my Champion."*

"Nay, fair maiden. I have done no more than any hero's sworn duty," he said. She smiled up at him, as beautiful as ever.

*"Oh how can I ever repay you?"* she asked.

His heart stilled as her silken lips drew nearer to his own...

As Kulbit dreamed on that night, a contented smile resting upon his purple face, not a worry dared enter his funny colored head.

# Chapter 2

Theodore was frightened. He was trapped once again, and none would come if he called. Not if they were able, as he was so deeply hated. They had every reason for it, of course. But the fact did not stop his fear.

*Not here again...*

He ran to the fan light windows gilded in silver. The glass was barred in rusted wire mesh. Digging his thin fingertips into the mesh, he knew he would see nothing outside of the window. The cold white lights were neither from sun nor moon. They were unnatural; bars of lightening trapped in tubes of glass. The light of the Pale Room.

Theodore was once more buried alive. A cold foreboding returned at the sound of the buzzing lights. He hadn't noticed that he had already begun to scream. He pulled and pounded at the wire mesh, a beast in a cage, his young boy's screams shrill like that of a bobcat. His knuckles became raw and bloodied as he raged his fists against the rusted grates. His heartbeat pounded in his ears. He needed to escape. Not here again. He could not bear another eternity underground.

*"Someone please! Let me out!"*

His screams would never be answered. The longer he fought the inevitable, the longer eternity would take to begin in the Pale Room. He knew well the ways of this place; screaming and carrying on only made matters far worse. Yet he gave in to blind panic each time he awoke to find himself here.

After hours of crying out to no one, Theodore finally sat upon the white damask chair that was placed before the mantel, exhausted. The lights buzzed. Sweat gathered in beads upon his upper lip. He was left alone with his memories.

He had seen these lights years before as a child visiting Nubinx in secret with his royal father and mother. They lined the ceilings of the underground tunnels that the foreign kingdom used for pathways. In the lights the strange people mulled about silently in the underground streets, all dressed the same in their gray colored uniforms that reminded Theodore of nightclothes. He hated the eerie fixtures of the tunnels' lights, with their constant din of buzzing sounds like that of a bee's wing. And within the walls of these underground pathways and chambers, a stiller, deeper hum could be heard that reminded Theodore of the low growl of some hungry beast.

He wished very much to return home that day when he saw the horseless cart that was sent for them. It would travel along a track into the bowels of the dark cave entrance that would lead them into the mountain of the underground kingdom. The thought of going into the darkness made him tremble.

Father insisted upon this visit as an act of diplomacy and forbade him to cry. He had said that the must come to inquire of the ruler of Nubinx the natural philosophy called *science*; a word that seemed so foreign yet so familiar. Father had spent many hours at the scholar's tower for weeks prior, trying to learn more of the sciences, but he was not satisfied. Finally, he declared that they must secretly attempt to extend friendship to the kingdom of Nubinx, in hopes that they might share their knowledge.

But he declared that the Seigneurs Du Cordovan must not know of his plans, for they would not permit such an extension without the blessing of the church. And the church had already declared that too much knowledge of the sciences lead down the road of heresy.

Mother blessed herself when she heard her husband speak his secret desires. To go against the will of the church was to go against God. But Father dismissed this and declared that they will go to Nubinx in the guise of praying at the abandoned Holy Citadel, as is custom to ask God to deliver the kingdom from war. And as custom, the royal family must pray in solitude.

Once within the caves of Nubinx, their guide had said that the glowing bars overhead were lit by a thing of science called *electricity*; lightening caught within a glass. Mother had said it must be some sort of witchery as they rode underneath them. Father called her a fool and ordered her to be quiet, worried their guides might be offended by the Royal Family's apprehension of their strange customs. Theodore despised the kingdom of Nubinx and hated Father for forcing them to come along.

*He never gave a care about how we were. All that filled his mind and heart were "matters of state". His precious Thom...*

He recalled Mother whispering in his ear as they rode back across the moors to ThoBromis not to worry, that they would never again be made to return to the strange underground kingdom. But despite her promise, a small piece of the prince's mind remained in that dark place, and the sound of the buzzing lights would always haunt him.

And so here he was once more under the hateful glass lights, in the Pale Room. He could see wisps of his breath swirl before him. He clasped his hands between his knees and leaned forward, staring at the elegant white door at the far end of the room. He awaited his punishment.

The silver doorknob turned, and the door opened silently. On the other side was a thick curtain of darkness.

"Theodore," echoed a woman's voice.

*No...*

"Theodore…"

Theo shut his eyes. He did not wish to see.

"Look at me, Theodore."

He opened his eyes and saw amidst midair in the doorway a painting framed in white filigree. It was of a graceful lady. Her intricate gown of white lace seemed to tremble with a breeze, a single black tendril blowing across her brow. Behind her in the painting lay a bright Thomish countryside. She tucked the dark ringlet behind a bejeweled earlobe and smiled. A faint scent of perfume filled the room.

"Theodore."

*Mother.* He raised a shaking hand over his mouth. The woman in the painting stood, and the countryside behind her darkened as if on the verge of a summer storm. Her face changed, her dark eyes filling with tears. The skin on her smooth cheek began the wrinkle like a wilting rose petal. Slowly, a thin stream of blood trickled from her nose and left a dark trail down her chin.

"Theodore, why have you done this?"

"I-I did not wish for this. It was a mistake. I was merely playing…
Please…"

"Theodore, why have you killed me?"

Theodore covered his ears, his thin fingers digging into his damp hair. Tears blurred his sight. His palms pressed tightly against his head, but her voice rang from within the very center of his mind.

"My son, what harm have I done that you should harm me in turn?"

*"Forgive me, mother…"*

He watched her lovely face continue in its rot, the fragile skin growing transparent with thinness over bone. The skin about her mouth stretched and shrank back to reveal her perfect white teeth. The tightness of it forced her grinning jaws open, and a long red tongue flopped out over her chin.

Suddenly, with a wet sucking sound, her entire face began to crumble inward, crushing the tiny bones of her nose and cheeks. Her dark eyes were forced unnaturally close together, and grew wider and wider in their sockets as if in utter surprise until finally, one of them burst. The other popped out of what remained of the socket, the orb hanging free for a moment on a red string before it was also sucked inward, inward, inward. Inward her face continued to cave, from the top of her forehead to just above her upper lip. Her pale skin stretched and split, blood spilling down the front of her frock. The skin about her neck and shoulders became a sickening yellow, with red and purple blooming underneath.

The side of her head burst open with the cracking sound of a summer melon, ribbons of whitish meat spilling out of the chasm. Soon there was none left of her face but a fleshy red and black hole that began at the base of what remained of her hairline to the bottom of the jagged, tooth studded shelf of her jawbone. White maggots writhed within the recess of her head.

"Kiss me, my son…" The faceless woman leaned out of the frame as one might lean out of a window. Her thin arms reached out for Theodore across the pale room, longer and larger than the room itself. He pressed his back against the damask armchair, shutting his eyes.

"No! No, no, no!"

His screams became muffled by squelching sounds as the ruined head of the dead Queen of Thom came upon him. Wet meatiness smothered his face. He could feel the jagged teeth that had lined his mother's jawbone drag warm and wet under his chin, a writhing tongue worming and wriggling against his throat and chest.

He struggled, panic and revulsion flashing over his mind like the strange white lightening inside of the tubes; like *electricity.* Above the wet sounds of raw meat and flesh, he could still hear them buzzing, trapped in their glass coffins.

His feet spasmed, thudding and scraping the chair backward. Sharp, tiny bones within the meat thrust against his nose and lips, shattered bits of what was left of the structure of her face. He gasped for air. Hot pulp and liquid were pulled into his nostrils and mouth. He could not breathe, drowning in his mother's blood.

He finally kicked hard and the white chair tumbled backward. He grasped his face, coughing and sputtering. He was covered in dark crimson with blood and meat. His teeth had bits of his mother's flesh stuck between them.

Her face was broken. Her blood tasted of sticky, sweet rust. He wiped away at his mouth with the sleeves of his nightshirt.

*Her face was broken. Meat in my teeth like raw venison of the hunt...The finest steak tartare in all the kingdom of Thom.*

He wanted to cry, scream and vomit all at once. But all he could manage was feeble sputtering.

At once it was all over. The painting of his mother's broken, caved-in face sank away into the darkness of the empty doorway. All was once again silent. Theodore was rubbing away at his own mouth, but there was nothing there. No blood. No bits of bone and flesh stuck to his lips. His face and hands were clean. He was sitting in the ground as if nothing had happened at all.

He buried his face in his hands and wept for hours. When there were no more tears left in him, he gazed at the empty door of darkness across the Pale Room. He rose and sat once more in the white damask chair.

The next vision was to come soon. No sense in seeking it out. It would come when it wished. All was silent, save for the sound of the buzzing lights. He watched the wispy coils of his breath rise from his mouth.

He found himself dozing when he finally heard a faint sigh behind him. He whipped his head about and leaped to his feet with a start. His father stood behind the chair, his hard black eyes striking in contrast with the paleness of his skin. His beard swayed with the same ghost breeze that had played with his dead wife's hair.

"Father."

"And now I shall join her," his father said.

"*Father*...Please, stay with me a moment longer..." Theodore reached a shaking hand out. "Do not leave me."

"You are bitter poison to the royal lineage. I am glad that I have died. For only death can console a great king who bears so pathetic an heir. You were meant to be my legacy. You have stolen my queen from me. You cowered from the mysteries that could have changed my kingdom and brought our enemies to their knees. You now sully my crown, that which you have so hated. And in the end you shall join us forever here at the torment of Haddus: The Great Fallen Angel; Lord of Hell and the Enemy of God. You shall live here in this Lake of Fire and Ash, for you are damned."

"Father. Stay with me...Please..."

The dead king began to advance upon the boy. Theodore reached out to him, but he passed through Theodore's body like a mist, and on through the open doorway, sinking into the darkness. Beyond Theodore could begin to hear faint screams of torture elsewhere, where the rest of the damned repaid their debts.

"Father...Come back."

"*Your Highness! Your Highness, wake up, little one!*"

Prince Theodore, the future boy king of ThoBromis awoke bathed in cold sweat, sitting up straight as a poker in his rich bed of velvet, silk and satin. Magdolyn, his royal nurse, stood over him in her ruffled night gown with a candlestick. Theodore blinked at her, eyes wide.

"Ahhh…poor poppet was having another nightmare again, wasn't he?" the old woman clucked. "You poor little mansie. They said you were screaming in your sleep again. Was it the bogey beasty man? Does His Little Highness want Maggie to chase the bogey beasty man away?"

Prince Theodore clenched his teeth. He wished to be alone.
"Magdolyn, bring me hot milk."
"Why doesn't poppet tell Maggie all about the nasty dream first?"

"Hot milk! NOW!" shouted Theodore, slamming his fist upon the night table.

"All right, poppet. Don't fret. I shall be right back." Magdolyn left, humming to herself. Moments later she returned with a tray.
"Put it by the fire and get out." Theodore stood.
"Doesn't poppet want Maggie to sing a lullaby first?"
"Get out!"
As he sat in front of the fire in the red velvet armchair of his extravagant bedroom chamber sipping hot milk sweetened with honey, he'd forgotten entirely about what he had seen in the dream.
As far back as he could remember Prince Theodore had always had nightmares. Every night. He did not know the reason, nor did he care. To him there was no chance of finding sense for it, so he abandoned reason all together. He hated going to bed, and usually spent most nights in a similar fashion as he did this one; sipping hot milk in front of the fire, wide awake.
When he finished his drink, he sat at the beautifully carved double harpsichord that once belonged to his mother. It sat by the great windowed wall, white and intricate and looking as if it were made of sugar lace. From this he could see the lay of not only the great palace proper, but the street lamps of all of Post shining warm yellow in contrast to the cold lights in the dome of stars above. The streets were mostly abandoned at this hour, void of all that may

distract the eye from the loveliness of the royal city. In the distance he could see the spires and domes of the great church and the ancient halls of the libraries and the shining scholar's tower. The land stretched out before him as a great sheet of strewn colored jewels across dark velvet.

The view would steal the breath of any who looked on from the vantage of the royal estate, and a soul that bore a poetic nature might have grown solemn and sentimental at the sight of the kingdom at night. But for all of his kingdom's loveliness he hated it all the more. It was his father's one and only truest love, more so than Theodore himself. More so than his angelic mother, whose beauty could put to shame thousands of glittering kingdoms. But he did not wish to think on that.

Heavy thoughts burdened his mind. He pushed them away. He shan't worry himself about them. The silence of night unnerved him. The thought of all in the quiet palace fast asleep except for himself frightened and angered him. He detested them for it. They abandoned him every night. None cared of what terrors he might come to. He was to remain always alone.

On most occasions he would wake everyone. He would call for the jesters to awaken and entertain him. The buffoons would then come drowsy and puffy-eyed from their beds, and they would fumble with their juggling balls and stagger and stumble in attempt to perform their tricks at three hours past midnight. He relished in their exhaustion. It served them right for their ability to sleep soundly while their prince must suffer alone.

But he would not summon the clowns on this night. Not even laughing at their misfortune could cheer him. The King and Queen were both dead. He was now alone. All was left to him now; the Crown Prince Theodore Ulysses Trydus of Thom. And on that very morning he would be king, left to care after the kingdom that his father loved more than himself. Nothing would bring him comfort from this.

Perhaps other ordinary boys would remember why they were suddenly so frightened from waking in the night, and cry to their mummies and daddies for solace. But princes are never granted such luxury. And on his last night of being a Prince of Thom, he was to be alone. He would battle the quiet on his own.

*Very well, then.*

His thin, pale fingers brushed skillfully over ivory keys as he began to play delicate strains of music on his mother's harpsichord. The piece he played was of his own composition, twiddling in a way that reminded him of the twinkling of the stars. It echoed hauntingly across the empty palace halls, disturbing those who were asleep in their beds nearby. Many heads were thrust angrily beneath pillowcases as the lovely music played on and on.

Theodore finally fell asleep despite himself at the harpsichord with his head resting upon his arm, and soon after his private dreams filled his mind once again with worry and a pain he willed himself to never remember upon waking.

*     *     *     *

In the thick brush, a darkness spread, cold and black. It was searching for a warm spot, a new sleeper. One who may bridge the realms to be combined. It knew where it must search, but it did not know whom. It needed a new mind. A haunted mind. One that will fear, and in fear make it stronger.

In the center of the small sleeping city, the darkness settled by the Meeting Post, listening and curling its wisps around the opulently sculpted pillar. It listened to the soft whispers of the sleeping minds in the darkened windows, and somewhere not much farther off and even softer still, the faint music of someone playing a harpsichord. It knew the dreamer was close. It merely needed to be found.

In the still of the night, a stray cat wandered among refuse heaps, yowling for a lover. Wind rustled through the leaves of the trees that lined East West Road. In the Royal Stable House, Kulbit dreamed happily, bits of hay poking from out of his blue curls. The darkness was repelled from the stable houses, frightened of the thick stench of a dream-flipping mind.

But not long after, a haunted mind was found. The chosen dreamer kicked and moaned, sleeping fitfully in a royal bedroom. The old clock tower by the tailor's shop struck midnight. And the darkness began to move again, its search now ended.

*     *     *     *

# AUTHOR'S NOTE

*"What the heck is this?"* you may be asking yourself.

What kind of writer interrupts the flow of their book with random author's notes anyway? Pretty annoying if you ask me. But think if it like this: when someone has a mental illness that makes them hear voices, it's kind of like these notes: Out of place and invasive, interrupting your train of thought. I'm sorry to have to do that to you all, but that's just how this thing seems to be coming together.

I don't think I'm losing my mind. No, if anything it was gone long before I knew I ever had it. They say it's hereditary. I've always felt like this. It comes and goes from time to time. It's not an everyday thing.

But every now and then it happens. Things feel alien to me. I look at my hands and they aren't mine somehow. As I type, these fleshy sticks structured with bone are conveying my ideas into text, and painting a picture of what is within my mind's eye. How can anyone even know what I'm thinking?

*Because they're always watching you, judging you, thinking it'd be better if you never were born* says the voices. Ah, the voices. I try to ignore them most of the time. And then the dizzy spells come. The dizziness is the worst, for it's always the last thing to leave me. I find myself tipping over or walking into walls.

There are the intrusive thoughts that come with the voices, as if the voices have control of a picture screen in my head. Images of violence and all sorts of bloody things a normal person should not be thinking about. What it would be like to be buried alive. If when your throat has been slit, if you might be able to breathe out of your neck for a moment just before you begin to drown in the wet saltiness of your own blood.

When I was little, I was obsessed with the death of my parents. I have a vivid memory of standing in the parking lot of our old Miami apartment building, crying until I had the hiccups. I had to be somewhere around 4 years old. My mother had short puffy black hair, 1980's stripes of pink blush streaking across her cheeks, and my father was wearing a dress shirt. I think we were coming home from church. I remember my parents laughing, telling me not to worry because their deaths "won't happen for a looooong time…"

I think I've always been afraid of everything that had anything to do with existing here in this world. But the things that scare me most of all were the eyes I would see watching me from the darkness of the closet late at night, or the deep, rumbling voices I would hear speaking under my bed. When you're really little, you can't tell the difference between reality and dreams, and I guess in that sense I'm kind of still the same. Some of the time.

### END NOTE

The next day at high noon, the royal court assembled at the Meeting Post in all their finery; a striking array of opulent white wigs and hair. The ladies were a rainbow of pastel silks and satins, their corseted gowns looking like a row of intricate cakes and macarons. They stood on the dais with graceful poise, fluttering laced and feathered fans. The men stood at stiff attention with frilly collars and white stockings, their cheeks and lips reddened with rouge.

The Priests from the big church at the far side of North South Road came in tall hats and white and gold robes, much fancier then the scarlet capes they wore at mass. The church bells rang, echoing across the city of Post and to the valleys beyond. Trumpeters in crisp yellow jerkins gathered in two neat rows on either side of the dais, and fanfare pierced the brisk spring air.

The Royal Guard assembled on horseback and raised gleaming swords in a silver arch. The princes and princesses of the High Blood walked underneath in a grand procession, and at the very end of this The Crown Prince himself rode beneath the blades on a pure white horse.

But hardly any of the villagers attended the ceremony. Most of them bustled about business as usual. Only a handful had stopped to watch the crowning of their new king.

Kulbit had come, for the white horse that the Prince rode in on was none other than his good friend Roger. He had given Roger a special rub down that very morning, bathed him in milk and perfumed him with sandalwood oil the night before. He even washed his own purple face especially for the occasion. It was not every day a new king was to be crowned at the Meeting Post. And besides, it was a chance to steal away from old Bugger, who had seemed to be in a foul temper that morning. He smelled of whiskey, and said that the bright color of Kulbit's face was making his head ache.

Kulbit climbed the nearest tree to get a good view of the procession. Roger's white pelt shone almost golden in the morning light, and Kulbit beamed with pride at his work. He may have imagined it, but Roger's large brown eyes locked with his own as they passed under the great camphor tree from where he was perched. The horse winked at him.

Prince Theodore stood atop the dais and looked out among the sparse few people. When the high priest placed his father's heavy golden crown upon his head, only three or four people clapped. One old man had fallen asleep under a tree with his hat over his face. The prince clenched his fists so tight his knuckles turned white. Here, this moment in time would be written down in Thomish history; the crowning of the youngest king since the reign of King Aguste III, four hundred years prior. Yet no one cared.

In the market place by the Post, a fat woman hollered at the top of her lungs of fresh meat for sale over the First Blessing that the Priest spoke as he anointed Theodore's forehead. Two old women began a rather noisy argument over the baker's last loaf of bread as the Orb of Thom was placed in his right hand.

A boy was trying to pull at the bridle of a balking donkey and swore vilely as the Royal Crest of Thom was fastened to an ornate livery collar and placed over Theodore's shoulders by the High Lord of Cordovan. As the Priest blessed Theodore the last time, his words were drowned out by the clanging bell of a horse drawn trolley car and the conductor hollering for all passengers to board. None seemed to notice the great event that was happening at the Meeting Post.

*I hate them. Someday, I will repay them all for this.*

# Chapter 3

The king turned out to be quite a disaster, as to be expected. His many advisers became more or less reduced to babysitters. If they attempted to guide him in the grown up matters of kingship, he would rant and rave and throw things and they would have to send for his nurse. Lord Chauncey, who had been chief adviser and High Lord of Cordovan to the late King Leonard, had never in all his years had seen such tiresome chaos. He was becoming more and more convinced that kings should never be crowned under the age of eighteen.

But unless the future king could be proven to be of ill-health and unable to perform duties as monarch, there was no denying his sovereignty.

The king was quite pleased with himself. He made ridiculous demands in the palace, and a mockery of the crown. He decreed that if the royal cook ever prepared spinach again, she would be hung for treason. As for matters and meetings of state, he could never be made to attend; for he spent most hours alone in his chamber, only his old nurse permitted entry to bring him his tray.

In time, the members of the court began to murmur that perhaps there might be something amiss in the head of their new leader. He knew of their whispers and hated them more and more as the days became the passing of seasons.

Meanwhile, things had gotten quite disagreeable for Kulbit ever since the new king had been crowned. Because of the king's spending, funding was reduced all around. The Royal Stable House took a turn for the worst, as King Theodore did not much care for horses, and Bugger and Kulbit were forced to take a cut in wages. This put the fat old man in the foulest of tempers on a regular basis now, and of course Kulbit was made to suffer the brunt of most of it. His work days were long and hard.

What's worse, since King Theodore also retracted much of the funding for the Libraries of Post, the great library kept odd hours usually only open when Kulbit was hard at work, so it was difficult for him to find new things to read. Luckily he had been able to keep a collection of his favorite old books. He would escape in his strange purple head with these whenever things were at their worst to raise his spirits.

Very little fun was to be had, so as you can imagine the servants of the palace became quite excited when word was spread that a foreign diplomat from the Copplean Islands would be visiting His Royal Majesty.

The hay wagons had come in full on the day of the Copplean Diplomat's arrival. Kulbit grunted silently to himself as he began pitching the last of the four hay wagon deliveries that had arrived at the royal stables. He had unloaded three carts full of hay so far by himself. They had a very good harvest that year. Kippers was a growing foal, and very soon he would be fully weaned. This surplus in hay would be quite useful.

Old Bugger came stumbling out of the stables, his head thrown back in a raucous guffaw. Once again, he smelled foul with ale. He held a piece of parchment in his hand.

"Come down from there, youngster. We've got ourselves an official correspondence 'ere, sent straight from the Master of the Household." He thrust the paper in Kulbit's hand, laughing.

*His Imperial Grace, the Duke of Gridde shall be spending the summer holiday at the Royal Estate in Post. He will be accompanied by his daughter, Lady Alise Di Gridde, and her young cousin, Contessa Elisabetta Di Marcheris. The foreign nobles are esteemed guests and shall participate in the Summer Solstice Festival. His Grace spares no expense to please his daughter and has requested thus. The young Ladies have brought their fine blood mares to be cared for in our royal stables. See that they receive the best of care. Her Ladyship has grown accustomed to a daily ride through the countryside, and shall require a page to escort and attend to her. The strangely colored boy named Kulbit has been chosen as charge of the mares, and will entertain the young Ladies' equestrian interests. His appearance will appeal to the young Ladies' fancy. He shall report to the Head Seamstress at once to be fitted for a uniform that he must wear while serving as page in the presence of the two Ladies. For his services he shall be rewarded an extra gold coin a day.*

"Looks like Lil'Cupcake is gonna be a nanny to a pair of little girls! *There's* a job that suits ya, fancy fine! Now you go up to the

Head Tailor to get yourself all nice and pretty! Lilac Lily Maid!"
Bugger gave Kulbit a hard slap on the back.

*Blast! Why must I be the one to pander to Lady Whatever-her-name-is? I'm not a house servant. An extra gold coin a day is good enough after the wage cut, but to be paraded about after some rich, spoiled palace-girls as some sort of spectacle isn't going to be any fun at all. For goodness sake, why must I be so bloody purple?*

Kulbit plodded up North South road to the main palace proper. He came to the palace gates and found his way to the Royal Textile Chambers. It was a vast room filled wall to wall with all sorts of fabrics of every hue and pattern. There was a great table in the center of the chamber, and around this sat several chattering women, each sewing or knitting some frilly thing or another. Off to the side, a young lady worked an enormous loom. The chamber seemed very busy.

The Head Seamstress was a thin, sharp-eyed woman covered in freckles, pins and needles sticking out from the corner of her mouth. She seemed too much in a rush to deal with Kulbit at all, and very much put out.

"It's about time you've gotten here! And Her Ladyship will be wanting a ride tomorrow. As if I hadn't enough work to do, what with His Grace ordering three new dresses for her upon her arrival, not counting the weeks' worth of mending and repairs we are to do on her already ridiculous wardrobe. What a fuss he's made over her! That man spoils that child rotten, it's a wonder she won't end up just like His Royal Wretchedness someday. But you didn't hear me say that... Step up on this stool, I've got to measure you right away. Boy, don't just stand there, take off that shirt for pity's sake," she said, and to his horror she roughly unlatched the straps of his dungarees and yanked his dirty oversized work shirt over his head. He stood shirtless on the stool, blushing furiously and holding up his britches to keep them from falling down. The seamstress balled up his work shirt.

"And the girl's cousin! She's just as terrible as the older one, what with her wanting all new lacing on her already..." The seamstress sniffed the air, then sniffed the shirt.

"Bless me, what a stench you have, Boy! Hadn't you been told to bathe before coming here? You smell like a horse's ass!"

This made the ladies around the room chuckle. Kulbit wished he could disappear into the ground. He shook his head.

"Well get down off of there and get yourself washed up! I'm not about to have you fitted in fine satin only to have you smear the stuff with dirt. Iris, take him to the washing room and get him some good strong soap. And hurry!"

The young lady at the loom took Kulbit's hand and led him to a small room in the back that was filled with laundry. There was a tub of cold water and soap waiting for him. When he was finished washing up, the seamstress had him shirtless and up on the stool once again.

Kulbit thought that there must be nothing more embarrassing in all the world than to have a strange woman poke and prod all about your person, measuring all of your bits in front of more strange women. (In this he later found that he was terribly wrong.) After he was measured and dismissed, he returned to the stables with strict orders not to get dirty again. This wasn't so bad, for he contented himself to lay in his hay bed and read for the remainder of the day.

The next morning, when Bugger bawled at him that he was to get ready to meet the noble Ladies and accompany them in their daily ride, he returned to the seamstress. As he stood in front of the great mirror in the Linen Chamber, if he could speak he would still be rendered speechless.

His breeches were a puffy mass of yellow lace. White tights covered his legs, and pink ruffled boots with tiny brass bells at the toes tinkled at his feet. His shirt was a collection of bows and frills and pompoms, and his pink jacket was made of a sparkling fabric and adorned with hearts and bauble fringe. On his head he wore a frilly tricorn hat. Pink, of course, and all a-fluff with yellow ostrich feathers. This in combination with his complexion and hair was all together so sugary and bright that he looked as if he were a walking bit of candy. All the ladies crowded about him and giggled and sighed, pinching his cheeks and chucking his chin.

"Ohhh what a darling!"
"Isn't he precious?"
"What a dear Little Man!"

*Why, oh why?* This was all he could think to himself. *Why me?*

"Now off you go. To the stables to get Their Ladyship's horses saddled. Then meet them at the main gates. For heaven's sake, try not to get too filthy."

Kulbit dreaded going back to the stables. He would have hated for Old Bugger to see him dressed as such, and knew he would never be able to live it down. But the ladies were waiting, and it wouldn't do to anger the Master of the Household, who was in charge of Kulbit's pay. When he arrived at the stables, he was pleased to hear that Bugger had gone off to the hay fields to quarrel with someone about something or another.

Jared was waiting for Kulbit. He was another stable page; a tiresome boy some years older than Kulbit himself, with beady eyes and whom always seemed to be chewing tobacco. When he saw Kulbit approach, he burst out laughing and almost choked on his chaw.

"I will say I was a mite envious when I hear that you'd be waitin' on those lady folk. I could've used the extra coin...But now I don't envy you at all, Lilac Lily! The ladies' horses are down in the third stall from the right. And 'ere; Master sent a note for you." Jared handed Kulbit another piece of paper, spat in the dirt and sauntered off.

The note had further instructions to the care of Their Ladyship's horses. Kulbit read these as he shuffled into the stables, the bells on his pink boots tinkling. The mares were to be bathed using milk and perfumed with lavender oil every other day. Their manes and tails brushed and braided with pink and yellow ribbon in a specific color pattern. Fresh white roses were to be twisted in among the ribbons as well. And they were to be saddled and bridled with Their Ladyships' special saddles.

Kulbit sighed as he approached the two young mares. Snowdrop was tall and pure white; a graceful creature with a soft pink nose and bright blue eyes. As Kulbit came to her, she let out a disgusted whinny and turned away from him. In his head he heard a delicate whispering voice, dainty as a rosebud.

*What a repulsive little boy-creature. This stable is atrocious. Where is my Lady? I wish to go home.*

The other mare, a lovely chestnut brown, was named Maple. She regarded Kulbit with a bored snort, her ears tilted back. Kulbit could hear nothing of her voice at all in the center of his mind. Behind the two mares, hung upon the wall were their saddles. Kulbit set to putting them in place. Snowdrop's saddle was bright pink, with intricate scroll work and embroidery and ruffles. The bridle also seemed to be made of sugary lace, a string of silver bells along the reins. Pale purple jewels and filigree etched across the brow band, so that it looked more like a tiara than anything else. And when Snowdrop's mane and tail had finally been braided with ribbons and posies, she looked more like a princess than a fine blood mare.

Maple turned out to be the more difficult horse. Her saddle was bright yellow, glittering with gems and laced fringe. When Kulbit attempted to saddle her, she kept turning her flank away from him so that he finally had to tie her to a post. Her bridle was also yellow, with silk roses across her brow band and more lace fringe at the reigns. She whinnied and grunted at Kulbit when he attempted to put this on her, and even snapped at him twice. When he was finished with her, she shook her mane at him with disdain.

*I don't like this anymore than you do,* Kulbit said to her in his mind. He led to two mares out of the stable, and Jared was waiting for him with a bridled and saddled gray mare.

Kulbit had always thought of this particular mare as Margret, but Bugger and the rest of the stable workers called her Silver. She was a gentle beast. Not the fastest by any means, but calm and very affectionate. She was to be the horse that Kulbit would use to accompany the Ladies with. When she saw Kulbit she gave a soft whinny and nuzzled his neck. He smiled into her big, sad eyes.

*Oh Margret. I am glad it's to be you. I would so very much appreciate a friend.*

She nuzzled him once more as if to say, *Not a worry, little one. I'll look after you.*

The boys led the three horses to the palace gate, where there was a small crowd of servants waiting. A tall, graceful girl with dark brown hair and eyes stood fanning herself. She was in a yellow gown so bright and intricately laced that Kulbit immediately knew her to be one of the Ladies; most likely the Lady Alise, with her affinity for yellow.

Beside her, with her back to him stood a smaller girl with long, golden hair all the way down her slender back. Her dress was a delicate pink, and lovely enough that Kulbit thought she looked more as if she were going to a wedding rather than out to the countryside for a ride. White roses adorned her curling locks, and as she turned Kulbit felt his heart begin to flutter.

Her face was a perfectly shaped heart, her skin as white as porcelain. Her large blue eyes were bordered with long, thick lashes that were never still. She looked all together so lovely and delicate that she reminded him of a doll. When she saw him, her beautiful face burst out in to such a bright smile that he felt himself grow quite dazzled.

*She's the most beautiful girl I have ever seen...*

"Oh cousin! Look at the charming little stable boy! Isn't he positively *darling?* I say, what pretty colors he has! And there is my dear sweet Snowdrop, looking as lovely as ever in a new saddle!" The Contessa squealed, tugging her older cousin's arm.

Lady Alise stopped fanning herself and began to giggle along with her beautiful cousin. As he drew closer, he felt his face grow hotter, and suddenly wished very much to be wearing anything but the fluffed nonsense that he was to wear right now. The girl's giggles didn't cease when he finally approached.

"You dear, dear little man! Why, you look just like a little sugar tart! Did not I tell you that His Majesty is a most gracious host? He spares no expense on amusing his guests. Oh, we're in for such a lovely time, Cousin. I *am* glad that your father has agreed to allow you to attend the holiday this year," Lady Alise said. She handed a servant her fan and began to remove her gloves.

"M'Lady, this is Kulbit. He's charge of Your Ladyship's horses while you're a guest at the palace. He'll also be your personal page, and should you need him send word for him at any time." Jared bowed.

"Pleased to meet you, dear Kulbit! What a delightful color you are! How come you to be such a lovely shade of lilac?" asked Lady Alise, pinching his hot cheek.

"Begging pardon, M'Lady. But he's a mute. His ears work well enough though. He takes orders just fine," explained Jared. Kulbit smiled weakly and bowed.

"Oh, what a shame. Such a dear little thing, too. I'd be tempted to ask father to permit me to take him home with me as a playmate!" the Contessa giggled. Kulbit swallowed hard.

"Elisabetta, you are so tenderhearted. Always trying to take in a new poor soul. Though he *is* an amusing thing to see, I grow bored of waiting. Shall we be off? I do so love the Thomish countryside."

"Oh yes, do lets. Dear Kulbit, you *are* coming with us, are you not? Come along." The Contessa once again smiled at him and he wondered if perhaps this was what the angels spoken about in the Holy Book must look like.

Kulbit rode behind the two ladies on Margret's back. The girls tittered and chatted endlessly as they trotted along, exclaiming at the beauty of the land that rolled out before them. Lady Elisabetta's musical voice reminded Kulbit of the tinkling of fine crystal.

The hillside was fresh and not yet too hot in the very beginning of the summer. They came to a little stream that twisted through a shady patch of willow trees.

"Cousin, is this not sweet? Let us have a rest and refreshment here. The weeping willows are so wonderfully romantic; don't you think so, Stable Boy?" Lady Elisabetta dismounted Snowdrop, took up her skirts and began to wander about.

Lady Alise followed, and the two girls sat by the river while Kulbit also dismounted. He tied the three horses, and took down a large basket from Margret's back. He lay out a lovely picnic cloth (pink of course), with yellow lace and pearl beading. It would seem that the Duke of Gridde was very much intent on surrounding the girls with beautiful things at every turn, isolating them from anything commonplace.

*It is no wonder,* Kulbit thought with a sigh, gazing at the Contessa. *Why wouldn't anyone wish to surround such a beautiful girl with anything that is not as equally lovely?*
Margret snorted at that with disapproval.

He lay out fine golden plates with brightly colored pastries, cream berry tarts, sliced pears and cheese. The girls sounded like cooing doves in the near distance. When Kulbit was finished, he stood by the horses and waited for them. After a short while, they came chattering over to the picnic cloth and settled down by the refreshments, their great skirts circling about them like giant blossoms.

"How scrumptious. You know, the Kingdom of ThoBromis is quite famous for its desserts. I'm quite pleased to see that they have kept their tradition. Dear, you must place the salted cheese *atop* the berry tart, like this. See? Strange, I know, but it is how it is served...." Lady Alise bit into the berry tart with cheese, offering her cousin a bite.

"Oh, but it tastes simply *gorgeous*, does it not?" said Elisabetta licking her fingertips delicately.

"I say, perhaps a bit of bubbled wine, another Thomish specialty...Boy, come. We shall have some wine."
Kulbit quickly brought out the bottle of bubbled wine, and opened it with a loud pop. He was unaccustomed to doing house service, and when the cork came loose, a good deal of foam went splattering into the grass. He went about pouring it into the glasses quite awkwardly. The girls tittered at him, but in the end were sipping wine from crystal and quickly grew merry. Kulbit returned to his place by Margret.

"This *is* the loveliest of holidays. I do so love ThoBromis. I wish that we could stay here always! Dear, dear Stable Boy, come and sit with us. Have a glass of bubbled wine! Sit, sit! Do you not enjoy wine? Pour yourself some!" laughed the Contessa.
Kulbit bowed stiffly, and came forward again, blushing. If the Master of the Household were to find out...But one look into Elisabetta's bright, merry eyes and he knew he could not resist her.

He poured himself a glass of white bubbled wine, and sipped timidly. He had never tasted wine before, and smiled with surprise at its sweetness.

"Oh mercy! I think he likes it quite well!" Lady Alise laughed. This set both the girls into such a fit of giggles that made Kulbit feel quite warm all over. Or perhaps it could have been the wine.

As they rode back to the palace gates, Kulbit decided that perhaps this whole venture was not as unfortunate as he originally believed. He was going to get extra pay, and then of course, he would get to see more of the Contessa. That night, as he dreamed he imagined that the Contessa Elisabetta Di Marcheris was under an enchanted spell that made her sleep for a thousand years. She was locked away in a beautiful silver castle atop a high mountain, waiting for one who truly loved her to break the spell with a single kiss.

*       *       *       *

Kulbit rode with the Ladies of Copplea every afternoon that summer, and it became the highlight of his day. Even if he did have to wear ruffles and lace. He and the two girls would ride out to the willows and have wine or chilled tea. Elisabetta taught him how to play a game of cards, and he had even won once. The girls laughed and jested with him as if he were an equal; Lady Alise twisting little white posies in his blue hair.

*So this is what it must be like to be one of the palace people...*

Kulbit had often read many books about falling in love. But he had never dreamed that it should feel so wonderful. Even old Bugger's teasing that summer could not seem to dampen his mood.

One afternoon he rode out with the Ladies to a great lake that shone like diamonds. Kulbit was sitting under a tree, watching Elisabetta pick wildflowers, and Alise called them over.

"Oh, how lovely. Cousin! Do come quickly! It is a family of wild swans. Are they not *sweet?"*

Elisabetta grabbed Kulbit's arm and pulled him towards the lake. Kulbit thought his heart would burst at her touch as he followed along after. The swan's cries echoed over the lake as the graceful birds glided across the glittering water.

"Oh, dear Kulbit. Are they simply not the most beautiful?"

The Contessa rested her head on his shoulder with a sigh. Her hair was scented with lavender, and the smell if it so near to him made his head swim. The end of her curls brushed lightly against the back of his hand like cool ribbons of silk. His skin prickled with goose pimples.

*Yes...Beautiful indeed...*

Kulbit used his first extra gold coin to buy a tiny writing book and quill with an ink well. He had never had one of these before; a book with blank pages, and something about being able to fill them himself thrilled him to no end. He remembered how Miss Elsie taught him to write in verse; poems that rhyme and such. But she had once told him that not all poetry must rhyme. Kulbit wanted to write something special.

The Contessa Elisabetta Di Marcheris had brought him so much happiness, he simply had to express it. He found himself lying alone in one of the fields, one evening after her daily ride, writing her a secret letter as the sun set in the horizon, bathing everything about him in red golden light. As his quill scribbled over the page, his heart began a wild and happy rhythm, his cheeks aflame and his head dizzy.

*To my Dearest Contessa,*

*You shall never know the depth of affection I bear for you. I am but a humble servant, eager to please Your Ladyship. But within me burns a love for you so steadfast that I fear neither time nor the grave shall quell its flame. If I might die within your gaze of crystal blue, I know that I will be holy and content, for within your eyes lie all the grace and virtues of heaven. Your lips are as delicate as a rosebud; as sweet as cherries. Your cheeks are like the finest apples of Thomish orchards; you fair skin as soft as the apple blossoms that bloom therein. Elisabetta, my forever, cherished beloved. How I wish I had the gift of speech for a chance to whisper your name to myself. My lips are silent, but my heart sings within its chambers only the single song of you; fair Elisabetta Di Marcheris of the Isles of Copplea. You shall never know the secret, silent love that I bear for you, but in the veil of our dreams I will ever be foresworn to love another, and to be eternally devoted as your Knight and Champion...*

He wrote many letters such as this that summer, filling the book's pages with sonnets and words of devotion. He wrote of how he dreamed of touching her golden tresses once more, only this time would not be an accident. Holding her delicate hand in his own. And he swore upon his own life that he should never share this book of letters with another single soul. It would be a sacred secret, and if he ever were to fulfill his dreams of becoming a wandering knight, in his heart he would conquer beasts and battles in the name of the *Contessa De Marcheris*. Perhaps he would someday die in a grand duel, and his final words in the center of his mind would be to utter her sweet name.

And each afternoon he would ride out with the Ladies, thinking of more and more wonderful ways to describe his feelings for her. Deep and secret as his own flipped dreams, but yet real and warming as the sun upon his skin. These were the brightest days he had ever known. But this was not to last.

One evening near the end of the summer, the Ladies had finished off an entire bottle of red bubbled wine, and had become quite intoxicated. They were laughing and falling over each other for such a long while that Kulbit realized that he would be responsible for bringing them back to the palace.

He packed away the refreshments and smiled to himself at the sounds of the girls' silliness. Elisabetta had placed a garland of flowers in her hair, and it had fallen over her eye as she raced her cousin to and fro.

"But what have I fallen upon? What is here? A secret book! Perhaps in it is a map to some buried treasure, or a witch's diary!"

Kulbit spun around quickly, feeling his pockets. His writing book was gone.

Alise was lying in the grass, holding a book above her face. "Why cousin! I do believe that this book is a letter addressed to you! From our very own dear Stable Boy..."

Everything inside of Kulbit felt as if it were falling down and out through his feet. His felt his face grow pale. His hands covered his mouth in horror. He fought the impulse to run and grab the book from Lady Alise, for the idea of a servant grabbing anything from a lady of such high rank was out of the question. Instead he stood in silence as Lady Alise flipped through his most guarded secret thoughts. He bit his lip, fighting the impulse to run and hide, or burst into tears.

"Why, it would seem our dear little Kulbit is quite the romantic. It would appear that he is dreadfully besotted with Your Ladyship!"

"What? Let me see, let me see", Elisabetta snatched the book and read. Kulbit thought he might faint. The Contessa burst out into a fit of laughter.

"Oh dear me, do listen to this: '*The skin of your hand is softer than the petal of a lily; how I wish that I might hold such a lovely flower within my palm, placing upon its elegant petals a summer's dewdrop jewel that will make you henceforth and ever more my most cherished bride...*' Oh! Oh my goodness! His *bride? Oh! Oh!*"

Elisabetta and Alise laughed and laughed. Kulbit was frozen in his place with terror. His nose stung as he forbade himself from weeping.

"What say you, cousin, to this fine suitor? Shall you marry him, abandoning your highborn state and become a Stableman's Wife; a maudlin quest in the name of True Romance?"

"Oh that would be just *beastly,* wouldn't it? Married to a stable boy. But how terribly funny!" Elisabetta's laughter grew shrill. "Can you imagine? I suppose my wedding bouquet will have to be a bundle of hay."

"Yes, and the barn mice will bear witness and carry your train!"

"Oh yes, yes! And for the wedding feast, we shall serve carrots and oats!"

"And I suppose the barn cat would perform the ceremony?"

"Oh no, cousin. Do not be crude. It would needs be none other than Snowdrop herself!" And the girls began dancing about, singing an old melodramatic romance ballad as Kulbit stood silent. He stared at the ground.

> *"...He thought for to devise*
> *How he might have her companye,*
> *That so did 'maze his eyes.*
> *'In thee', quoth he, 'doth rest my life;*
> *For surely thou shall be my wife,*
> *Or else this hand with bloody knife,*
> *The Gods shall sure sufiiiiice!'"*

Finally, the two girls were so consumed with laughter that they could no longer sing. There was nothing more for Kulbit to do, but finish packing things away. Moments later they were on horseback and on the way to the palace. As they rode along, the young ladies resumed their light chitchat about what they were to wear to the Festival, and whom they planned to dance with.

He rode a pace behind them, now forgotten all together. And only then did he allow the tears to come. And as he watched them far ahead he realized that the Contessa saw him as nothing more than a curious plaything; an item to amuse her fancy until something else more interesting came along. She brushed away the idea of his love for her as easily as one might brush away a gnat. Moments later, the book was as forgotten as himself, and Kulbit saw it fall to the ground as the girls talked during the ride. He did not bother to retrieve it. It was not important enough to be remembered, you see. As he had been.

\*     \*     \*     \*

The King, on the other hand, had but one love known to only himself and the nurse since receiving his crown. The love of games. Card games. Board games. Games with intricate little figurines carved from precious stones. Many did not find it to be such an unusual thing, this pleasure of the king. To play games was often believed to be fair practice for battle stratagem, declared some of the gentlemen of the court.

But to be so enraptured with these toys, and yet dismissive of matters of state? And to play alone for sometimes a few days on end, never emerging from one's bedchambers? He's becoming quite mad, gossiped the ladies of the court. One must remember his mother...

Fires crackled within the large fireplace of the king's bedchamber, candles burning late every night. He was usually cold, but was unaware if the fact. His mind felt glowing hot, and this was all the warmth he wished for. The jade chess pieces before him stood out in bright green defiance. He moved the onyx piece as easily as he would change thoughts in his own mind.

He played games alone for hours on end, until the sun rose and shined its bright yellow beams into his royal bedchamber. First he would play onyx, then he would play jade. Hours would pass. He would then bring out his elegant deck of cards. Soon the whole world was none but cards black and red squares, and even as he stopped to rub his eyes he saw them spreading onward and onward into the darkness that was his mind. Jade pawn on Black Square. Queen of Hearts. Onyx knight on red square. Lord of the Spades. It was at this time the portrait painting of his mother's eyes hanging over the great fireplace did not seem to follow him in the darkness.

When his mind was glowing hot, he feared for nothing. In time his games became the only subject he would speak of. He would go about with a dour expression, his black eyes staring at the ground. If a lady of the court were to say to him:
"Your Majesty, is it not a lovely morning?"

He would reply: "My king was conquered last night by a pawn...A filthy, low-blooded pawn...Spit on the morning..."
Or if one of his gentlemen in waiting were to say:
"Sire, shall there be a hunt this season?"

He might smile and say: "The king of hearts is a dirty sod, and hunts no matter what the season. But *that* is the reason why he always wins. That is the true way to win."

On his sixteenth birthday a ratty card trickster came to the palace. She was an old woman with gray hair, so dirty and matted within itself it looked like ropes growing out of her skull. She would flip the cards with eerie swiftness, her fingers a blur. He was mesmerized.

The old hag laid out the cards to be selected, and after one of the cards were chosen, she would shuffle them again. Then one must try and guess which card was the first chosen. What he cared about were her hands. Watching her hands made his mind glow again. After watching, he discovered her trick. Her hands were fluid. None of the men could guess the right card. But Theodore could. Because of the boy king, the old crook ended up leaving the palace far poorer than whence she came.

Playing his games put his mind in a strange state of euphoria. And if ever he felt himself growing cold, or wondering if perhaps there was not such a thing as a Pale Room somewhere out there, he would remember the look on the hag's face and feel warm and again at ease.

By the following winter he had begun an extensive collection of tarot cards. He learned tricks of his own, and in the loneliness of his sleepless mind he would play and play and play. He became sullen of appearance and soon after began to only speak to others in order to get them to gamble with him, and on these occasions he would make fools of them all. The higher the stakes, the better the game. Cards and chessmen. Red and black squares. That was all that mattered.

The king began to spend great amounts of the royal treasury. He would gamble endlessly. The kingdom of Thom sped dangerously in the direction of debt, but their king was indifferent. He spent much on bringing in fortune-tellers and tricksters. He knew that they were all false, but he brought them anyway. Because it was not what they did that he enjoyed, but the actual act of figuring out *how* they had done it. This became his obsession.

He kept everyone up at all hours of the night. He bossed and bullied to no end, sending many to the stocks out of mere spite, especially if they made the mistake of winning him at a gamble. Losing was not what bothered him. It was not having the ability to decipher *how* they could have won, and it usually came only as a result of his eyes burning for want of sleep. But sleep did not matter to him. All that mattered was the game. The people of Thom hated their king. And he hated them back every bit as much.

It was at this time that word reached King Theodore's ear of a powerful foreign Wizard that had been traveling through the *LeBois* of the west. Rumor was told that this Wizard was a fantastic magickian and fortune teller, and that he could even summon the dead from the Underworld. King Theodore had by then seen hundreds of old wizards, witches and psychics, all fakes and tricksters performing for the coin and the entertainment of gullible minds. But for one to be able to summon the dead...that would be impossible. Not that King Theodore had any interest in speaking with the dead at all. (Somewhere in that wretched mind of his he remembered a vague image of a raven-haired woman in white lace.)

No, he did not care for that. However, he was curious to know *how* this game was played, if so many fools were to believe in it. It was so that soon, it was all he could think about. In time he sent for the old Wizard.

The season's change mattered little to the boy king. He noted nothing but the passing of each game, each time alone in the darkness. When on one night a silent cloaked figure appeared in his doorway, he did not notice. In the center of his chamber lay a tall castle made entirely of cards. The young king was sitting by the fire, a deck of cards in his hand as he gazed at his masterpiece.

*This castle is my true castle. This game, my true kingdom. These cards...shall be my weapon...*

He fanned them out skillfully, and flipped them into order with one hand as he stared at the castle in the candle light. The room was silent save for the soft whirring sound of his cards and the crackle of the great fire before him.

"Greetings, Your Majesty."

Theodore gave a start. The castle of cards fluttered to the ground. He leaped to his feet. "Who is there? How dare you come into my presence unbidden?"

"I beg your pardon, Your Majesty. I did not mean to frighten you", came a rich voice. It carried a strange accent. Perhaps from the icy islands of the North East...
"You have sent for me, and so I have come."
"I have done no such thing. Who do you think you are, coming into my chamber...at this hour? I shall send for the Royal Guard," Theodore stammered. His heart had just about burst in his chest.

The cloaked figure stood in the doorway in heavy silence. Theodore swallowed hard. He stared at the man expecting him to speak, but the man said nothing.

"Well?" Theodore said finally. "What have you to say for yourself?"

The stranger made no reply, nor had he moved. He stood in the entrance of the royal bedchamber, his face hidden in the shadow of the gray hood. He was stock still. Still enough to be a painting in the doorway.

Theodore shivered. "Who… Who are you?"

"I am Craddosche," said the man, stepping into the chamber. He removed the hood of his thick gray cloak and stepped into the light of the fire. His face was strikingly handsome, with a highborn brow. His golden hair was pulled back with a black ribbon. An elegant lace collar could be seen at his throat underneath the cloak, a brooch with a dark red stone winking beneath it. His eyes were a rich sort of brown in a hue that Theodore had never seen before. They almost appeared red in the firelight.

"C-Craddosche?" Theo repeated, thinking. "Ahhh, I remember. You are the Wizard from *LeBois*. The one I had sent for earlier in the year."

The strange man said nothing.

"I was not expecting you so late," said the boy, sitting back down. He took a deep breath to steady his nerves. He motioned to the chair opposite himself awkwardly.

"Please, sit down. I will ring for tea, if you like."

The man remained standing. Theodore bit his lip.

"Tell me your will, Your Majesty."

Now that this Wizard was here in his room, Theodore could not quite remember why he wished to see him. He suddenly felt that perhaps it was not such a good idea after all. With a graceful motion the man brought out an opulent hand mirror. He held it out before the boy, the gold scroll work around the looking glass studded with rubies. The rubies also seemed to glow red in the firelight. Red as the smiling eyes of the stranger. Theodore gazed into the looking glass and saw his own thin face.

"I simply wanted…" began Theodore. *I just wish to know how the trick is done...*

"Do you wish to speak with the dead?"

Suddenly the reflection of Theodore's face in the mirror changed. It aged before his eyes, the lines about his mouth and eyes deepening, the hair at his temples graying; a thick, black beard spilling down his chin and onto a deep, burly chest. He found himself looking into the face of his father.

Theodore looked away quickly, squeezing his eyes shut. "No. I do not wish to see that. Take it away."

"Very well," said Craddosche, and the mirror disappeared somewhere in his cloak. The stranger moved in front of Theodore's chair and cupped his face in an oddly intimate fashion, tilting the boy's chin to look up into those strange reddish eyes. Theodore did not like the feel of the Wizard's graceful fingers across his skin. The gentle caress made the tiny hairs on the nape of his neck stand on end.

"Tell me then. What is in your mind?"

In an instant, angry thoughts came flooding back into him. How he despised the townspeople. How they in turn despised him. How he loathed his cold, heartless father even still while in the grave. And how he loathed himself most of all.

"You are a very angry boy," said Craddosche, "with a very angry mind. You are angry at those around you. They pander to you, they fawn on you, but they care nothing for you. They swear loyalty to you, but are absent in the darkness of the night, when your mind is poisoned and alone."

Craddosche's long fingers began to stroke Theodore's cheeks in time with the rhythm of the smooth words he spoke. To and fro, to and fro. Something deep within the boy's chest twisted at the Wizard's touch. And yet he was soothed. As if falling into a deep, dreamless sleep. A sleep more peaceful than he had ever known.

"Where are they when you are drowning in your thoughts of misery for endless hours until the morning comes? They are asleep. At rest. But not you. Never you. You are abandoned. You are alone. You have no rest, for you are damned. With none but your games and chessmen to witness your wild visions of torment in the Pale Room."

Theodore could not fight back the tears that filled his eyes at these words. He was alone; penance for the harm he had done. For what had happened to his mother. No one dared say so to his face, but he saw the accusation in their eyes. And in the eyes of his father as well.

"You despise them," said the stranger.

"I despise them," he murmured.

"You wish to punish them."

"I wish to punish them."

"I can give you the power to do so," soothed Craddosche, "They will share in your pain. In the night, they shall be hexed and alone as you have been."

Something pricked in the back of Theodore's mind. "But...*How?*"

The Wizard brought out a glass vial from his wrappings. In it swirled what looked like water. "Pour a drop of this potion upon the Royal Crown of your forefathers, then lie in the bed of your birth as you sleep for one night. Then they will suffer in the fall of night as you have suffered."

The stranger's smile faded. Theodore started as one disturbed from some deep slumber. Craddosche tipped his head slightly to one side, the potion that would seem to end Theodore's torment (or else share it) in his extended palm.

"Is this not what you have wished for in the night?"

The boy eagerly took the little vial from the stranger, putting it in his pocket.

Everything in the room stilled as he gazed back into the red eyes of the Wizard Craddosche. The pain in his heart dulled and disappeared. He was meant to be alone, but it no longer seemed to matter.

"Good sir...your payment," he said suddenly. He stood, scurrying to the night table drawer to fetch a small sack of gold coins. When he turned back, the stranger had vanished. The room was empty and silent, save for the soft crackle of the fire.

He stood amidst his fallen castle of cards, gazing at the vial in the firelight. The liquid glimmered crystal clear as ordinary spring water. He may have just been deceived, he supposed. But then, stranger took no payment.

As King Theodore Ulysses of the Throne of Thom lie down to sleep, his father's heavy gold crown upon his head, he did not even question himself once as to what would become of any of this.

*　　*　　*　　*

*"Tear for tear and bone for bone*
*Wounded minds will bleed alone;*
*Waking moon and sleeping sun*
*Thread by thread combine to one."* - A Night Hex, carved into Ferrious' tombstone at Haveny. It is unknown who carved the verse into the stone, but it is believed that its purpose was to foretell the return of the Warlock King from the land of the dead, to seek his revenge. The King and Queen had the verse immediately removed, and relocated the dead warlock's corpse to a secret location.

*"A man that is deaf and blind sees not nor hears not the voices of the dead. And in this, he may defeat them."*- A Hero Thou Art

*　　*　　*　　*

It was a quiet night when the strangeness of the reign of the new King of Thom began. And years later, Kulbit would always remember the nightmarishness of it in unexpected little snatches. He had never had a nightmare before that night, so the event was to be a novel one etched in his memory forever.

He was snuggled up nicely in his bed, dreaming about capturing leprechauns. Funny little things they were, with their riddles and their sparkling pots of gold. Even in his flipped dreams these creatures seemed to outsmart him. The day's work had been a hefty one, and settling into sleep was like sinking into a deep warm bath.

He suddenly awoke with a start. Outside came a shrill scream. He sat up straight in bed and fumbled to light the lantern, then stared about himself puffy-eyed. All was silent, but moments later the scream was heard again. With a silent grunt, Kulbit wriggled out of bed.

Looking down from the hayloft window, he saw Bugger outside, lying on the grass in his nightshirt. He was babbling to himself, rolling and rolling across the ground.

*Blasted fool must be choking, or else his old heart finally failed him. Or perhaps he's had too much whiskey again and has at last gone mad. In any case it's to be more work for me, I'll warrant.*

Grumbling silently to himself, he quickly climbed down the hayloft ladder and rushed outside. As he came to the place where the old man lay, his steps slowed. Bugger was rolling in the grass, his fat arms and legs flailing about, batting and swatting at himself. He was clawing his throat, his dirty fingernails scratching at the skin on his neck, drawing blood.

Kulbit stared. *What the devil...*

"Help me! The Spiders! Get them! Get them!" Bugger was screaming. Kulbit froze. What spiders? Kulbit stepped closer to see that Bugger's white nightshirt was crawling with hundreds of tiny black things. *Spiders indeed! Dear me!*

Kulbit recoiled, his blood running suddenly cold. He did not care much for spiders. The man's red and silver hair and beard seemed a nest of them. Bugger opened his mouth to scream, and spiders came crawling out of his throat, spreading across his face and neck in black waves. The ruddy skin seemed to move, odd shaped lumps rolling about beneath, deforming his face; the spiders escaping from out of his nose as well.

*Good gracious...They're under his skin...*

*"Please! They're behind my eyes! It hurts! It hurts... Help meeeeerrggh..."*

Bugger's screams garbled away into wet gurgling as his throat filled. He began to heave and choke, vomiting spiders and food and mucus onto the grass. The expelled spiders scurried from the grass back up his arms and the front of his nightshirt, scrambling for a way back in through his eye sockets, his mouth and his nose. Bugger clawed madly at his face.

Terror tore through Kulbit's chest as the old man's fingers broke through his own eyelids, and he began to tear away at his own face. His fingers found their way into his mouth, and he pulled at his cheeks harshly, turning his mouth into a ghastly grin. There came a tearing sound, and the sides of his mouth tore apart.

Underneath was a grotesque grinning mask of teeth, muscle and bone. Shards of the old man's cheek fell into the grass like pieces of uncooked pork. Spiders' legs began emerging from the holes of his eye sockets like a bird hatching forth from an eggshell.

Kulbit felt a familiar dizziness settle over him, as if he was watching himself from the outside as he rushed into the barn and grabbed a bucket from the hook on the wall. He hadn't the faintest idea of what exactly it was that he was doing. But something inside of him knew that it would not matter what he did as long as he had done *something*.

He filled the bucket from the horses' water trough and sprinted back out to the front of the stables. Bugger was lying on the grass, a struggling black mass of blood, torn flesh, nightclothes and spiders.

*WAKE UP!*

Kulbit heaved the full bucket over his head and splashed the cold water onto Bugger. The spiders instantly began to scatter, disappearing into the grass. Kulbit ran back to the horses' trough and refilled the bucket, splashing the old man a second time. By the third bucket of water the spiders were gone. Vanished, as if they had never been. Bugger sat dripping wet and trembling in the grass, coughing.

His face was whole and unharmed. There was not a trace of blood or flesh to be seen anywhere on the ground. Kulbit dropped the empty bucket and collapsed next to him in the grass, panting. After a moment, the two stared at one another with wide eyes. Kulbit helped Bugger to his feet.

"I-I was sleeping, and I've no notion where they came...How did I get out here? I thought I was dreaming, I really *was* dreaming at first. But they was real...You saw them, didn't ya now...They was *all real,*" Bugger gasped. Kulbit nodded slowly. He offered the shaken old man his arm. His own heart was still throbbing in his chest.

Old Bugger suddenly froze, holding Kulbit's shoulders. His face leaned toward Kulbit's, his cloudy blue eyes staring deeply into the boy's. Kulbit had never seen him look so old and frail before, standing there in his soaked nightshirt.

"Boy...Y'saved my life...Thank you. You're a good 'un, really. I know you never seemed to add too much before, but I see you're really a good 'un all in all. I mean that, from the bottom of my ol' heart," he said thickly. Bugger grabbed the sides of Kulbit's face and leaned in so close the boy could smell a thick stench of whiskey (and vomit) in his dirty red beard. He kissed the boy's forehead. Kulbit smiled weakly, patting Bugger's arm.

His mind could hardly comprehend what he had just seen let alone the old man's words, and all he could think of now was how much nicer it would be indoors and out of the eerie moonlight. He eagerly tugged the old man in the direction of the cottage.

Kulbit sat Bugger in front of the fire wrapped in a warm blanket. He put the kettle on for tea. *What is happening here? What is the meaning of all of this? Am I dreaming?*

"There's witch's trouble afoot," said Bugger, staring with wild eyes. The light of the fire made sharp shadows across his face and beard that deepened the wrinkles about his eyes and the pockmarks of his drunkard's cheeks. White lightening flashed silently outside. "Mark my words, boy, there's a night hex in the air. I feels it in my bones."

Kulbit merely shrugged vaguely in reply. He knew nothing of night hexes and witches and whatnot. Nor did he wish to. Ideas like those made his stomach lurch.
*This is like a dream...Perhaps I am still in bed...*

"Best to stay in. Stay in and stay alert. Virgin bless us, Father have Mercy. The devil's on a romp tonight; old Haddus Half Foot's dancin' in his merry round."

Old Bugger babbled and blessed himself as he sipped his tea. Soon after, Kulbit was helping him ease into his bed.

"Y'saved my life. I dunn' want no harm to come to you, boy. You're a hero...You saved me...You saved me..."

After a bit Bugger's mouth sagged, his head tipping to the pillow and he was soon fast asleep, snoring loudly. Kulbit closed his eyes. What had happened? Exactly what had he just seen?

As he hastened back to the hayloft, his mind flailed helplessly like a blind man in the dark. Where on earth had all of those spiders come from? And where did they disappear to? And what of the old man's wounds? His face was entirely peeled clean off the bone, his eyes none more than red, wet holes. Kulbit had seen it. Perhaps he should keep the lantern lit and read while snuggled under the nice warm covers. That would calm his nerves a bit. This was all far too strange for reason. Night hexes, spiders. He did not wish to think on these things. He'd run away into his imagination as usual. He chose a book from the makeshift book shelf over his hay bed.

*It was merely a phantom dream. In my waking my mind was fast asleep, and in that I thought I had seen the horror...A mere phantom dream...*

Without meaning to, he fell asleep with his face pressed between the pages of the book as the light of the lantern eventually sputtered and died.

The next morning greeted him with a stiff neck. Wincing, he sat up as the pages of his book peeled off of his cheek. He rubbed his face and gazed bleary eyed about him, then froze. He could tell by the light streaming in from the window that the morning was far later than he realized. He leaped out of bed and dressed. He was sure to catch it this time. He rushed down the ladder and out the door tucking his shirt into his dungarees and fumbling to pull his boots on. *Blast blast blast!!*

It wasn't until he came to the main lobby of the empty stable house to get his list of morning chores that he remembered the strangeness of the night before. *But it was a dream...It was not truly real, of course.*

Bugger was nowhere to be found. Jared and the other stable boys must have gone off to mess about their own business without the Head Groom. It was not uncommon, for the old man was known to lose himself in a bottle or two of whiskey and go missing the morning after. But as Kulbit stood beneath the gray morning sky, a current of worry washed through him. The image of the old man peeling his face away in the grass danced within his mind's eye. Perhaps he had better go and see if Bugger was all right.

He arrived at the head groom's cottage and raised a purple fist to knock on the door. He heard a loud snore from within and eased. If Bugger was well enough to make a sound such as that, he would be well enough indeed. Kulbit thought of the eerie shadows that played across the old man's face, and the even more eerie words he spoke of about the devil and midnight hexes, and decided it was best to leave Bugger be.

He went about the chores on his own, all that morning his mind lost in a fog. He did not know what he had seen the night before, or if it was not entirely a thing of dreams. But there was no use sitting about wondering when four of the horses needed re-shoeing, and three of the eastern stables were due for a mucking.

*     *     *     *

*"Fear always outnumbers dangers"*- A Hero Thou Art

*     *     *     *

Kulbit had finished the long day's work alone. He had grown so weary that he did not bother with pumping and heating water for a bath. After taking his supper, he decided he would prefer to retire early. He climbed ladder to his loft yawning widely and nearly jumped out of his skin with fright.

Snoring loudly on the other side of the loft in a pile of hay was Bugger, curled up like a child. When the light of Kulbit's lantern shone over his face, he awoke with a start. His eyes were dark rimmed and sunken as he gazed up at the boy pleadingly.

"You saved me...I-I wanted to be close by in the night...in case the spiders come again..."

Throughout that dreary, quiet day Kulbit had tried to push the night before out of his mind, but at the mention of the spiders a dizzy rush of strange sensations gripped his heart.

*Drunk again...That is all...And now he's gone and had a fright, and expects me to look after him...*

Kulbit did not fully understand the sense in it, but he was so weary and the night so still, he simply nodded, put out the lantern, and lay down on his own bed. He forced his mind to think of merry things and dropped off into a heavy sleep in moments.

He dreamed of standing on the prow of a sailboat. There were seagulls overhead, their rusty screams piercing the clear blue sky. Where was he sailing off to? He did not know, but he was ready for the adventure. *This is how dreams are meant to feel. As if they're under your control,* he thought. Nothing so much as the night had been before.

The cries of the birds grew. He suddenly realized how much the cries sounded like that of a screaming woman. The great ship rocked more and more, the sounds of the waves crashing loudly against the starboard and port. Kulbit got the sense that something was not right. This dream was his own, and yet it was pulling away from him as the ocean pulled at the ship.

To and fro, to and fro. He was losing control of it. The dream would not *flip.* The sun grew too bright for him to see anything, but the screams of the white birds overhead intruded in his mind and grew louder and louder.

Kulbit jerked awake, surrounded by the darkness of the hay loft. He started at two glittering points in the dark, then remembered the old man. Bugger sat awake in his pile of hay, the light from the moon outside reflecting in his eyes. He was trembling.

"It's happenin'...It's happenin' again... Another night of hexin', another night of dreamin'...Best to stay here," he whispered. Kulbit thought he had never seen the old man look as pale as in the scarce light of the moon shining in from the window. The heaviness from Kulbit's dream had yet to fully leave him.

It took him a moment to realize that he could still hear the cries of the gulls. But they were not birds. It was a woman, real and screaming outside. He lit the lantern and gazed out of the window into the silence of the night. Perhaps he had imagined it.

Moments later, his blood chilled at the sound of another scream. He held the lantern high. It seemed to be coming from the old gravel lane south of the stable. That was the path he took to visit the Butterberry Estate. He liked the wealthy Butterberrys, and often earned himself extra coin babysitting for the Missus.

"The night hex isn't coming here, boy, no need to fret," came Buggers voice so close to Kulbit's ear that he nearly dropped the lantern. "We'll be the lucky ones tonight. Let the devil bother someone else a while. 'S none of our business. None of our business. Virgin bless us, Father have Mercy..." Bugger walked stiffly back to the pile of hay and sat, blessing himself, and fell back asleep.

Kulbit bit his lip, wondering if he should investigate. There was a dreamy strangeness in the air that reminded him of the calm before a summer storm. Old Bugger's warning echoed in his ear. He supposed that whatever was happening at the Butterberry Estate was indeed none of his own concern, and in the stiffness of the air there was something larger than even his strange dream-flipping mind could comprehend. The night before Bugger had called Kulbit a hero.

Hero. Such a delightful word, despite it coming from the old fool's mouth. It was this word that he thought of as he pulled up his dungarees, laced his boots and began finding his way down the ladder, past the sleeping horses' stalls and outside.

He stood with his lit lantern, straining his eyes to see down the lane as it sloped upward into darkness. All was silent. The air was still and strange. Kulbit shivered as goose pimples grew up his arms and down his back. Perhaps they *had* imagined the screaming. After a longer moment had passed, he turned back to the stables. He was nearing the back entry when he heard the cold sound of distant screams once more.

*Go to bed. Simply turn and go to bed, as Bugger said to do. It is not your business...*

*You're ma' hero, it all be true...*the fat old groom had also said. What kind of a hero would run to bed and hide under the covers when someone is in of need of assistance? After that idea came to mind, he could not turn back.

*Oh blast blast blast and bother the stupidity of it all. This is not a silly adventure book. I should just go back to sleep.* So of course, Kulbit slowly began to walk down the gravel lane. He quickened his pace when he crossed the little board bridge over the creek. By the time he reached the elegant farmhouse estate, he was running. The screams grew louder.

Mrs. Butterberry was standing on the lawn in her nightgown, wringing her hands anxiously, her golden hair loose and disheveled about her face. When she spotted the light of Kulbit's lantern, she came running across the lawn looking like a wild banshee. Kulbit recoiled as she grabbed his shoulders.

"Please help! My baby! He's falling! He's falling!" she cried. Kulbit followed her gaze to the roof.

Little Bertrand was suspended in the air above the roof of the farmhouse, kicking and screaming. His hair and nightclothes fluttered upward, as if he were plummeting from a great height. But he was not coming down. He hung in midair, spinning and crying. Kulbit rubbed his eyes twice before he could understand exactly what he saw. Mrs. Butterberry was right, in a sense. Her little boy was falling, and would be falling forever... for he was *falling in place.* The child's screams made his skin prickle.

Familiar dizziness enveloped Kulbit's head, the same he had felt it the night before as he filled the bucket with water from the horse's trough. He hadn't known it then, but knew this feeling well now. It was a *him* feeling. A purple feeling. He was outside of himself, watching once more. It did not matter what was done, as long as he did *something.*

*This is...A dream to be flipped...Perhaps it is a bit different from when I am in repose, but I daresay I may be able to do something to assist after all...*

Kulbit ran into the farmhouse and clambered up the stairs. He dashed to the window of one of the bedrooms and could just see little Berty. He reached out for Bertrand's foot but could not come close. Mrs. Butterberry watched the purple boy climb out onto the gabled roof. He reached again for Berty, but couldn't quite get at him.

Kulbit had always had a good head for heights. But of course this was an altogether stranger sort of situation, and he felt his head swim. He tried not to look down but told himself this too late. He could see how high he was and make out Mrs. Butterberry on the lawn, looking like a tiny doll.

*Steadfast, now. Tread lightly,* he told himself. Kulbit reached, stretching as far as he could, standing on his toes. His fingers just brushed Berty's sleeve. He reached again...

Mrs. Butterberry screamed as she watched Kulbit lose his balance and tip forward. He fell, just catching the edge of the roof with one hand.

Kulbit shut his eyes as he dangled from the three story farmhouse by his fingertips, shocks of fear racing down his spine. His hands moistened as the rusty edge of the roof bit painfully into his fingers. He was going to fall, but not like the little Butterberry boy. He was going to hit the ground. *Fear not, be a hero and flip it. Be a hero. Just as I have always done in my dreams. Flip the bloody scene over...*

He swung his other hand up and grasped the roof. The metal of the roof's edge bit cruelly into his fingers. He heaved his arms up over the edge, bloodying his elbow, and after a moments struggle managed to get a leg over as well. He pulled himself up and flung his body at the window. Mrs. Butterberry watched Kulbit's boots disappear within her bedroom window.

In a moment, he returned with a rope. Tying it in a loop, he swung it in a large circle above his head, as he had done many times working in the stable. With a skillful pitch, he cast the loop of rope at the floating child. It landed neatly about Bertrand's waist. Bracing his foot against the gable, Kulbit pulled and pulled and little Bertrand Butterberry was yanked from the air and into the older boy's arms. Kulbit then awkwardly carried the frightened child into the window. Moments later Mrs. Butterberry had burst into the bedroom and was sitting between them on the bed, hugging her son and crying.

"Oh Monsieur Kulbit, how can I ever repay you!" she was saying. She threw her arms around Kulbit's neck and much to his surprise began kissing his face, hugging his head, and almost smothering him in her bosom. He gave her a red-faced grin when her gratitude finally began to ebb long enough for him to breathe.

"You saved my Berty. Blessed you, boy. The hand of God is upon you!" she cried, kissing his aching fingers. She led him downstairs and dressed the tiny cuts on them and bandaged his elbow.

It was not until after Kulbit found himself sitting in front of a plate cookies and chilled milk in a crystal glass at Mrs. Butterberry's kitchen table that he came aware of his mind, the pleasant dizziness lifting. She was sitting across from him, staring in silence. There was a strange glow in her dark eyes that made Kulbit worry. Berty was sitting very close to Kulbit, nibbling on a cookie.

Finally, Mrs. Butterberry spoke. "There is something quite wrong. I felt it all today, since the night before; something odd has happened that I simply cannot fathom. Or perhaps I am going mad...Am I going mad, do you suppose?"

Kulbit stared at his hands, grateful for once for his silent tongue. There was nothing he could say to this, for he had felt it as well. The spiders. The strange heaviness in the gray sky. Mrs. Butterberry began to weep softly, and Kulbit looked up. He caught her eyes with a steady gaze. He shook his head slowly.

*If you have gone mad I suppose I have gone along with you, Missus. As well as Bugger. This is all in the air and so very much like one of my dreams. Only...I am not fully in control. Perhaps the old drunk was right. Perhaps there is a hex in the night.*

He looked out the frilly kitchen window, which overlooked the lay of the town. A silent streak of lightening made a momentary crack across the yellowish black sky. He closed his eyes and sighed, and just then something, a coil perhaps somewhere in his deep mind shifted. Something in the air seemed to fade. He smiled and looked again at Mrs. Butterberry's confused face. She had felt it as well. Something had changed.

*I have seen this change many a time before. If in a dream this night has faded, in this moment it would be about perchance to shift and blend anew. This dream of falling in place has finished; a new dream in rebirth. For dreams live only in a moment, and in a moment's breath be at an end. Perhaps the next is to be another adventure, stranger than the two before it! Spiders and climbing a farmhouse roof are all well and fine, but not so much fun as slaying one's adversary, or some big horrible monster of a sort. If I have gone mad, and she has gone mad, and old Bugger has gone mad...I suppose it is best for one to have a merry time at it...*He smiled at her tenderly, and in his strange state of mind had quite forgotten that no one can hear the thoughts in his head but himself.

He rose from the table and patted Berty's fluffy blonde head with absent affection, bowed and started for the door. Mrs. Butterberry grabbed his arm fearfully.

"Wait...Do you mean to leave us? Please...Where are you going?"

*Not to fret, dear lady. I am certain all of this will come out in the wash at the end of things. In the meantime, I have become quite weary and would do well to rest me. Perhaps tomorrow night shall lead us into another adventure! Good night, little Berty. Mind your mother.*

He hailed them merrily and walked from the door and warm glow of the Butterberry estate in the same mental fog that seemed to keep him afloat all that day. The two silhouettes of Mrs. Butterberry and her son stood still as they anxiously watched him disappear into the night, the Missus wringing her hands once more.

*I say, this is more exciting than any flipped dream, is it not? I wonder how any of this is truly happening at all? And perhaps at any moment I shall wake and find that morning has come.* As Kulbit strolled he grinned to himself. When he returned to his loft, Bugger watched him eagerly from the darkness.

"What was it? What didja see, boy?"

Kulbit ignored him, his mind still lost in that light and purple calm, lay down and promptly fell asleep. This night spared him no dreams. For after all that had transpired, he needed none.

\*     \*     \*     \*

Theodore was in the Pale Room once more. He sat in the chair, waiting. He did not weep or scream this time. The room was bitter cold, and Theo's skin grew numb from it. But he sat still, barely breathing. His father's crown was upon his head; his father's dagger hidden at his side. He had done something dreadfully wrong, and he was full aware of the fact. Such a strange thickness in the air. Night and day passed over his mind like a distant dream of a dream. The electric bars overhead buzzed as he tried to remember the days that had passed.

Had they ever happened at all? What had he done with himself all that day? He locked himself in his bedroom the night after he slept on his royal bed with the king's crown upon his head. He could remember nothing...All that came to his mind's view was the two red eyes of the Stranger. The eyes of the Devil Haddus. He had sinned against God and The Virgin. His punishment would be harsh, but he was prepared to pay the price. This was the Pale Room. This was his room. His Hell.

*"Mea Culpa...Mea Culpa...Mea Culpa..."* he muttered, blessing himself.

*If I appear to accept the punishment, I may win at this game yet...*

The door burst open and his father stood in the darkness. Dirt clung to his royal robes in muddy patches. His hair and beard were white. The skin on his face was rotted, pocked and full of decaying holes. Theodore could see jagged teeth through some of the patches of cheek that were missing. His eyes were like the cold silver discs of a fish.

Flies filled the room, as the smell of rotting fish caused Theodore's eyes and nose to smart.

"Theodore, why have you done this to us?" But the dead king's rotting lips never moved.

Theo shut his eyes, waiting. Every muscle in his body was poised and ready.

"We will punish you, Theodore."

In a blink the king was standing before him in the pale room.

"You will pay for what you have done."

*"Mea Culpa..."*

"You shall die one day. And on that day, you shall be in Hell of Haddus."

Suddenly, the dead king's royal robes were a mass of shadow that filled the room, the air thick and loud with the buzzing of a thousand flies. The shards of skin making up the king's rotted lips pulled back into a grotesque grimace that seemed to cut his head in two halves, his teeth in rows of hundreds of spikes like that of a biter fish. The deathly entity that was once in the image of his father quickly advanced upon Theodore, a thick dark wave.

Distantly, he heard a voice whisper. *"Where lies the Phantom Dreamer...the Dreamer is Lost..."*

With a scream, Theodore drew his father's dagger and lunged forward from his seat, thrusting the bright blade into the darkness that was the entity's chest. The shadows that filled the room seemed to ebb. The dark demon's decaying body fell to the ground of the pale room like a doll of rags.

*"You are not my father, Devil of Haddus!"* he hissed, pulling the blade from the creature's chest.

He stood over the shriveled body triumphantly, watching it bleed. The demon writhed and wailed, its eyes black and staring up at Theodore. He spat again.

"You're nothing but a room. A pale room, and I will not fear you."

Suddenly he heard a soft creak as the door opened again slowly, warmth and sunlight filling the room. The smells of summer caressed his senses. He heard sparrows in the distance.

"Theodore, come outside to the garden and play with me," came his mother's voice as clear and alive as he remembered it when he was very small. He looked at the door and saw it was no longer dark, but looking out into one of the lovely palace gardens.

His mother came trotting into the room, holding his favorite golden ball. She stood before him, as beautiful as he recalled, wearing in her white muslin summer dress. There were flowers in her hair, and her cheeks were flushed from frolicking. She was laughing, tossing the ball in the air, but when she saw him she froze. Her smile disappeared.

"Theodore? What...What on earth has happened?" she asked, breathless.

King Theodore stood in front of his mother, a hands dripping red with blood. He looked down and saw his father sprawled on the floor, alive and breathing, but clutching his bleeding chest. His eyes were filled with tears and disbelief as he gazed up at his son.

"What have you done?" Theodore's mother cried. The golden ball bounced away, the musical chimes within singing merrily. Theodore felt time slow as he watched it glimmer in the air for a moment, bounce, then disappear under a table. He turned his eyes to his mother in horror, afraid to look yet not able to resist. She cried out as she rushed to her husband's side. She clutched him and kissed his face. His dark blood stained her lovely white dress. Everything inside Theodore seemed to spiral downward. He dropped the dagger.

"Why have you done this?" his mother sobbed. "You brought a dagger here in this room? Why?"

"No… No mother…He was different. He was not Father…He was a demon! I saw him! I-I believed-" Theodore fell to his knees. This was not the way it was meant to happen. This was not what he had planned.

"My son. My son…" the dying king gasped. He reached his hand out and in caressing his son's cheek, left a smudge of red. His eyes closed. After a moment of agonized breathing, a wet rattling came in his chest, he was dead. The queen wailed clutching her husband's corps to her. Her screams made Theodore's ears ring. He held his head.

*"Murderer!"* The queen rushed at him and slapped Theodore's face. He fell back into the white damask chair, staring in wide eyed terror.

*What have I done?*

King Theodore awoke from the dream with a cry. Shaking, he dragged his fingers through his dark, dirty hair. He reached for the golden bell over his bed.

"Magdolyn! Hot milk!"

## AUTHOR'S NOTE

*She closed her eyes and allowed her fingertips to tap across the keyboard of the computer, the words spilling from her head onto whatever media was there to catch it.*

I've always wanted to be a character in a novel. I used to scribble across notebook paper little descriptions of myself; the bandage on my knee, the way my nails were always bitten down to the raw pink meat. What my room looked like, or the sounds I can hear in the moment. The people around me. Then I'd write about the things that were on my mind, but say them as if I were talking about a stranger. Instead of "I", say "she". It's easier. Makes you hate yourself less.

I can think in words when I write. Normally I have a head of guttural instincts, vague feelings and impressions too base to be understood. Images and sounds flutter about in the murkiness of my Waking Mind, disturbing the silence of the Sleeping Mind below. Rushing thoughts like butterflies in the wind.

*She typed. Now she was getting fancy and descriptive. Maybe she could be a writer someday. Or at least, do a pretty good job of pretending to be one.*

These worlds are too much for me. Writing about them is the only way to remain properly in this one, even if I'm not really good at realizing where I am.

26.1224° N, 80.1373° W

**END NOTE**

# Chapter 4

That night as Lord Chauncey stepped down from the carriage in front of his private estate, his eyes strained to see if the lights of the bedroom chambers were lit. They were darkened, and that was good. He stole silently through the servant's entrance, and crept into his study and locked the door. He remained late at the palace proper intentionally. He was hoping the Lady of the House had long gone off to bed. He sat down in his great stuffed chair and shut his eyes. Carolene had been at him again that morning. It seemed to be a ritual as of late.

He was tired and all he wished for at present was a drink. Lord Chauncey stood from the large desk of his private study and crossed the room to the elegantly carved bookshelf that was the east wall. Beneath the shelf second to the bottom he pressed a latch, and a little compartment disguised as a book slid open. He pulled out a crystal bottle filled with amber liquid. This was his secret. No one knew anything of it. He placed the bottle to his lips and felt goose pimples prickle his skin as the burning liquor poured down his throat. He shivered with satisfaction as the familiar warm glow began in his belly.

"Now, do let's be civilized," he scolded himself. He opened his desk drawer and found a tall glass. He filled the glass to the brim, and sat down, sipping thoughtfully.

Why did Madame Carolene hold him in such contempt? He did not know why in most cases, but to silence her he would simply apologize, and that seemed to stop her tongue wagging. It was for this reason he would always apologize. Yet he had grown tired of it.

He tracked ashes from the hearth. He had forgotten to let the old cat into the bedroom. His breath stank of corn whiskey. He would beg forgiveness for all of these petty crimes, even if he had not committed them. He knew that he must do penance. Penance because he was no longer a father. And because he had failed Ana.

He poured himself a second drink. There was a cold strangeness in the air this night. He was trying to warm himself up. It was merely a little something to help him sleep, he had always said, and being such a powerful man filled the mind with such never ending worries. It was near impossible to quiet his thoughts.

"Time for a sip, for a nippy nip nip, for a drippy drip drip for the Sandman's Ship..." He muttered the old drinking rhyme to himself before downing a third glass. A rusty cough erupted from his throat, and some bone between his shoulders gave an odd *ping!*

He removed his white wig, passing a hand over his bald head. The room seemed to blur slightly. He felt old. He placed his palms upon his oaken desk, gazing at the great mirrored armoire across the room. He looked harder that he had ever looked. What was he?

In the oval reflection across the study, a small old man sat at an oversized desk, his scrawny arms spread across the dark wood. He was a sad looking thing, older than his years. His thin frame swam in his Statehood Robes. His hard black eyes stared back at him. They filled with un-spilled tears, and his face crumpled like a child's. What was he?

He was the High Lord of the Seigneurs Du Cordovan, Head of the Parliament of Thom. He was a very great man. He had worked quite hard to come to this position of power, and decided the fates of many men, sending them to the stocks for treason, or awarding them titles of nobility. There were those who feared him. There were those who honored him.

He was also a father...once. He had also been a grandfather, but only for a moment. That moment passed as quickly as it came. And the twenty-two years he enjoyed calling himself a proud father passed along with it. At once, all was gone from him. His little girl. His grandson. Both gone. There was a light tinkling sound as the bottle poured into the crystal glass once more.

She died giving birth to her first child. The boy died two hours later. He had blue eyes. Midwife said that his eyes might turn brown like his mother's someday. But that day was never to come. Chauncey stared at the tired old man in the mirror. He would apologize to Carolene. Apologize forever if need be. Not for any one transgression, but because he was not a father anymore, great and powerful man that he was believed to be. He could not save his only daughter. His legacy would die with him.

"Ana..." His own voice startled him. He cried silently, burying his face in his arms.

*     *     *     *

No one had heard from His Royal Wretchedness the King for two days. He had locked himself alone in his room, and even Magdolyn was sent away. He would see no one, and all supposed he had been feeling ill. No horrors came to the city of Post that night. A thunderless storm threatened in the night sky, a thick blanket of clouds hiding the silver face of the moon. The king was wakeful.

Theodore cowered underneath his bed, bits of dust and cobweb clinging to his hair and cheeks as he lay upon the cold stone floor, sucking his thumb and crying bitterly. Strings of mucus hung from his nostrils. He hugged his knees with his other arm, shivering violently.

*"Theodore."*

"No," he whimpered under his breath. "No, no, no, no, no. I cannot hear you, I cannot hear you."

The large painting of his mother flickered red from the glow of the fireplace. Silent lightening cracked across the sky, filling the royal bedchamber with a flash of cold brilliance.

*"Theodore."*

"No, no, no, no, no you are dead, *you are dead* and I am awake. This cannot be possible. I cannot hear you, I am awake…"

His nightmare from the night before had followed him. The Pale Room had followed him.

*"Theodore."*

"Stop it."

Theodore jammed his fingers deep into his ears, his long fingernails digging painfully into the tender canals.

"I am awake. I am awake, I am awake, and you cannot be here! This is not your room. This is not the Pale Room! *Mea Culpa, Mea Culpa, Mea Culpa…you cannot be here!*" he babbled.

*"Theodore,"* came the voice inside his head. Plugging his hearing did no good. The voices of the dead are never heard by the ear. They tormented the young king throughout the night.

*     *     *     *

His second day of being a hero proved to be more of a challenge to Kulbit than he had realized. Kulbit awoke to a silent flash of lightening that raced brightness across the sky and into his window, and opened his eyes. The tiny blue hairs upon his forearms stood on end. The night before once more seemed like a dream. Kulbit felt a grin spread across his face. He turned to his side and if he had not he been a mute, what a frightened yelp he would have given. Standing over his bed with a wooden tray stood Bugger. Old Bugger smiled his gap-toothed grin, oblivious that the wide-eyed boy was clutching his chest to steady his heart.

"Good mornin'! Good mornin'! How's my hero feelin'? Got ya some nice breakerfest here for an early start on the day!" he crowed.

Kulbit swallowed, blinking up at the fat man who stood grinning at him. Kulbit smiled back at him feebly and rose. After a moment of staring in silence, he realized that Bugger had no intention of leaving the loft so the boy may dress in private. He undressed awkwardly under the gaze of the old drunkard, and reached for his dungarees, which were hanging in their usual place on the support beam by his mattress of straw.

"Here now lemme get that for ya," said Bugger, snatching them and handing them to Kulbit. He slowly took them and realized then that this was to be a very long day indeed.

Bugger followed him about, "helping" him with his chores for the rest of that day, but mostly made the boy stand and watch while he did them himself. Kulbit never realized how strange it might be to be among people who fancy you a hero on an ordinary day. How they would stare at you with adoring eyes and not allow you to go about your own business.

He wished the old fool would let him alone. He enjoyed his work. It gave him a sense of usefulness. He managed to steal away from Bugger when several wagons of hay arrived from the King's fields and was grateful, if anything at least to have the chance to hear himself think a moment. And he had plenty to think on. His mind drifted to the past two nights.

What he imagined as only a dream was indeed real. He could not explain it, but what was there to explain? He would not have been able to make sense of it. But it had happened. And even after everything, after all the outrageousness that had occurred, the hay still needed pitching, and Kippers was the last who was in need of a new set of shoes.

As he filed smooth the bottom of the foal's hoof, he wondered in his mind to the young horse if perhaps this was all magick.

*Magick? What is a magick?* asked Kippers in the boy's mind.

*Well it's...to be precise, it is...well goodness, how am I to explain magick to a horse? It is a thing that is mystical and difficult to understand...*

The young horse snorted. *I find it mystical and difficult to understand why you humans insist upon putting funny bits of metal things on my feet...*

Kulbit chuckled silently. *I had read about magickal things before; tales where magnificent things happen to ordinary people.*

*Are you an ordinary people then?* Kippers asked. Kulbit paused.

*I've always thought so.*

He was only a stable boy after all, even if he was purple and held imaginary conversations with horses in his mind. Sweat began to trickle down the small of his back as Kulbit finished up Kipper's shoeing and headed outside to begin pitching a wagon load of hay into the loft of the south stable. It was hard work, but he welcomed the simplicity of it in contrast with the stranger sorts of ideas like magick.

Bugger had been so tiresome that morning he was glad to keep busy and away from him. It was the old man's eyes that disturbed him the most. He was little accustomed to being stared at in such a way, as if he were the Arch Angel Gabriel or Saint Anthony come down with sacks of gold from the gates of heaven, as some of the country folk still believed would happen someday. Kulbit whistled to himself as he worked hard until supper.

*       *       *       *

The sun was setting in the horizon, but the regular beautiful sight of it sinking into the west could not be seen. The only light that came from the murky sky was an occasional flicker from what seemed a rainless silent storm. Cats stared fixedly out the windows as they crouched on sills, ready to leap and hide at a moment's notice. The air was thick again, and though no one in the palace proper said so, there was a tension that could only be described as ominous. None had seen His Royal Majesty for a time now, and this enough was a frightening thing, especially to his old nurse. She had been paid to worry, of course, and was determined to do the best at her duty as she could. Not a sound came from his locked chambers. Finally, after working up as much courage as she could muster, Magdolyn rapped timidly upon the king's door.

"Poppet?" she called hesitantly.

Silence.

"Poppet, you must come out. Haven't you had anything to eat? Maggie knows Poppet feels icky, but Poppet hasn't sent for a tray in almost two days now."

There was no reply.

"Please, Poppet. Open the door. Let Nursie in."

Nothing.

"Poppet, are you sleeping? Haven't you slept enough?" she cooed. Suddenly, she heard muffled laughter on the other side of the door. It began slowly, and rose to a frantic shriek. The sound of it gave Magdolyn's bones a chill.

*"Sleeping?* You all believed I was *sleeping?"* came the shrill voice of the boy behind the door. "I was certainly not *sleeping! But mother thinks so, does she not? Mother certainly thinks so!"*

The shrieking laughter began again. Magdolyn stood in the opulent corridor, wringing her hands for a good moment as the king's laughter assaulted her from beyond the door. Soon it sounded like choking sobs, and she thought the king might be vomiting. But the sounds wouldn't stop. It shrilled on despite.

"Poppet, you're worrying Nursie. Please..." Magdolyn said. Moments passed and eventually the laughter ebbed away and died. Nothing could be heard from behind the door. "Poppet?"

The old woman stood listening for a long while before deciding perhaps the worst of the boy's tantrum had passed. "If it is best, Maggie will leave you now..."

No reply came.

"Well then...Be good, Little Man. Play your games! That always lifts your spirits," she said, satisfied that saying this would fulfill her duty. Little boys need their privacy, after all. The old woman did not admit to herself that the true reason why she returned to her own apartments was because she did not wish to be present if that horrible laughter came back. She pretended not to notice that she was near running as she hastened through her own door and bolted it shut.

*      *      *      *

That night, as Kulbit settled in to bed, Bugger came climbing up the loft steps. Kulbit stared at him in the light of the lantern. "In case...In case the night hexes come back..."

Lightening flashed again outside without a sound, and Kulbit sighed as Bugger settled himself in the pile of hay once more. The air had again become thick. Kulbit lay in his bed turned out the lantern. Moments later, a soft voice called up from the stables below. The light of another lantern shone up between the floorboards.

"Monsieur?"

Kulbit rose and stood at the top of the ladder. Bugger plucked at his elbow, startling him. "What if it's a trick? A magickal apparition, come to torment us!" he whispered. Kulbit shook his head and climbed down.

*Honestly. For such a horrid bully, what a ninny that old man is! Why, it's merely the voice of a woman...I say, it's Mrs. Butterberry...And little Berty as well. What on earth could they want here at the stables?*

Mrs. Butterberry curtsied humbly. "Please, Monsieur Kulbit. Berty awoke from a nightmare, and my husband is still away at sea. We were frightened that the night hexes may return. You are a Tool of God, and there is no dwelling safer than that in the presence of one of His Chosen Vessels...May we stay the night here with you? In case anything should happen?"

Kulbit blinked. In her eyes shone the strange glow that he had seen in them the night before. Little Berty gazed up at him hopefully. Outside, the silent lightening turned the strangely yellow sky into flickering cracked glass.

*It has returned. I feel it in the air once more, like a thick fog. The evil will come again this night. It is only a matter of when...and where.*

Kulbit nodded and followed them up the ladder to the loft. There were other piles of hay for them to settle into, and in a moment the four of them were huddled in the dour light of the two lanterns as lightening flashed, straining to listen for the crash of thunder but hearing none.

"Mama...What is happening outside?" whispered Berty.

"It's the Devil come to Thom, and by the purple boy is the only safe place. Virgin bless us, Father have Mercy," whispered Bugger, mostly to himself. The look in his eyes made Kulbit quite uncomfortable. The lightening flashed once more, and for a time all was silent.

Suddenly, the horses below began to whinny and stamp in their stalls uneasily. High up in the loft, the four of them could feel the ground quiver and shake. It was as if some great heavy thing was placing foot falls outside. The foot falls stopped. Kulbit felt his heartbeat throbbing in his ears.

"What is it?" came Berty's thin voice. Silence.

There came the loud cracking sound of a falling tree. Kulbit rose quickly with the lantern, and looked out of the window.

The wooded area east of the stable was silent. Beyond lay one of the lanes that twisted through the marketplace. Kulbit stared at the dark treetops, black triangular shapes against the starless sky. Suddenly, the treetops began to sway, as if some great thing was moving beneath them. It reminded Kulbit how tall grass trembled when the miller's cat was crouching in it out of sight, hunting field mice.

*What on earth?* Kulbit wondered. The ground throbbed with a loud rumble. Kulbit heard a low, deep grunt. The breathing of some great, horrid beast. The trees, cracked and swayed east.

Kulbit felt his heart sink as his thoughts from the night before haunted him.

*Well then. I did say some great and horrible beast or dragon of some sort should prove to be more fun, did I not? Bother me and my stupid sense of adventure...*

Kulbit felt the dizziness come again, the same purple sense of calm, and he knew the time had come. He must again play the hero. Despite his heart beating in his chest, he was smiling as he began to pull on his work boots.

"Wait...Please, Monsieur, where are you going?" Mrs. Butterberry asked feebly. Kulbit merely smiled at her, patting Berty's head.

Now was his time. He knew it more than he knew what was happening about him. He had been waiting for these moments his entire life, and now that the time had come he was in his own. He climbed down the ladder and moments later he was walking to the marketplace. At the sound of screams, he began to sprint.

*How frightening it is to be a hero! It is a horrid dragon, as I had foreseen upon last night. Dreams often follow a sort of pattern, and once you learn how to manage them it is not all that difficult to tell what is to come...Well, nothing more for it but to see it through.*

Kulbit reached the main road and stared at the chaos before him. The great beast was even more frightening than he had hoped. It was standing in the center of the crossroads, curling its great body over the Meeting Post, the townspeople scuttling beneath it like little mice. A long serpentine neck curved in the sky with scales glistening like bright steel. Its talons, each the thickness of a man's body, dug and cracked away at the cobblestone. It had the face and teeth of a biter fish, its large cold eyes seeming to glow silver. But the oddest thing Kulbit noticed about the dragon was its tongue. It whipped out of its mouth like that of a frog snatching at flies, stripes of black and white flashing. They reminded Kulbit of the striped stockings he would often see fashionable women wear. The fish faced dragon arched its neck to the sky, chugging steam from its nostrils. With the heat and glow of a blast furnace erupting from its maw, bright fire torched the sky, setting nearby rooftops aflame.

Kulbit stood staring up at the creature in awe. The fish dragon's disc-like eyes seemed to suddenly settle on the tiny purple boy standing in the middle of the road. Its gaping mouth opened wide in a horrific grimace, revealing hundreds of sharp, glittering spikes. It lowered its hideous face down right in front of Kulbit. He could feel the blast of its hot, moist breath.

**"What have we here? A Little Phantom Dreamer..."**

Kulbit thought he heard the fish monster speak, but could not be certain. He gazed into the face of the monster, and in the shining wet glare of the silvery eye he saw his own reflection quite clearly. He saw his purple face, his comical blue curls. He could even make out the stitching on the collar of his shirt.

*"Albert! Albert, come inside!"*

Mr. Bonnaire, the fish merchant, stood a bit away. His wife's screams came from the doorway of their shop. He was also staring up into the face of the dragon. Its cold eyes turned from the purple boy to the old man, its red lips pulling back from daggers of teeth.

*Run...Run!* Kulbit screamed at the old man through his mind, but the merchant was frozen in his place. Without thinking, Kulbit ran toward him. *Be the hero, be the hero, he is going to be killed, he is going to die-*

In one swift motion, the top half of Mr. Bonnaire was caught up in the monster's tongue and between its teeth. With a cracking sound, his struggling legs fell limp, and the bottom half fell to the ground in a red spray. Kulbit stopped in his tracks as crimson rained down upon him from above. Mr. Bonnaire's head and shoulders were neatly clipped off of his body, with red streamers of flesh and innards splattering blood across the cobblestones like a wet mop.

Mrs. Bonnaire screamed as the long, striped tongue whipped out of the monster's mouth and snatched up the rest of her husband's remains. Kulbit watched, awestruck as the old man's boots flopped then disappeared down the dragon's gullet.

Everything around him seemed to slow. His hearing seemed to plug up and none could be heard but a faint ringing in his head. People rushed about, falling all over themselves and trampling each other. But to Kulbit, all was silent. Someone had knocked over a cart of fruit, apples and tomatoes spilling everywhere, a few of them rolling into the crossroads.

In the strange stillness of the chaos, Kulbit stared at a few tomatoes at his feet. He suddenly remembered a good dream he had not very long ago. He reached down and picked up a tomato, the dizziness of the night once again coming to him. A stupidly bemused smirk found its way onto his lips. He was about to do *something* once more.

*You're no monster.... You're nothing but a silly fish. A spoiled, selfish, rotten prince who desperately needs to be taught a lesson in respect and manners.*

**"Little Dreamer…Fear us...We know of you..."**

*I will not. You're a dream and nothing more. A dream to be flipped...*

With a smile, he hurled the tomato into the air, and it flew into mouth of the fish monster. Instantly, all was silent. The dragon had disappeared. As did the flames upon the buildings. Kulbit blinked, staring at the empty space the monster had occupied. There was nothing there save for the empty starless sky and the unharmed rooftops.

*It truly was nothing at all, really. Fancy...*

Huddled on the ground before him was Mr. Bonnaire, whole and alive and screaming with his arms over his head and his knees bent to his chest. The old man's shouts died and he gazed up at Kulbit, confused. Kulbit grinned at him with a nod.

"Albert!" Mrs. Bonnaire came running, pulling her husband to his feet. She dragged him away towards the door of the shop. He was babbling and pointing at Kulbit.

"The boy, Edna...That little purple stable boy...H-He saved my life...*Bless you, boy...God bless you!*" He had said more but the door of the fish shop had closed on the rest.

(Albert Bonnaire, who had once been rumored to spice and salt rotten fish and call it fresh caught, became an honest man since that night, and years later after he had long since sold his fish shop to join the Holy Church of Srye Harbor as a vicar, he would tell all who cared to listen of how God's chosen often come to us all in the unlikely shade of purple.)

Everything in the market place was untouched, as if nothing had happened at all. After a moment or so, the townspeople realized this and stopped screaming and running about. Everyone stood in the moonlight, bewildered. Lightening flashed silently overhead. Kulbit gazed at the empty space in the starless sky where the great monster had been.

*I daresay that had been a right jolly thrill, had it not?* The dreamy grin never left his face. He did not understand most of what had happened, and was certain it had something to do with the Devil Haddus and all a manner of midnight hexes and something to do with the end of the world. But for goodness sake, he never dreamed bad magick could be so bloody satisfying. He dug his hands into the pockets of his nightclothes and strolled back toward the Royal Stable Houses, whistling.

As he walked past, the townspeople gaped at the strange mute purple boy who was sometimes called Lilac Lily All Nice and Frilly, and had once been hung by his underpants at the Post…the strange purple boy who had just slain a terrible fish faced dragon with naught but a tomato and saved all of their lives. When Kulbit returned to the stables, Mrs. Butterberry and Bugger watched silently as he took off his boots. No one bothered to ask any questions, and it was not as if the mute could give any answers. Kulbit settled into his cozy mattress of hay, smiling to himself. This was a splendid dream flip, even if it wasn't truly a dream in the strictest sense. Perhaps the best he had ever had yet.

*A Hero. A true Hero…*

\*     \*     \*     \*

The sky was so dark outside, one could hardly believe that it was the eighth hour of the morning, but the grand clock in the main foyer sang its deep throng at the time of day, and breakfast had long been served to the rest of the High Bloods. Magdolyn had a cart sent to her chambers with the fixings to make porridge. She would not have trusted any of the servants to prepare His Majesty's porridge the proper way, and so as always she made it herself in her own apartments.

Poor little Poppet hadn't eaten anything for days now. He came out of his chamber earlier that morning to go for a walk in the nearby wood, his hair hanging before his face as he gazed at the ground. Maggie had seen him from the garden, and watched as he walked briskly into the brush. She wondered if she should go and speak with him, but at the sight of him muttering to himself, that dark look shadowing his gaunt face, she decided he would not like to be bothered.

*It's hard business being a king, and the poor little mansie just wants some fresh air alone,* she told herself, and turned her attention back to her needlepoint. When the young king came out of the foliage carrying a bundle of dry sticks, she smiled to herself. "Little boys love to play at making forts and such. Poppet must be feeling much better now."

It was at this time that she decided to bring him a nice hot bowl of her special sweet porridge. The boy would be certain to work himself up into an appetite after his playtime. Perhaps now he would find time to take some breakfast. She spooned the steaming hot mixture into a bowl and sprinkled it with chocolate shavings. She poured hot milk and honey into an elegant tea cup, and stirred it with a golden spoon. She hummed to herself as she carried the tray to the king's chambers, happy that Poppet felt well enough again to play outside.

"Little Man, I've brought you your favorite..." She stopped short when she noticed wisps of smoke coming from underneath the door. The tray left her hands and crashed to the ground. She frantically pulled at the brass door handle, but it held fast. The King had bolted it. She rushed down the large corridor screaming for the guards.

"His Majesty's rooms! They're a-fire! They're a-fire! Someone *please help!*"

Three armed and uniformed men came running down the great hall. The largest of these rammed his shoulder against the cherry wood door of the royal bed chamber. The door held true, and the wisps of smoke were now clouds floating up to the high arched ceiling.

Magdolyn's skin crawled as she once again began to hear the shrill sound of King Theodore's laughter.

The guard lifted his heavy booted foot and kicked with all his might. The wood groaned, his boot leaving bright scuff marks on the dark finished grain, but the door remained solid. The piercing laughter of the boy inside the chamber continued throughout their efforts, frightening Magdolyn to tears.

Before long, one of the guards brought an axe and violently began chopping away at the entrance to the royal bed chamber. When the wood was broken, the guard lifted his big black boot again and kicked. The door crashed and tumbled inward in splinters. A wall of smoke and flashing orange light greeted them, and they all coughed and sputtered as they rushed into the chamber. Magdolyn drew her apron up, covering half of her face as she staggered in behind the guards. The smell of burning wood and fabric stung her eyes and throat.

"*Poppet! Poppet!*" she screamed, muffled through the fabric of her apron. She could see nothing but smoke and hot light. The laughter attacked her ears as it echoed from somewhere within the murky room. As the black smoke wafted out into the corridor, her eyes adjusted.

The king's enormous bed was a mass of flames, the great crimson curtains that hung about it bright with large tongues of fire licking away at the blackened ceiling. Atop the bed in the heart of the fire were stacked chairs, a night table, and the sticks of wood he had gathered that morning from the brush, as his nurse watched and worked her needlepoint. Perched at the very top of this was the great painting of Her Royal Majesty, the deceased Queen Mariah of ThoBromis. The queen sat calmly in the painting as her face bubbled and blistered, succumbing to the fire.

King Theodore stood next to the blazing bed. He was naked from the waist up, wearing naught but a pair of black riding breeches. He was bouncing excitedly on the balls of his bare feet, laughing and pumping his fists into the air.

*"I have been awakened, mother! I am awake!"* he was screaming. *"But not for much longer!"*

Magdolyn stared at him through the smoke. Icy horror curled itself about her old heart. This was her Little Pet, her Poppet; her Little Ducky who could do no wrong. He was her king. And he was the Devil.

*"We shall all be together! You and Father and I and the whole precious kingdom will burn and burn forever!"* The screams echoed in the grand chamber. He held his hands up in the air, joyfully spinning round and around.

One of the guards was filling a bucket from the water pump by the lavatory, and the others followed his lead. They began dousing the flames of the royal bed, the hissing sounds of the dying fire almost drowning out the king's ramblings.

Suddenly the king stopped, and noticed what the guards were about in smothering the flames.

"No...*No!* What are you doing?! She must burn! We must all burn together!" he shrieked at them. He began to weep. But the guards ignored him, and after a bit the flames were gone. The young man gazed at his royal bed. Pools of brackish water stood within the blackened bed sheets. The burnt image of his mother sat atop the scalded furniture in charred bits.

"What have you done?" he wept. Magdolyn came to him despite herself, offering a comforting arm around his shoulders, as was her duty. She was given good wages for this, and she meant to earn them. Her skin crawled at the clammy feel of his hot wet shoulders, yet she stroked them as a mother would.

"It's alright, dear one," she cooed as she tucked a damp forelock away from his face. "The fire is all gone."

"You fools..." he whispered. "You *FOOLS! You took her away from me.*"

He swung a fist at Magdolyn, and it struck against her cheek with a fleshy smack. The old woman fell to the ground. He flew across the bed at the nearest guard, his bared teeth glimmering behind a film of foam. He screamed, clawing and biting at the man, who fell back as if attacked by a rabid dog.

The guard screamed in pain as Theodore's teeth sunk into his raised forearm. He kicked, sending the boy spinning across the great floor. Theodore crashed into a small table by the fireplace, but was instantly bounding back rapidly toward the guard on his hands and knees, dark streaks of blood smearing his mouth.

"Your Majesty, *please*-"the guard began, holding his bleeding arm and struggling to his feet. But the boy was advancing jerkily at him across the room, his face crumbled hideously into a bloody snarl, his eyes glittering like two lit coals. The guard swung out his huge fist into the king's face. The strike hit solid and true. The boy lay sprawled on the floor, unconscious. His nose was broken and bloodied. The guard stood over him in horror. He had just struck the King of Thom.

"Bind him quickly, before he wakes." After seeing poor Magdolyn to her feet, the guardsmen came to the king and bound his hands and legs.

"Send for High Lord Chauncey. The King is not himself. He...He has gone mad."

Lord Chauncey arrived immediately. The boy was lying on the stone floor of his bedchamber with his hands and feet tied behind him. He had finally come to himself, and was lying motionless upon the ground, his nose a bleeding, pulpy mass. Lord Chauncey knelt down before him.

"Your Majesty."

The boy lay still, staring blankly at Lord Chauncey's boot.

"Your Majesty, please speak to me."

Nothing.

It was as if the boy had fallen into a deep sleep with his eyes open. In his dark rimmed brown eyes there was nothing but vacancy. Lord Chauncey regarded him for a long moment. He slowly reached for the king's bare shoulder.

Theodore suddenly snapped at Lord Chauncey's hand, his teeth clapping together with a loud click. Chauncey recoiled. The boy's boney face wrinkled, his dark eyes cold like those of a shark. He thrashed wildly, yowling like a cat. He hissed and spat, spraying bits of foam and blood.

"There is nothing to be done," concluded Lord Chauncey.

Shortly, the palace physician arrived, and after attempting (and failing) to examine the wild snarling creature, he ordered that the boy be restrained in the dungeon to save him from harming himself.

\*       \*       \*       \*

Lord Chauncey took a sip from the crystal glass, grimacing as the liquor stung his throat. In the past, he had guided the royal family through many dilemmas. When the farmers of the small village of Collines had led a protest against the necessary raise in taxes to improve irrigation, and King Leonard had lost his temper and put a fist through a wall, Lord Chauncey had been calm. When the Queen of Tirfan had paid a fleet of pirates from the Indigo Sea to raid ThoBromish trade ships on route to Diamonius, Lord Chauncey had been clear minded. When the wheat famine had the people of Thom go hungry in a year of bitter winter, Lord Chauncey had been collected.

But today, the Royal Advisor was at a loss. That morning the king was declared by the Royal Physician to be mad. Had he not been royalty, his head would have been shaved and he would've been branded with a hot poker and sent to the island of Cachot just off of the coast of Srye; the island where the Kingdom of Thom place those plagued by madness to be forgotten.

Lord Chauncey sat down at the great oaken desk in his private office and rubbed his tired eyes. He removed his tricorn hat and customary white wig, running a liver-spotted hand over his head. News traveled fast in the small city of Post; gossip even faster. Tell of the madness of the king would spread throughout the kingdom. Soon after, it would reach their enemies. ThoBromis would appear weak in the eyes of Tirfan, and they would attack the borders of Ende by the end of the season.

\*       \*       \*       \*

Kulbit's eyes had opened slowly and gave a start when he gazed upon something moving at the opposite side of the loft. It took him a moment to recall that Mrs. Butterberry and Berty had come to spend the night there. Bugger had gone. Kulbit sat up and stared at them.

Berty was curled into his mother's stomach, her arms protectively resting over him. When he returned from dealing with the fish dragon over at the market place, it seemed to most natural thing in the world for them to all sleep in the loft, the only light the occasional flash of brightness in the static air coming in through the window.

He gazed at the woman and child for a long moment, looking like two lost vagrants spending the night in a pile of hay. One wouldn't know that they were Butterberrys; one of the most powerful and wealthy families in the nation of Thom. He wondered if a rich, graceful lady like the Missus had ever spent the night huddled in a barn loft before, and felt a strange pang of pity.

And then of course there came the question of *why* they had come. The lady was afraid to be alone, the air full of night hexes. These things sounded senseless and mad in the dreary light of the morning. But it was true, and here they were.

Berty shivered and snuggled in closer to his mother for warmth. Kulbit took the worn quilt from his mattress and gently placed it over the two of them, gathered his boots and dungarees and climbed down the ladder to the stables, where he washed and dressed as fast as he could.

*There is no sense to be made of any of it. But even still, there are chores to be done, and I have had a dreadful start of the morning. Goodness, it must be the tenth hour! It is a wonder that Bugger had not yet sent for me, but I expect he is going to treat me differently...for a time. That is what comes of being hailed as a hero.* He rushed to the palace proper in hopes of finding some breakfast.

The royal kitchen was deserted; breakfast for the palace help had long been served and put away. Kulbit wandered to the larder, wondering if he would get caught lifting a bit of cheese and a hunk of bread. He froze when he heard soft sobbing coming from within.

Mrs. Templeton and the washerwoman Franny were hiding inside, the door slightly ajar. Franny was weeping and Mrs. Templeton was trying to comfort her.

"Are you certain you weren't merely dreaming, dear? Perhaps you'd eaten something disagreeable," Mrs. Templeton was saying.

"I most certainly was *not* dreaming. You know that I'm a practical sort, and I never tell tall tales...It was he, I tell you. My old Granda come back from the grave...He said he was in Hell...that he was saving a place for my brother Henry and I..."

"Hush, now, don't say such things so loud! It'll bring bad luck," said Mrs. Templeton. "As if speaking about seeing an apparition from the grave is not blasphemous enough."

"Blasphemous indeed. Mary, do you think it might be true? Why has Granda gone to Hell? He was...an upstanding member of the church...He served as custodian for thirty years," She began to cry again, tugging at her graying braid.

"Of course not! Any man or woman who serves the church ensures a place by the side of the Virgin. It says so in the Holy Book, as plain as day. Haddus comes in many forms, dear, and it is written that he is a deceiver and a perverter of truths. What you saw was not your Granda, but some vile thing in the service of the Devil," said Mrs. Templeton, though Kulbit felt that she did not sound so certain of herself.

"But *why* has he come to torment me? What evil have I done?"

"None, to be certain. If there is any evil in ThoBromis, it would lie in the hands of the Seigneurs Du Cordovan...The manner in which the death of Her Majesty was dealt was unholy to say the least. But that has none to do with you." Her voice lowered so that Kulbit had to press his ear against the door.

"There is something evil in the air...I've heard it said that the king himself has been lost to madness. The Seigneurs all say the fire in his chambers was an accident; that he had knocked over a candle. But why then did he stack bits of wood upon his bed? It *was* lit by his own doing, just as we all suspect. He went wild and bit one of the guards when they tried to put out the flames. I've heard that he even struck poor old Maggie to the ground. His Royal Wretchedness had always been a little blighter, but this? It was said that they may send for the High Priest to see about him...that perhaps his body has been possessed by a demon..."

Franny began to weep again. Kulbit did not remain for the rest of the conversation. The subject matter was far too much for him to stand about pondering at. Better to simply think of what needed to be done, and set about doing it. The air hadn't changed; he knew that much. And truth be told, that was all that mattered. He wasn't nearly as hungry as he thought.

He busied himself long and hard that day, and when the work was finished, he returned to his loft and swept it clean. Without asking himself why, he lay out extra bed clothes upon the piles of hay. And as the sun set, the Butterberrys and old Bugger returned to the loft to sleep.

They came up the ladder silently, each carrying a lantern and extra pillows. They settled in to the makeshift beds of hay that Kulbit had set out for them. No words were exchanged, save for a shy "*Merci*, Monsieur Kulbit," from little Berty as Kulbit blew out the last of the lanterns.

Kulbit could not tell them that they were welcome with words, of course. But they knew it just the same. After all, it was the duty of a hero to be there when he is needed, is it not? Even if the hero is afraid and does not understand very much himself.

The four of them lay wakeful in the darkness of the hayloft until very late that night, awaiting any sights or sounds of the night hexes' return. When sleep had finally come, none of them were expecting it.

\*     \*     \*     \*

The darkness had found a new home. Many, in fact. Soft and warm were the minds that lived in this kingdom. The land had many secrets. Poisoned thoughts were hidden deep within these hearts. And the constant lightening was ever silent, as if the thunder could only be heard in the sky of another world.

\*     \*     \*     \*

"Almighty God,
We beg you to deliver this child of the evil spirit that torments him.
At your command, O Lord,
May the goodness and peace of our Lord Jezu Christu, the Redeemer, take possession of this servant of the Throne of Thom."

The words echoed in the dungeon chamber as the Seigneurs looked on. The elderly Priest stood before Theodore, creating the sign of a cross over his head with two gnarled, shaking fingers. The boy sat on his rumpled cot, staring at nothing.

"Virgin bless us, Father have Mercy..." intoned the Priest. A page boy, clad in crimson ceremonial robes, raised a golden bowl. The old Priest dipped two fingertips and a thumb into the water, and began sprinkling it over Theodore. The Priest and the page stood aside, and Lord Chauncey approached the king.

"Your Majesty."

Silence. Theodore blinked.

"Your Majesty, please. Speak to us..."

Nothing. Lord Chauncey gazed at the Priest, who simply shook his head.

*    *    *    *

*"Bogey-Fran, Bogey-Fran, running from the Bogey Man,*
*Bogey beasties of the worlds, gnaw the bones of naughty girls..."*

The washerwoman's eyes were closed, but she was awake. She prayed that she would never hear that old rhyme again. The words her Granda would say to frighten her when she misbehaved. With those words came sights and sounds that she had buried in her mind for forty years. One would believe that after such a long time, she would not fear them any longer. That they would never again draw images of his cracked, yellow teeth grinning at her through scant silver whiskers, or the creaking sound of the leather belt he'd use to whip her with. The smell of the harsh soap he used to wash with before church. Franny pulled the blankets over her head like a child.

*You're dead, Granda, and I'm asleep, and this is simply a dream. And good riddance...* The silence of the room grew heavy, and she felt herself sinking into sleep.

Suddenly, she found herself flung into the air from her bed and crashing into the mirrored bureau. She lay writhing in the broken glass, too out of wind to scream, jarring pain in her ribs. When she was able to open her eyes, she saw two bare feet.

They were pale and gaunt and covered in filth. She did not need to look above to know that it was her Granda standing there. They were dirty from climbing out of the unmarked grave he had been buried under, down by the old oak tree.

"I used to sweep the floors, Franny. I kept everything in God's Temple tidy...I was a good servant, but they would pay me a pittance. I had to care for you and your ungrateful brother...The Holy Book says that the Virgin shall look after the poor...but none would look out for us, Franny. Do you not see? I *had* to take the money from the offering box...It was rightfully mine...I was not hiding it from you...It was my reward...I was a servant of the Lord..."

Franny struggled away from the apparition, cutting her forearms and bare legs as she dragged herself across the broken mirror glass. She refused to look up at him. She would die first.

"You knew where it was hidden...You and your brother watched me bury it under the chicken coop by your favorite climbing tree...You took it, Little Franny. You knew I would not be able to ask you where it was...You knew that it was a secret...You made it your own secret then, did you not? And that is where you and Henry buried me. Under the old oak tree. Hoping that you could forget. But the wandering dead do not forget. Franny, I am in Hell, for all hearts that bury secrets are sent here...and so shall you be..."

None heard her screams that night. And in the morning, though they each lived in separate parts of the city of Post, Franny and her twin brother Henry were both found hanging from the rafters of their bedrooms, bedsheets tied about their necks.

\*     \*     \*     \*

"Poor, Franny. I would have never dreamed she'd do such a thing," said Mrs. Templeton. Edna Bonnaire's brown eyes had dark circles under them. She seemed to be very much out of sorts. She flinched and started as one of the cooks began to chop a few carrots. Mrs. Templeton eyed her suspiciously. She did not expect Edna would take the news of Franny's death so casually. But there was clearly something else on her mind.

The early morning proved to be the same as the last. Grey, moist, and strange. The streets of the royal city were quiet. The two women sat at a small desk the loading door of the Royal Kitchen, and as Albert and the two Bonnaire boys carried in the last barrels of fish, Mrs. Templeton and the fish merchant's wife gossiped over a cup of tea, as was their custom. Yet Edna's tea remained untouched.

"She was so very frightened, and I couldn't think of a thing to say that would ease her mind," said Mrs. Templeton. "I daresay I can't imagine what had come over her. Saying such things as seeing the spirit of her Granda come back from the dead, and after all what's happening with the king...I wonder has everyone gone mad?"

"Oh, w-well..." muttered Edna. She twisted her handkerchief, her eyes darting to the door. Beads of perspiration dotted her forehead.

"For goodness sake, Edna, what is the matter with *you*? Here I've just told you that dear Franny has been found dead, and all you can say is 'Oh, well.' You look as though you've danced with the devil himself. What is wrong?"

The boys set the last barrel down among the ice blocks, wiping their foreheads. Mrs. Bonnaire quickly rose. "I-I'm sorry, Mary. I really must be going..."

"Now, hold off. Edna, you and I have been friends for eighteen years. I see when something is amiss. Has something happened?" Mrs. Templeton placed a hand on Mrs. Bonnaire's shoulder, and the fish merchant's wife bit her lip.

"Come, into the larder. I'll not frighten the boys..." The two women hastened into the larder, nearly shutting the doors behind them. Edna Bonnaire burst into tears, suddenly grasping Mrs. Templeton's hands painfully in her desperation.

"What on earth is wrong, Edna? You're frightening me."

"It was Albert...The night before last, something terrible had happened. Or rather, was *meant* to happen...The Devil *has* come to Thom, just as everyone has been saying. It is true as life itself. Albert and I... We may be both going mad together, but there is no mistake in the evil that was seen..."
"What evil, my good woman? What have you seen?"

Edna blessed herself. "A thing of Hell...but we were shone mercy. Mary, you must listen to me. There is safety from the fires of Haddus. We have seen the Tool of God; His Chosen Vessel. Only in his presence will we be shone grace..."

"What on earth are you talking about?" Mrs. Templeton felt a wave of fear wash over her. She was a stout-hearted woman, and was unaccustomed to this. "Edna, if you don't stop babbling nonsense and say what it is you mean to say-"

*"It's the purple boy,"* Mrs. Bonnaire said thickly. She grasped the back of Mrs. Templeton's neck and whispered fiercely in her ear. "He comes as a child in the stable, just as our Heavenly Savior had come to the stables under the Beacon of the Blessing Star. It is strange, but true, and Albert and I will be spending the night near God's Chosen Vessel. I believe it is God's way of teaching us humility in these End Times...We will stay as near to him as we can. You should come as well, Mary. For your own safety..."

"What? Where are you going?"

"Haven't you heard a word I've just said? To the stables, to be near the Purple Boy. Only he can shield us from the midnight hexes..."

"Purple...why, do you mean little Kulbit? The dear little Cupcake mute?"

"I'm telling you, Mary, he has the power to protect us from the night hexes. He is the Tool of God. I've seen him do miracles with my own two eyes. He saved my Albert after I watched him die, just like the story of Lazar. The Hand of God is upon him. I must go."

The two women came out from the larder, their faces somber. Mr. Bonnaire and the boys were loading up the wagon. Suddenly, Mrs. Templeton threw her arms about Mrs. Bonnaire' neck in an embrace. She then blessed herself. "I knew it all along. I knew there was a reason why he was so strange looking, and such a dear, sweet little thing. I believe you, Edna. There is evil in Thom."

"Come to the stables tonight. Tell as many as you can. It is a place of protection."

"I will." And Mrs. Templeton meant it.

# Chapter 5

A meeting was held at once in the Statehood Wing.

"The King," said Lord Chauncey, "has been ruined by madness. And as a result is no longer fit to rule. According to the law a king can be deposed when his health hinders him from his royal duties." The committee of gentlemen muttered among themselves.

"Parliament will govern the kingdom until either the king's health is restored, or the next in line for the throne can be decided," Lord Chauncey continued. His voice spoke steadily, but his hands shook and sweat beaded his brow.

"But my Lord!" exclaimed Lord Feldin, "Hostility among the forces of Tirfan have escalated. Without a royal head, the people will panic. ThoBromis is vulnerable to her enemies' attacks. The Queen of the Tirfan has just garrisoned troops no more than two weeks' journey off the borders of Ende. They know of the depleted state of our Royal Headship since the death of King Leonard. She is a serpent waiting for the right time to strike."

"And how much weaker still shall Thom be with a boy king who has gone mad?" asked Lord Chauncey. "It is for this very reason we must relieve His Majesty of the crown while we still have some control over our Headship. We must relieve King Theodore of his sovereign state until he can be either cured...*or replaced.*"

The men clamored among themselves raucously. Lord Chauncey rang his silver bell to quiet them.

"I agree with Lord Chauncey's proposal," said Lord Marsen, much to Chauncey's surprise. "However, perhaps such measures will not be necessary. Providing a cure for the king is discovered. What's more, the magickal matter of the rumored midnight hexes have not yet been resolved. The people are frightened. Many speak of visions of the dead. Therefore, I myself make a proposal that may aid in both situations."

All were silent, waiting.

"The heathen nation of Diamonius has ever been our friend, though in our own devotion to the ways of the church, we have failed to make a formal alliance. And with them we may share a common, yet unlikely ally, who has in the past assisted Diamonius in times of great need. Perhaps it is our turn to beseech assistance as well, if only to ingratiate ourselves to the King and Queen of Diamonius," Lord Marsen hesitated. "We must extend a friendship with Lord Nelios, Head of Caramoox."

Lord Chauncey once again had to ring his silver bell to silence the shocked din of parliament.

"Nelios? He whom calls himself, 'The Good Wizard of the Moon'? That is preposterous! Utter superstitious nonsense!"

Much had been told of this "Good Wizard." He was a mystic who lived upon a remote tropical island somewhere in the southern Indigo Sea. He was the leader of a commune of fortune-tellers, outlaws and charlatans that called themselves scholars of the supernatural. This ragtag group proclaimed themselves the "Caramooxen Court"; sort of a strange religious sect comprised of outcasts. Many of them were exiles and criminals from all over the known world. Some were even said to be fallen nobility, or defunct royalty. The King of Diamonius and his wife were very superstitious people. They had arranged an "alliance" with this spiritualist and his "Court", and often consulted him in matters of state.

Lord Chauncey had recalled a time when in visiting Diamonius, having to be subject to much of this sacrilegious nonsense. The Queen had commissioned a talking board to be made so that she could have the old soothsayer speak with her long deceased sister. Lord Chauncey had feigned a head sickness and had thankfully been able to avoid attending the séance.

"Perhaps this is ridiculous, but Lord Nelios is reputed to be a man of utmost wisdom in the matters of magickal medicine. If there is a cure for madness… or any other sort of magickal trickery, he would be able to identify it," replied Lord Marsen. "And if not…The throne of Thom has no allies. We have been strong enough in times of war without them. But our strength has lessened with the death of King Leonard."

"We are in dire times, My Lord," said Lord Rexmeyer. "We must try to see all ends. Besides, what harm could it do to cordially invite a trusted friend of Diamonius? Perhaps doing so might please the King and Queen. We need them to agree to give us reinforcements, should the occasion arise. If this wizard man advises them to send aid, no doubt they will obey without question."

"Here, here", chimed in the other members of the court. This was true. For if Thom had even a single ally, perhaps the Queen might think twice before waging war. Of all the other arguments, this one rang true to Lord Chauncey. Never mind the magickal nonsense. An added ally that would do quite well.

"Very well," said Lord Chauncey tiredly, "Send for this Nelios of Caramoox. We shall have an end to this one way or the other. In the meantime, I move to send men beyond borders of Ende, and prepare for an oncoming skirmish. The Queen of Tirfan will see that there is still bite left in the jaws of Thom."
"Here, here", agreed the men.

The following day, troops were sent off the borders of Ende, and an invitation was sent to the Good Wizard of Caramoox.

## AUTHOR'S NOTE

I was so damn hungover this morning. Went club hopping last night. I wasn't quite feeling sociable. But everyone said it might help me blow off some steam and relax. I'm not certain how vomiting in a parking lot in stilettos is relaxing. But my lipstick didn't smear, and while I probably smelled like a New York City public bathroom, I looked pretty hot, if I do say so myself. If that means anything anyway.

*She opened her eyes. The sun made golden stripes across the ground through the vertical blinds that felt like daggers being forced between the plates of her skull. Very soon the weekend would be over. She'd better get some semblance of writing in while she still could. Even if her murky, liquor soaked mind refused to cooperate.*

**What was I talking about? Oh yeah...**

Ever hear of Krokodil? It's a drug, otherwise known as desomorphine. People take it to get high, and when you get high sometimes you can hop on over to the Darka like skipping rope, break on through to the other side. The Waking World is so hard sometimes. I get it.

I saw these pictures of what that drug does to you. Don't Google it, unless you have a strong stomach. Your skin starts falling off, and there was this one lady whose arm was half that of a skeleton. She must have had a hard time in life to have to go that far just to run away from it. But if it's gotten that bad, I'm certain you won't find what you're looking for in the Darka. The Darka can be better than heaven or worse than hell. Running too hard will bring you face to face with the thing you're trying to avoid most. I seriously need a drink, dammit.

## END NOTE

That night, Mrs. Butterberry and her son, as well as Bugger had come to the loft. The night seemed that it would be a quiet one, and the four of them settled in without a word to one another.

They had all fallen quite fast asleep before long. It was little Berty that awoke with a start. Outside, he heard voices. The horses below shifted and stirred uneasily in their stalls. He crawled from under his mother's arm to look outside of the loft window.

"Monsieur Kulbit...Wake up." He shook the older boy's shoulder. "There are people outside..."

Kulbit sat up and lit the lantern. The four of them crowded around the window. Below, camped out in the grass lawn beside the stable house was a number of people sitting about a collection of small fires. Many of them had brought blankets and beds of straw. They were settling in as if they were going to spend the night there.

"Mother, what are they doing?" asked Berty.

"Perhaps...they are doing the same as we are. They are here to spend the night." She gazed at Kulbit affectionately, placing a hand on his shoulder. "A night free of hexes. Close to the protection of the Tool of God."

The four of them stared out of the window for a while longer before one by one going back to their beds. Kulbit was the last to go.

*The Tool of God.* He wasn't all to certain how he felt about being anyone's tool.

## PART II:  There's Witch's Trouble Afoot
## Chapter 6

Emily Marie Osterling sat on the front step of the cottage, wrapped in so much fur and wool that only her two brown eyes could be seen through a slit of dark fabric wrapped about her head. Her mother had been worried that she might catch a chill, as sometimes happens when little ones are underfed, and so she always told her religiously to bundle up before going out. Emily didn't consider herself to be very much of a little one at all. She was thirteen years old, but when you are the second to youngest of a family of five daughters, thirteen years might as well be thirteen weeks. Mother was asleep anyway, and would not know where she would be going that night. But perhaps either out of guilt or habit, Emily dressed just as Mother would have had her.

Daniellia had turned sixteen this past spring. As custom, all of the young men in the village came knocking at her door early in the morning of her birthday to offer her Lover's Stones, each one painted with a happy birthday wish underneath. Daniellia would keep the Lover's Stones in a tiny box inside of her hope chest, and on the day she would be married she was to bury all but the one given to her by her true love. That stone would be hidden under the bed of the newlyweds for good fortune.

What a terrific fuss Daniellia had made that morning, rushing about here and there with rouge and hair combs and frocks. How she bossed and bullied her younger sisters about like some sort of spoiled princess out of a fairy tale.

"Emily, hurry up and boil my bathwater! Carrigan, you shan't embarrass me with your silly pet turtle today! Take the ugly thing out of the house! Mother, where is my blue hair ribbon? I need my blue hair ribbon! Jon Hannigan says it brings out the color of my eyes!"

It was awful. Marian and Rose, the eldest twins of the five Osterling sisters at six and twenty years old, both now married and Marian big bellied with her first child, were all motherly smiles and sage advice. Mother had baked her special cream puffs for the young suitors, and none of the girls were even allowed to taste a single one. It was bad luck, mother had said, and would chase the good suitors away.

Emily and her sisters never had any birthday parties. Papa was not a rich man, but a very skilled carpenter, and while he created the most beautiful things, since the death of the King his business had been slow. He and Mother could never afford to shower the girls with birthday affairs, like Betty Robinson's father had done for her and her two brothers every year. So as you can imagine, when one of the daughters turned sixteen it would be a family event to remember. After all of the boys came in the morning to deliver the Lover's Stones, Mother and the rest busied about preparing for the birthday feast. Most everyone in the village was to attend, and all would bring gifts of food, wine, and gold. All for Daniellia's hope chest.

Emily Marie didn't have a hope chest, and neither did her younger sister Carrigan. Papa was going to make them each one when they turned thirteen. Emily's fourteenth birthday was coming at the end of that winter. That year, it did not look as though she would be getting a hope chest after all. The entire town was going hungry. Papa had sold all of his timber to buy the last bit of grain in the general store just before it shut down, which was owned by the Robinsons. Richer families like theirs had sold everything and moved on the greener pastures. It would seem like the little town of Keppington Valley was going to be deserted come next spring; and forgotten all together. One of the many nameless hamlets of ThoBromis that had come and gone over the years.

She didn't quite understand why all of this was happening. She heard Papa and the other men talk of how the young King Theodore had stopped buying things from his own kingdom, and had begun to order them from other countries. This hurt Papa a great deal, for most of his wares sold to the royal city of Post. In the meantime, there were tales of night terrors attacking the kingdom's capital. That some horrible magician had cursed them, and that evil spirits were now roaming the streets of Post every night. This, Papa had said, was a tub of female superstitious horse wash. Carrigan, who only believed in facts, figures, and the breeding cycle of damsel flies, said only ninnies believed in magic anyway.

Papa and Carrigan never believed in fun things like magick and witches and spirits. Mother did, but was terribly afraid of it all, and forbade any of the girls to speak of such things. But Emily believed, and thought they were very exciting. In fact, she almost hoped it would be true. What a thrilling adventure it would be, if something magickal were to be the reason for the town's struggles. So much more interesting than economy and politics.

Far away in the edge of the valley lived an old lady by the name of Grenna. Old lady Grenna was a recluse, and had hidden herself up in the mountains for years. Everyone believed that she was really a witch, and there were many stories of folks seeing her flying over the valley in the dead of night on her broomstick, as the wolves of *LeBois* howled up at the full moon. When Grenna had finally died, no one had known of it until a week past. It was said that her old, wrinkled corpse was full of worms, and her face had first swollen and then burst.

Ever since she was small, Emily held a strange fascination for Grenna. No one would ever see the woman all year round, except on the day of the Full Harvest Moon, she would come down to the village and sit on a stump in the middle of the marketplace. There she would be seen sitting and tying knots into old rope, while singing strange songs to herself. No one would speak to her, and no one would look at her, for the rumor was that if you spoke to a witch during the time of the Harvest Moon, she could spoil your crop. Carrigan had always said that this was ridiculous, for how could a silly old woman have anything to do with crops?

"If we should be worried about anything, it should be catching some sort of plague from her. She smells as if she hasn't had a bath in ages, and I once read that diseases spread most from unhygienic hands," she sniffed, pushing her spectacles up her nose.

Mother still told all of her children to stay away from the old woman if they ever came across her.

Emily had seen the old witch, and even spoken to her once. The aged hag was sitting alone by the grocer's. It was the week before Harvest. Mother had gone to the grocer's stand to complain about buying a bushel of apples that had been full of little green worms.

Grenna had been sitting alone on her old tree stump, and everyone in the marketplace was trying to avoid her, walking a wide berth away from her as they had done every year. The crazy old lady had been singing and mumbling aloud, rocking herself slowly, her glittering eyes staring off into nothing. Emily could see the piece of rope being worked in her gnarled fingers.

Her face reminded Emily of the wrinkly little shrunken apple heads Mother would make at this time of year. Mother made the dolls' heads by carving faces into the apples, and soaking them in brine. She would then let them dry on the doorstep for two weeks. Then she would hang the heads on a garland over every window and door. This was supposed to keep the spirits of the terrible Moonsmen at bay. Autumn was their favorite time of year to haunt the houses of the living, and snatch your breath away as you sleep.

Something about the old woman drew Emily. Something horrible and ugly, yet fascinating. She stood in front of Grenna. The hag's hands stopped working the knotted piece of rope. She looked at the little girl. The flesh on Emily's arm prickled, as the witch spoke to her.

*"Witchie-me is witchie-see, do I spy a witch so wee?"*

The low, creaking voice reminded Emily of a rusted hinge. Grenna smiled and held out the knotted rope to Emily.

"Take it, child. It is a gift, from old Granny Grenna...*For nine nights after the full moon, untie each knot one by one, just before bed. By knot of one, your spell's begun. By knot of nine, what's done is thine. Make a wish, and wish come true. And soon your wish shall come to you.*"

Emily hesitated, then took the knotted rope from Grenna. And because it seemed the polite thing to do when speaking with elders, be they a witch or no, she gave a half curtsey and said softly, "*Merci*, Madame Grenna."

Just then, her mother came out of the grocer's. Emily quickly hid the rope in her pocket. But that didn't stop Mother from scolding her for standing so near to the old hag.

Just as the witch had told her, Emily untied one knot in the rope for nine nights straight, and hid it under her bed. Each night, she wondered what she should wish for, knowing full and well that she must decide by the ninth night.

Emily had never owned a store bought doll before. Actually, there had never been one anywhere in their little town. Not even

Betty Robinson owned one. She saw one earlier that month. A band of gypsies set up camp along the side of the road. One of which was a peddler who sang funny songs and sold all sorts of things. He had a huge covered wagon with the words "DR. MOUNTEBANK'S TRAVELING MEDICINE SHOW AND CIRCUS" painted on the sides in big, curly red letters. Her mother wished to buy a new pot from the peddler, and he had given Emily and her sisters' fizzy drinks to lift their spirits.

Emily spotted the most beautiful doll she had ever seen hanging among the lovely fabrics he had for sale. She was a doll from the Far East, dressed in a rich green gown embroidered with golden thread. Her hair was made of spun silk, as red as strawberries. Her skin was made of a fine glazed porcelain. She had one blue eye and one green.

"A doll fit for a princess," the Doctor had said when he caught her eyeing it.

"Well, we have no princesses here. Just simple townsfolk interested in a new stew pot," her mother cut in bluntly, sweeping Emily aside. And that was that.

As long as she would live, Emily thought she would never again see such a beautiful doll. So as the nine nights crept past slowly, she set her mind on what she would wish for. On the morning of the tenth day, she awoke early, excited. Before dressing or even washing her face, she rushed about the house, searching for her wish come true. She checked the kitchen table, the pantry, and even under her bed. But no doll fit for a princess was to be found. Mother told her to quit running about like a ninny and to dress and fetch the milk for breakfast. When she ran out to the milk shed, sitting proper as you please on top of the milk bucket was her precious doll, looking lovely as ever in the morning sunshine. Pinned to her frock was a note:

*"To Dear Little Emily Marie,*
*Just a reminder that any little girl can be a princess, if she's*
*clever enough and sets her mind to it!*
*Truly Yours,*
*Doctor Mountebank"*

Ever since that day, Emily knew that Grenna was indeed a witch, and became more and more curious about magick and sorcery. Unfortunately, she had no way of learning much more about magick, for her mother forbade such things with such vigor that if ever she were to try the knot spell again, she would be sure to do it in utter secrecy. And at the following full moon, she in fact did try the spell again, wishing for a basket of rare oranges even in the middle of the fall, when not only trade ships that would carry fruit from exotic tropics of the south would still be at sea, but their poor family would never have enough money to buy any if they were to come to their small village in Ende.

But even despite all of these things, the next morning after the night of the last untied knot, a kindly neighbor had gifted the family a small basket of oranges. Emily was thrilled to no end by the rare sweet fruit, but even more thrilled that she might have found a way to do magick at will.

She craved to learn more, but had not the nerve to venture out to Grenna's cottage to ask the old witch for more secrets. If her mother ever found she had been seeking the witch, she would turn her out of the house for thinking about such things. When she heard news that the witch had died, she grew wild with curiosity to see if perhaps she had left some sort of clues of magick behind. And as the months after Grenna's death rolled past, little Emily could hardly sleep at nights, her mind full with wondering. The run down cottage was now abandoned, and many of the children of the village began to tell tales of the witch's ghost haunting the wood above the valley.

And so on this current night, the night of the Fall Equinox, when her family was deep asleep, Emily crept from the large bed she shared with her sisters. She finished bundling up and sat for a moment by the hearth, trying to settle her nerves. The fire was low, popping and crackling softly. As she adjusted thick woolen scarf about her neck and face, she could scarce believe that she was actually going to go through with it. Why was she so set on going to the old witch's cabin anyway? She did not know.

*There will probably not be anything worth seeing anyway. Just a musty old cabin with spiders and rats...*

She shuddered at the thought, and decided thinking about rats and spiders should best be saved for a time when she had not set her mind for courage. She stole away outside, and through the cold of the night, under the white blue light of another full moon, she journeyed to the cottage.

When she had finally arrived, her hands and nose and ears red and tingling from a cold wind, and she thanked her stars she had followed Mother's advice on always dressing warm. The cottage door was open. It swayed lazily. Perhaps someone, a beggar or a runaway thief had hidden himself there? In that case, it would not be wise at all to consider going inside. She turned to go, but then stopped. Looking over her shoulder she gazed at the dark little building surrounded by brambles and unruly shrubbery. The cottage door swung back and forth in the wind like a beckoning finger in the moonlight. She *had* to go in. If she didn't, she felt she would go mad with wondering. After all, what magickal things could the old witch have left behind that might be able to help their poor family?

Emily rubbed her hands and stamped her feet. *Besides,* she thought to herself, *if anything it would be a good deal nicer to get out of this dreadful wind for a moment.* And so, she stuck out her chin, wrapped her cloak tighter around herself, and slowly stepped onto the creaking front porch. She walked into the darkness of the cottage, and started as unseen ghost's fingers reached out and brushed across her face.

With a cry, she batted at the air about her head and quickly saw that she had walked into a thick sheet of cobwebs. Brushing and swatting at herself madly, she hoped that the spiders had long gone. She stepped to her right and stumbled over a table. On the table was a tiny tinderbox and a tiny brass oil lamp. Fumbling with cold fingers, she managed to light the wick after a few tries, hoping the old cabin would look less frightening with some light. In that she was disappointed.

The little bit of warm light only served to create strange shadows all about her. The cabin was positively filled with cobwebs from the stone floor to the slanted rafter ceiling. The wind blew a draft, so that the webs swayed and made odd shapes. For a moment, Emily thought that she saw the figure of an old woman with long white hair standing by the filthy hearth. But it was only her eyes playing tricks.

"Enough wasting time, Emily Marie," she said aloud to herself. "Hurry about your business and be off."
She began exploring the cabin. Other than the ridiculous amount of cobwebs, there was nothing very extraordinary about it. Cooking

pots hung over the water pump. A small, rumpled cot lay in the corner wall by the fire. Over the fire was a shelf with all sorts of mason jars full of herbs and dried seeds. Upon this shelf there were also lovely little crystal clusters of purple quartz. Mother called these Faery Castles, and had often warned that if you see one in the woods growing out of a stone, don't dare touch it or the faeries will feel welcome in your house.

*I suppose if one were a witch, one might very well invite faeries into one's house if one needed to. There is no sense in being afraid of things like faery magick if you are trying to learn about them.*

And so Emily took the tiniest of these and put them in her pocket. Perhaps befriending a faery may come in handy. It was funny how frightened the townspeople had become of things of that sort when there might be a practical use for it. She would hide a crystal in Papa's wood shop. Maybe the faeries could help him with his work.

Atop the shelf, Emily noticed all a manner of strange carvings into the wood. Symbols of stars and eyes and letters that she couldn't recognize. The mystery of their meanings made her mind itch with excitement, and she felt an odd pricking in her fingers when she reverently dragged them over the carvings. She wished the old witch were alive so that she could tell Emily what all of these symbols meant.

She wouldn't be afraid. You hear all sorts of terrible things about witches in fairy stories, but Grenna didn't seem to be a mean sort of witch at all. Emily decided there and then that being a witch didn't always mean that one was going to be wicked. Perhaps witches can even help people.

Suddenly, an odd draft coursed through the entire cabin. It was warm, and something in it smelled of dried flowers. The tiny hairs on Emily's neck stood on end, and her eye was drawn to an empty bookshelf. Except it wasn't entirely empty. There was but one single book in it. The book was leather bound, the kind for writing in. Papa had one or two of these to do the mathematics of his money and their family budget and whatnot. What sort of family budget would a witch have?

Emily reached out for the book, but quickly pulled her hand back with a little cry. A large spider was sitting upon it. It wasn't like any spider that Emily had ever seen before, so large that each of its legs were as long as one of Emily's fingers. It was a black and shining, with a dark purple star burst mark upon its abdomen. She tried to shoo it away, but it didn't move. Then something suddenly occurred to her. It was strange of course, but this was a very strange night.

"Hello, Spider," she said aloud. "My name is Emily. I suppose it is you who is responsible for all these cobwebs. May I please have Grenna's book? I promise I won't harm it. I only wish to have a look."

As if the spider understood, it scampered away and out of sight in haste. Emily eagerly took the book and opened it. On the first page, written in trembling letters were the words:

*Grenna's Grimoire.*
*Book with cover black as pitch*
*Inward danger have a look*
*Learning only as a witch*
*Seeking magick in this book*

"It means," Emily said to herself, "that this book is only meant for witches to read and use...Well, I hadn't given much thought to that before. Suppose if regular people who aren't witches read this; something awful might happen to them! Well then, perhaps I should put it back then..."

It was here where a very strange thought occurred to her. Witches are people who cast spells and do magick...Which is exactly what she wanted to learn how to do. Did that mean that she was actually meaning to learn how to become a real witch herself?

Suddenly, the soft warm draft returned with the smell of dried flowers, and a terrible chill ran down Emily's back. She turned around and felt a white wave of fear hit her. She dropped the oil lamp and it shattered to pieces, and the flame quickly spread to the base of the wall. Standing at the hearth was old Grenna. Her gown was long and white, as was her hair, and her face so pale that Emily thought she could see right through it. The old witch smiled.

*"Witchie-me is witchie-see, do I spy a witch so wee?"*

A piercing scream escaped Emily's throat as she gathered her skirts and fled out of the cabin. The witch's cackles rang in her ears with the roar of flames that began to flicker angrily out of the little windows. She ran at full speed into the night, despite stumbling over loose stones and tumbling down steep slopes. Behind her she sensed the glow of the fire that quickly ate the old witch's cabin. She ran and ran, until she found herself running far into the woods, down the peaks and dips of the mountainside, and back to her own farm, where she collapsed right at her doorstep among the shriveled apple head dolls, panting wildly, her sides cramping.

When she finally came to her senses, she realized that she had something black and square clutched in her cold hands.

The witch's grimoire. She hadn't meant to take it with her...had she? She carefully opened the front door and sneaked back into her and her sisters' bedroom. No one had even so much as stirred since she had gone. She hid the book under her bed, wriggled into her nightgown, and slipped under the covers. Oddly enough, she was able to fall asleep right away, and had no dreams.

Early the next morning, an odd change had come over Emily Marie Osterling. She remembered the book that she had stolen, and had immediately begun to make plans. It wouldn't do at all for Mother to find her hiding it, and as Mother was a very industrious woman, she would most certainly find the witch's book if Emily were to try and hide it away in some secret place in the cottage. No, she must hide it in a place where no one would think it strange to find a black leather bound book. So she arose from her bed and put it in plain sight upon the kitchen table. Mother wouldn't think twice of seeing one of Papa's old accounting books sitting there, and would most likely not even bother to open it.

And just as Emily had predicted, as Mother set the breakfast table she mumbled to herself, "That tiresome man, leaving his things all about the house..." and saw that her mother had absentmindedly tossed the book upon the bookshelf among many other books that looked exactly like it.

And so, Emily went about her daily chores and lessons as usual, not a once giving a single glance at the bookshelf else her mother wonder at her interest. But inside her mind was hot with desire to begin to read the old witch's book. She waited all that day, and laughed and bickered with her sisters at supper as if there weren't anything strange at all in her mind.

After everyone in the family had settled down for bed, Emily Marie lie wide awake, waiting for the darkest hour of night so that all were properly asleep. Then she climbed out of her bed slowly and quietly, took the book, a few blankets and a stump of candle, and glided noiselessly out of the cottage and into her father's closed work shed.

It was bitter cold inside, and had been locked shut because he had little business as of late. She started a fire and put a few logs into the wood stove, pulled over his old stuffed chair close to the warmth and light, and curled into a tiny ball with her blankets, and began to read.

# Chapter 7

The Chosen One of Jezu Christu. The Blessed Child of the Stables. These were things whispered around Kulbit as he went about the everyday business of being a stable hand. He pretended he could not hear the things that were said, but hear he did, and it filled him with foreboding. In the morning, he didn't need to beg for his breakfast in the kitchens. A plate was already hot and steaming and set aside for him. Mrs. Templeton watched him as he ate.

He didn't like the look of her eyes. They reminded him of the strange look he saw in the eyes of Mrs. Butterberry; wide and just a tad too bright. Something was happening in Post, there was no mistake about that. But something was also happening to the people.

*Perhaps everyone is going mad...*

They all stared at him. And even Jared would hush up and watch him as he went about his duties. Things were being said about him. Things he was not so certain he liked.

That is why when news came that a group of foreign diplomats from overseas were to come as royal guests to the Statehood, Kulbit was more than happy that the focus had come off of himself for the time being. Everyone stopped standing about him, gawping stupidly, and had begun busying about for their arrival. It made for a lovely distraction.

The day they were to arrive, Kulbit was once again perched atop his favorite tree by the dais at the Meeting Post as the Royal Court of Thom assembled with much splendor. A great silken archway was arranged over the dais and a large red carpet rolled out from under, painting the North South road crimson for what seemed a good distance. Garlands of white and yellow flowers trimmed the carpet, the dais, the pavilion. Kulbit thought he had never seen so many flowers in one place before, nor smelled so sweet their perfume.

Atop the dais stood High Lord Chauncey in a white robe, and he was flanked by the Seigneurs Du Cordovan in deep crimson. That was strange, for usually when people of importance were to arrive in ThoBromis it was customary for the King himself to receive them.

*Hullo...No trace of His Royal Wretch...I wonder, has he truly gone ill in the head as everyone had said?* It seemed as if everyone was pleased not to think on this at the current occasion. It also seemed that everyone in the City had attended today's reception, so different in comparison to the coronation of their king.

The townspeople pressed in on either side of the red carpet, so that teams of guardsmen had to stand along it to hold them at bay. Some of the people even waved tiny flags, bright crimson with the Thomish Crest emblazoned across them.

*Apparently these Caramooxen foreigners are quite popular here in Post, though I myself have never heard tell of them before present,* thought Kulbit. He found this all quite fascinating, especially in light of his own recent experiences. Perhaps these Caramooxen have something to do with it all. Nothing of the matter was known, not even by the women of the kitchens.

The trumpets blasted fanfare, but that was quickly drowned out by the cheers of the people. An open carriage dripping with yet even more flowers, flags and silks came along the carpet, drawn by four white horses (Roger, and his equally handsome brothers Sam, Pickle and Bo. Kulbit waved at them madly.). Seated in the carriage were three oddly dressed people. The carriage stopped just before the dais, and they stepped out one by one.

The first was a rotund man with skin so dark a brown it was almost black. He wore a great orange robe with yellow stripes. Orange and yellow beads hung from the long, braided ends of his wooly beard. The big man smiled and waved at the people as he stepped onto the dais.

"His Esteemed Royal Majesty, King Nafari of the Unknown Nation of *Af-Ri-Cah*!" called the Herald.

The next to step off of the carriage was a woman, strange, beautiful and proud. She wore a long red satin robe embroidered with yellow silken roses. Her face was painted white and her lips very red. Pink blossoms dotted her long black hair, which hung all the way down to her knees. Kulbit had never seen a woman so exotic, so regal. She fluttered a pink fan in front of her face and bowed in a fashion that he had never seen before.

"The Arch-Duchess of Lann, Lady Azumi of the Eastern Kingdoms."

The next man to step off of the carriage was the strangest of all to Kulbit. It was an old man with a big black top hat perched over fringes of wild white hair. He had a white handlebar mustache and a pointed goatee. A shiny eyeglass sat upon his cheek. He wore a gray vest that had a golden chain draped across the front, and a starched white collar stood so high upon his neck it nearly covered his ears. An enormous gray cape hung from his shoulders. He held a tall staff that seemed to have a crystal ball on the top.

From somewhere in his cape the old man brought out a big red apple and took a bite before stepping onto the dais. He tipped his hat to the Seigneurs Du Cordovan and froze when he spotted Lord Chauncey. He spoke out in a loud, clear voice before the Royal Herald had a chance to announce him. The herald, who never interrupted his betters, held his peace.

*"Salve and Bonjourno,* my old friend Chauncey!" exclaimed the man. He had a funny manner of speech. Kulbit at once liked him very much. The old man embraced Lord Chauncey with a jolly chuckle. Lord Chauncey stiffened.

"It has been so long! How is your dear wife, y' old *tumble!* I hope things are far better between you now. My, what a lovely procession you have arranged for us! So many flowers! And how pleasant after such a long journey," the old man said. He took another big bite from his apple.

"Welcome, Lord Nelios," Chauncey bowed, "Lady Azumi, King Nafari. Shall we to the palace? We have a feast prepared, and many pressing matters to attend to."

"Oh yes, to the palace," said Lord Nelios, "I'm sure her Ladyship would like to rest." He rolled the *r* in the word *rest* in a way that made Kulbit chuckle.

The visitors and the Royal Headship proceeded to the palace on foot, following the red carpet to the royal gate. Kulbit could only wonder as to what was going on beyond.

\*     \*     \*     \*

The darkness shifted restlessly. Strange, unfamiliar magick would spoil its designs.

\*     \*     \*     \*

# Chapter 8

After a fine but formal repast, the guests were grandly escorted to their rooms. They would discuss the strange matter of the king's health the next morning, Lord Chauncey had said. The truth was that he hadn't quite the words to say exactly what it was that he wanted from these strange foreigners. He did not wish to give them too much unneeded information. Royal matters were private and meant to remain that way. A night would give him time to formulate the diplomatic means of asking for the assistance of these unholy people.

And of course, there was the brown bottle that beckoned him from his study. He simply needed to sleep on matters, he assured himself. And perhaps a nip or so might help. Carolene was asleep once more, and he sat alone in the study, the light tinkle of glass and bottle his only company. Before long, the bottle was nearly empty, but his head was still quite full. He was certain there were more bottles tucked away in the cellar somewhere...

"Papa?"

Chauncey's mind was growing old and stupid. How many times had he thought he had heard Ana's little shoes running through the corridor? Or hear her shrill laughter out in the courtyard. Nonsense. She was dead, and had died a grown woman. But his stupid old mind refused to remember her as anything but the excited little girl with the dirty face.

Carolene had always fussed at the girl for playing in the dirt and ruining her frocks. She said it was unbecoming of a young lady who would someday be married to a great courtier. But Chauncey did not mind. Not in the least. Children were meant to behave as such, at least as far until they are forced to become adults. There were times when he wished that he had joined her down in the mud, listening to her sweet laughter as she made mud cakes as one listens to the calming sounds of a gentle summer storm.

"Papa..." he heard the soft voice once and decided it was time for another nippy nip nip. He emptied the bottle into the crystal glass for the last time, and downed it with a soft belch. He wondered if there were any tiresome servants still hanging about near the entrance of the cellar. He was certain they had all gone to bed. He rose slowly and his head swam. He would refill his secret bottle and Carolene would never know. No one would.

He froze across from the mirror in the armoire. Behind his chair in the reflection he saw a small figure. A little fluffy blond head, a round little face. Ana, standing behind his desk. He whirled about. The room was empty.

"Papa..."

He heard the voice far much more clearly. It was not merely in his own head this time. It was coming from the corridor. His study door was ajar. Through the crack of the doorway he saw a flash of white moving past, and heard the clicking sound of little shoes.

Chauncey's head throbbed. He was finally going mad. He leaned on the door frame. The darkness of the corridor was a thick wall before him. The end of the hall was dimly lit by the dying torch lamp at the far side. The air about him grew cold. His breath became thin ribbons of steam. The torch light flickered, only allowing a small patch of the rich red carpet to be seen below it. Faintly lit in this feeble pool of light, he could make out a figure pressed up against the far wall. Two little stockinged legs. Silver buttoned leather boots. A small white frock.

"Ana."

A thin voice wept at the end of the hall. The figure had its back to him, face and hands pressed against the wall, as if playing a game of Hide Me Seek Me. Chauncey staggered into the darkness, swaying on his feet. He thirsted after that bottle of whiskey down below. But first...

He came to the little white figure, standing in the cone of light. His vision blurred, as he reached out his hand, half believing in what he saw, half wondering if he had been dreaming. He placed his hand on the small shoulder. Slowly, the child turned, and as he saw her small chubby face, everything within him seemed to collapse. He wept loud wails of grief as he pulled her into his arms. They fell back, she kissing his face and wiping his tears, he digging his old crooked fingers into her golden hair. The empty glass in his hand had fallen and shattered into glittering shards across the carpet. He did not take notice.

*My child, my child, my poor little girl...*

"Oh, Papa. I've missed you so!"

"Ana girl, my dear little Ana girl..."

He held her in his arms, as he had so often done in his dreams, only this time it was real, she was warm alive and real, and his own little girl again. They both cried on the corridor floor. His whole body quaked with his sobs as he rocked her as if she were a baby again. He held her close, his eyes shut tight.

"Papa...*it hurts...* " Her voice became low and oddly deep.

"No, my little Ana, I shall not let you ever hurt again. Never never never."

"But...I am bleeding..."

He opened his eyes. She was no longer a child, but now a grown woman sitting on her knees before him, her belly swollen and round. She turned pale as paper, doubling over in pain.

Suddenly, crimson bloomed on the front of her white dressing gown between her thighs. She began to cry out in pain as the blood spread in a dark puddle on the carpet over the shards of broken glass. Her hands were red with it. She reached out and clutched at him, spattering him with hot stickiness.

"Papa, please...Save my baby...He is dying..." She fell back.

"NO!" He scrambled over, holding her in his arms. Her dark eyes looked up at him in fear and confusion.But in moments her gaze grew blank, and her body fell limp. He held her dead, swollen body to himself, threw his head back and howled.

Carolene was dreaming. A Banshee had come into their bedchamber through the window, screaming Ana's name. But as she sat bolt upright in her bed, the screaming continued, and she rushed from their richly decorated room into the stairwell, still half dreaming, not remembering to take the candlestick with her. She ran down the steps into the main corridor, and stopped dead in her tracks.

The Banshee had come from her dream, and was sitting with its thin back to her, dressed in a white death shroud, surrounded by a thin pool of light in the darkness. She nearly turned and fled, but instead drew her wits about her. It was no banshee, but her husband. He was sitting alone on the ground, rocking himself in his nightclothes.

"Chauncey! Chauncey, what has happened?" She rushed forward then recoiled. His arms and the front of his night shirt was dark red with blood.

"Ana..." he whispered, dazed. "She is bleeding. I cannot make it stop." He fell forward on his face, sobbing.

She came to him quickly. Chunks of shining glass stuck out in jagged spikes from his forearms. His blood was spread about everywhere, but Carolene could see at once the wounds were not serious. She was very frightened, and being frightened always made her angry.

"You fool! Been drinking again, and now look at what you have done! Broken glass everywhere, it is a wonder you have not killed yourself! You have no business lying about on the floor like this! What do you mean by it?"

"But...where is Ana?"

She didn't answer. She roughly pulled him to his feet and led him to the bedchamber. She did not wish that the servants see the master like this. Tongues would wag, and it would reach the Statehood.

As she pulled the bits of the broken glass from his arms and dressed each wound before the fire, he told her everything that he had seen. Ana, alive again, her blood staining everything as she died a second death. Only this time it was in his arms. Carolene began to weep despite herself, which made her even angrier.

"You drunkard. No blood but your own has been spilled. And how dare you speak to me of Ana...This is black witchery...I shall not hear any more of it."

"You are the fool, woman. I saw her. I held her. Ana was here, in my arms." The strange light in his eyes made her blood run cold, and she said no more. Carolene went back to sleep in one of the spare bedchambers of the estate. But neither of them slept that night. The next morning, Lord Chauncey bid the old necromancer to visit the king.

*     *     *     *

As they passed the dark recesses of the royal torture chambers, Nelios said nothing at all. When they opened the doors to the dungeon cell that now served as the new royal bedchamber, they were met by the stench of sweat and madness.

"You shall pardon His Majesty. He has been a bit... agitated just this morning," explained Lord Chauncey.

The boy was chained to the stone wall of the roundish cell. He was slumped on the ground, his thin arms hung out by chains like two broken bird's wings. The room was dark, save for a few bars of light given through a tiny slit of window overhead.

When he saw them he rose, straining against his chains wildly and screaming. His jaws snapped together loudly and his damp hair clung to his cheeks and forehead, disfiguring his face. Lord Chauncey and the guards behind him took a step back. Nelios stood before the boy thoughtfully. He brought out a green apple from his wrappings and took a bite.

"Why is he chained?" Nelios asked finally. "Is it Thomish custom to treat their monarchy as a prisoner when they have fallen ill?"

"We chained him to prevent him from harming himself. Or others," explained one of the guards, struck by the obviousness of this.

"Set him loose," said Nelios. He cocked his head to one side and peered owlishly at the boy with one blue eye.

"But my Lord," said the guard. "He is dangerous."

"Yes, I know. All the same, set him loose," said Nelios. "All will be well." Theodore lunged against the chains again, screaming.

"Be still, Boy," Nelios said sharply, as if addressing a barking dog. The boy silenced. His eyes were there, but at the same instant not there. It was as if they did not see the room, nor the men about him. He was dreaming with his eyes wide open.

The guard hesitantly approached him and unlocked his chains. Theodore did not snap at him. He simply stared blankly. Nelios tossed the apple aside and approached the boy, kneeling before him. He put his hands on either side of Theodore's face. He brushed the boy's dark hair away from his forehead, and put his face so close to Theodore's that their noses almost touched. He stared into the young king's eyes for a long moment.

The wizard then took Theodore's hand and examined the soft webbing between the boy's fingers. The tiny network of veins shown faint blue under the white skin. He stared at these thoughtfully for a moment, then frowned. He raised Theodore's arm up before his face, balling the boy's fingers into a fist. He let go.

The Theodore's arm and fist remained in the air before him just where the wizard had left it. Nelios raised Theo's fist over the boy's head. Again, it remained in the air where the old man had placed it. The wizard closed his eyes and held is palm just over Theodore's chest. He began whispering strange words under his breath, and the boy relaxed his arm down to his side. Lord Nelios smiled with relief.

Nelios pulled out a piece of parchment and a bit of writing charcoal, rested it on one knee, and began scribbling words across it. Lord Chauncey and the rest strained their necks and read what was written, but could not make any sense of it:

*Tension insanity. Oneirophrenia. This is a thick one, indeed. It fills the air with its odor. There but not there. Awake yet dreaming.*

Nelios stood there, gazing intensely at the parchment at his knee for a long while. Finally, the old man cleared his throat.

"This young man is not truly mad. He is *incantata lacertis.* Under the power of a Darka spell. One that he has naturally imposed upon himself, it would seem."

Theodore's head slowly rolled back drunkenly, and he stared up at something on the ceiling, his eyes glazed. Lord Chauncey said nothing. He wasn't about to give the strange old man the satisfaction of knowing how curious he truly was to know what a Darka spell was.

"Theodore, look at me," said Nelios gently.

The boy only stared at the ceiling.

"Theodore," said Nelios, snapping his fingers. The noise seemed to catch the boy's attention, because his eyes followed the source of the sound, and was now staring that same blank stare at Nelios' fingertips.

"Look at me, boy. Look at my eyes. Can you see my eyes?" said Nelios, pointing to his own face. The boy's gaze followed Nelios' hand until he was made to look into the old man's eyes again. The wizard shut one blue eye, and when it opened again, it was brown. Lord Chauncey's skin prickled as he watched this, and one of the guards blessed himself.

Theodore's eyes cleared and blinked, as if he was finally seeing the face in front of him. He reached out a hand and touched the old wizard's beard with a baby's fascination.

"Good. Now, attend to me," soothed Nelios. "Someone came to you in the night, did they not?"

The boy's chin trembled as he cocked his head childishly to the side, still stroking the wizard's beard.

"Theodore, you must answer me. Who was it?" asked Nelios.

He stared at the wizard, his eyes filling with tears that began to spill down his cheeks. He shook his head slowly.

"Theodore. Please tell me, who came to you in the night?"

The boy finally spoke. "I-I am so sorry. Forgive me, I did not know what would happen. I did not wish to cause harm to anyone. Not...Not truly. Please. Please, get me out of here...She'll be coming back soon..."

"Theodore, answer my question. You are frightened, but you must be strong," said Nelios softly, cupping the boy's face. "Who came to you in the night?"

The boy did not answer at first, but after a long time came a soft whisper as his eyes began to glaze and stare once again into nothing.

"The Demon Craddosche of the Darka, Seventh Lord of the Hell of Haddus..."

"Theodore...*what* Hell is this that you are in?"

"She's coming...Oh dear Lord, she is at the door...Please, help me..."

"What door? Where are you now? Tell me."

"Mother is here...She's come inside now... She's going to hurt me again..."
"Theodore, where are you?"

The boy shut his eyes and screamed.
*"PALE ROOM!!"*

Suddenly, there came the pattering sound of trickling water on the stone floor. Nelios stepped back in time to avoid the slow spreading puddle of urine that spilled from between the boy's knees. Theodore's terrified screams echoed throughout the dungeon.

\*     \*     \*     \*

Lord Chauncey, Nelios and the Seigneurs Du Cordovan assembled at the Statehood Wing at once.

"My Lords," said the old mystic, "Your young king has made a very foolish mistake. He has performed black magick to curse the kingdom of ThoBromis using *Darka* enchantments. He is a child. He did not know of what consequences would come with tampering with such forces. He only knew of his own anger and pain, and this is what drove him to do such a mad thing. He must be forgiven. He must be saved." The gentlemen of parliament murmured among themselves.

"The boy is extremely disturbed. There are torments in his heart that he has kept hidden for much of his young life. Lord Chauncey, for the child's sake, tell me. What happened to the boy's mother? I saw her name in the wheel of his heart. He is greatly distressed by the manner of her death."

"Her Majesty had fallen ill. She passed in her sleep when he was a small child. I cry your forgiveness, Lord Nelios, but that is none of your concern. We did not invite you as a guest of the Royal Headship for the sake of exploiting private matters to foreigners," answered Lord Rexmeyer coldly. The two old men stared hard into each other's eyes, and the wizard finally broke the gaze.

"Please, Lord Nelios," said Lord Marsen in a kinder tone. "What is this black magick of which you speak?"

"Darka magick is the magick of the mind. It has been known throughout time and age, and gone by many names. Many men walk about the earth, free in body but bound by chains of the mind. Chains forged from the past, or in fear of the future, hindering the present. They lead to a slow death of the soul. Some men, though alive in body, are already dead.

"Men are of two minds, you see. The Wakeful Mind, and the Sleeping Mind. The Wakeful Mind is a mind that rules when a man goes about his life. The Sleeping mind...That is the mind where dreams and fears hide, where a man may cloister his deepest secrets to hide from all...Even himself. When madness arises, the Sleeping Mind is the one that is bound and dying in invisible chains; the Wakeful Mind oblivious until it has become too late. When the time comes for the final death of the soul, madness ensues, and the Wakeful Mind falls into the realm of *Darka*. This Death Fall of the Sleeping Mind is the source of all insanity."

"And where is this Darka Realm you speak of?" asked Lord Chauncey. He spoke vaguely, as if his mind were elsewhere. (Perhaps back in the cellar of his house, pondering over the last of the bottles of corn whiskey. He was unbearably thirsty.)

"The Darka has gone by many names. The Spirit World, the Further, the Realm Between, the Plane of Souls...but we all know of this place no matter what we chose to call it. It is part of the void *between* the Wakeful Mind and the Sleeping Mind; a place of angels and demons, where memories of the dead roam. It is the void between our thoughts, much like the blank spaces between the words in the pages of a book. It is here through which dreams travel and take shape, sent to us in Waking from the mind that is Sleeping below.

"This realm is the world to which all of our private minds become conjoined, and the place where the secret hell of madmen dwell. It is also in this realm that there is Light; a place where chaos fades into utter beauty, and the purity of heaven exists. It is through the Light that love and goodness is shared. The realm between locks worlds, realities and universes together in the eternal Web of Consciousness; that which connects us all infinitely. Your boy's Waking Mind has begun its Death Fall into the Darka Realm, and in his despair can see no way to reach the Light."

The old man held Lord Chauncey's gaze, and lifted a bejeweled finger in chide.

"You fret and squabble after the threat of one mere phantom beast beyond your borders in the so-called *LeBois*. But there are far worse horrors that lurk within the minds of the mad. The attack of Tirfan is mild compared to what will soon come. The Death Fall of Thom is on the horizon.

"The boy is trapped in the Darka. Yet in some way, the spell has locked the fate of this kingdom to that of his Sleeping Mind. When his Sleeping Mind has finished its Death Fall, so shall he be, and the Kingdom of Thom will collapse into the Darka Realm forever. *All fates are beholden upon the Mind of he who wears the crown.*"

Something in these words stood out to Lord Chauncey, and he forgot about the bottles of whiskey in his office or the stinging of the wounds bandaged and hidden beneath his robes of state. *Beholden upon the Mind of he who wears the crown...*

The old wizard ceased his speech as he saw the hungry, pained look in Lord Chauncey's eyes. His brow wrinkled as he turned to Lord Marsen.

"If I might be able to understand the deep secrets of the boy's Sleeping Mind, perhaps he can be persuaded and strengthened to fight against the Darka spell that he has used to condemn himself, and come to the Light. But only he can free himself from this curse.

"But there is *plenty* hope for those so are willing to try," said Nelios. There was a faint twinkle in his eyes. "But hope is only gotten by desire for it. My court friends and I will do what we can to assist, as long as we remain permitted to."

The Seigneurs Du Cordovan fell silent.

The strange old man in the top hat gazed at them, but none met his eyes.

"Tell me again about this purple boy of yours, this Tool of God. The people speak of him in whispers. Perhaps when all straw-be-a-gathered, a basket can be made."

Lord Chauncey told the tales of the common folk. Of the night hexes, and the visitation of the dead. As he spoke, sweat began to bead his face, and the hungry light in his eyes glowed so that even the Seigneurs began to stir restlessly in their seats.

As he spoke, he felt that it was all something out of a dream. One of those dreams one has after eating too many sausages and cabbage for supper. One of those dreams where nonsense makes sense and a simple thing can have endless meaning. Lord Chauncey's bandaged arm wouldn't let him dismiss it all so easily, however.

As the events were recounted, the old mystic listened raptly, the fine crow's feet creased at the corners of his eyes deepening. Lord Chauncey half expected him to burst out laughing.

But Nelios of Caramoox did not laugh. At the end of it all he simply asked,

"Where may I meet this purple boy?"

*     *     *     *

*The Tool of God. What a lot of nonsense.* Kulbit poured water into the horse's troughs angrily.

Earlier that morning, a handful of townspeople had still been hanging about the stables, and had begun following him as he worked. It was troublesome at the very least. When one young man came too close, Bolger, a nervous brown steed, became spooked and began to buck, knocking over the trough and leaving a lovely crack in the gate. Kulbit had decided there and then that he had quite enough of being a famed hero.

The worst of it was old Bugger's pandering to his every move. In the light of day, the entire affair seemed ridiculous. Kulbit fully expected that in time the novelty of it would wear off, the old man would eventually resort to his old ways. Very soon he would begin to call Kulbit "Cupcake" again. It was his habit. And why? Because people forget gratitude. Especially when the thing to be grateful for is something out of the ordinary, and life afterward remains *quite* ordinary. A mind might be able to forget the whole thing ever happened. Old Bugger's most certainly would. Wouldn't he?

*And for my own sake and sanity, the sooner the better,* Kulbit thought.

He never would've imagined that being a hero could disrupt one's routine so terribly. Little did he anticipate exactly how disruptive it would truly be. And when the King's armed guards appeared at the front of the stables to retrieve him, he learned there and then.

\*　　\*　　\*　　\*

Emily Marie lost herself within the pages of the old witch's book, for there were many mysterious things that set her mind to itching. She learned about different herbs and their uses for medicine, of how to read dreams as one might read an almanac. Of the different times of the year when it's best to do certain kinds of magick. In the book there were lists of symbols and their meanings, and some of the pages in the book rather read like stories. Emily read of the Goddess Dymm of the Moonsmen of Old, and how her mother is the earth; Mother Terra. She read of a certain dragon's venom that can be boiled and if used in extremely small amounts, can help one see and communicate with the spirits of the dead. She read of how to summon a demon, and how doing such a thing may have dangerous consequences. She read about using animals as familiars, and how these animals can aid in magickal learning just by their very nature. These things seemed quite high and intimidating for her to learn all at once, and she hoped that Grenna had put some smaller spells in the book for a newer witch to tackle.

In the book she came across a section of spells that were to be used for everyday things. A spell of how to find items that one has misplaced. A spell to help one to lose fat, despite eating as many sweets as they might like. A spell to calm a frightened pony. A spell for rain. And a spell that would make any woman immortally beautiful at any age. This last seemed to pique her interest. She had always wondered what it would be like to be beautiful.

Everyone said that Daniellia was such a beauty. She had been fortunate enough to get Papa's clear blue eyes and Mother's shining golden hair. She was small and her figure was nicely curved, her skin without a single freckle. All of the young boys in the village came on her birthday with Lover's Stones. Daniellia was very vain about her looks, and would never leave the house unless her hair was curled and tied with bright ribbons. She would always sneak a bit of Mother's rouge despite not being permitted to, and would refuse to even go to the grocer's without checking a mirror twice. Emily Marie and Carrigan always thought this quite silly, and would tease her. To that, Daniellia would pat her curls haughtily and say, "You're all jealous of me."

Emily Marie never had gotten any attention for her own looks. And while no one had said that she was homely, she assumed that she must be. For no one ever seemed to take notice of her very much. Even Carrigan, who also had blue eyes, golden hair and dimples, was called pretty on occasion, despite wearing spectacles and turning her nose up at such girlish things. Everyone said that someday she would grow to be quite charming, if she could only keep her face out of books long enough for it to be seen.

No one ever took much notice of Emily. It's what comes of being in the middle.

But now that could all change, she thought to herself. A beauty spell would be just the thing to start off with for someone who doesn't know much about spells just yet. If anything, the spell wouldn't work and nothing dangerous should happen...she hoped. Here was the spell, written as follows:

### Spell for Immortal Beauty

*On the night of a full moon, place a Bohemian Ruby stone out in the moonlight in a glass bowl of rain water. Leave it thus until the following night, so that both sun and moon may place blessing upon it. On a piece of paper, write down words of your desired beauty's praises, and burn the paper over the rainwater, letting the ashes fall within. Add a thimble full of corn whiskey, stirring with your writer's finger the way of the clock saying thus:*

*Roses pink and beauteous be,*
*None shall e'er be fairer than me,*
*Eyes be bright and hair so fine,*
*None compare to beauty mine.*
*I AM BEAUTY*
*I AM BEAUTY*
*I AM BEAUTY*
> *Take a saucer and fill it with salt. Sprinkle the beauty potion lightly over to make a thick paste. In the light of three white candles, within a drawn sacred circle, scrub your face with the mixture, and with shut eyes in your mind see all homeliness washing away. Rinse with fresh water. In the morning, you shall look into the mirror and see a lovelier face than was before. Repeat this potion whenever you feel your beauty fading.*

Emily was excited to attempt this spell, but knew it would be no easy task to gather the items needed. Mother had plenty of white candles and though salt was scarce, her family had managed to save a sack or two from Papa's last travels to Srye. It would be difficult to find the pink quartz stone called Bohemian Ruby, as mother was not rich enough to enjoy decorative gardening at their humble cottage, but with a trip to the market and some sleight of hand, she was able to snatch a small one from a pile of colored garden stones for sale and hide it in her stocking. There was plenty of rainwater to be had, and she discovered that Mother had left out a glass bowl in the shed. She found the cat's milk dish would work as the saucer to create the mixture. But the trickiest object to get at was the whiskey.

Her father had a jug of whiskey that he sampled from, only on special occasion. The large jug was kept high on the top of the cupboard, and as Mother's primary place was always in the kitchen, it would have to be late at night when she would be able to climb upon the counter to get at it. The night of a full moon was to be the very next night, and she knew she had but this one chance to get it.

That night after supper, while Mother was tucking Carrigan into bed, she crept into the kitchen in her nightclothes and climbed atop the counter by the washbasin. The top of the cupboard was still a bit over her head, and she had to stretch her arms awkwardly bending at the elbows to get it. It was quite heavy and she was almost unable to lift it.

As the heavy thing lifted from the dusty cupboard top, she nearly lost her balance. Gingerly, she placed the enormous jug by her foot on the counter, and turned to climb down. Something caught on the heel of her slipper. She bit her lip. It was a dish rag, tangled round the washbasin. With a clumsy twist, she slipped and tumbled to the ground, a handful of forks, spoons and two wooden bowls clattering after her. In a flash her mother came running to see her sprawled out on the kitchen floor, surrounded by a mess of utensils.

"Heaven on earth, child! What are you doing?"

"I-I...I was getting a cup. I was going to get a drink from the water pump," Emily managed. Behind the akimbo elbows of her mother, upon the counter sat the large whiskey jug. Emily held her breath, willing her mother not to turn about and see it.

"Well you needn't be climbing about on the counters like this for a cup. One might think you were a cockroach," her mother muttered, turning. She reached for a cup from the cupboard. The whiskey jug was right in front of her and she hadn't noticed it. Emily began to pick up the mess of things she had knocked to the ground.

"Here, I'll get those. Hurry up and get your drink. Then get into bed. Enough time has been wasted already," her mother said, shoving the cup in her hand. Emily fled outside to the water pump. When she came back, her mother had left the kitchen entirely, and the whiskey jug remained right where she left it on the counter.

With a thrill in her belly, she poured a drop of it into her thimble and scampered noiselessly outside to the barn. She climbed the hayloft and up there prepared the Bohemian Ruby Water. She then took the glass bowl out into a secret spot she had found in the old abandoned garden behind the cow shed (Mother never had the time or money to keep a flower garden. She was a very practical woman). It was upon an old tree stump hidden among a thicket of broom bushes. The bowl would not be seen by anyone who might pass by, but could still be shined upon by the light of the sun and moon. And if she sat very still and huddled low, no one would even be able to see her hiding in the brush. It was such a perfect little spot that Emily thought it might be safe enough to keep the rest of her magickal things, all except for the book.

Emily spoke the little rhyme to herself as she stirred the whiskey and water together with her finger. As she did so, she began to imagine what it would be like to be immortally beautiful. Would her face look different? Perhaps her eyes would turn sky blue or pine green, instead of boring old brown.

As her mind wondered over these things her finger stirred faster and faster, until soon within the glass bowl a tiny little tornado formed in the water over the pink stone. The silvery funnel spun faster and faster in the water, but she didn't even notice. She was too busy thinking all sorts of lovely things.

Of how finally all the boys in the town might begin to notice that she wasn't so much of a little girl anymore. Of how the people in the town would all smile at her and the ladies would all gasp and remark on how gracefully she has grown. Of her hair shining and curling in the sunshine, and twisting posies in it, no longer a plain dusty brown but now a luxuriant black. Or maybe her hair would change to a glowing shade of titian. No more freckles on her nose of course, which might be smaller and much daintier. Perhaps she would get a dimple or two, like Carrigan. Or maybe she might even find herself taller!

Her heart beat wildly in her chest as she thought of all the fun she might have once she became beautiful, and finally was startled to notice that she was still stirring. She stopped abruptly, watching with fascination as the little silver funnel slowed and disappeared in the clear water.

"I am beauty..." She whispered shyly. It felt silly to say these words.

"I am beauty..." She stuck out her chin. Perhaps being a witch meant doing silly things.

"I AM BEAUTY!" She shouted, raising her hands in the air gleefully.

"For goodness sake, Emily Marie, are you still outside mucking around with that water pump? Get back to bed this instant!" Her mother called out the window. Emily darted back into the house like a frightened cat.

The very next night she sneaked out of the house with the cat's saucer. In it was a little mound of sea salt. She held three white candlesticks in her other hand. She snuggled down among the broom bushes in her secret spot, sure that she would be hidden in the darkness, but worried that the lit candles might be seen from the kitchen window. It was very late at night, and she had heard the sounds of both Mother and Papa sleeping before. Still, she was quite nervous. Her little tree stump worked very well as a table, and she drew a chalk circle around the edge of it.

"To the spirits of all up, about, and around. Here is a circle of magick, peace and protection. None who wish harm may enter here."

She lit the candles, created the salt and Bohemian Ruby mixture, and began scrubbing her face. The mixture stung the skin of her cheeks and nose, and the night air was bitingly cold, but she scrubbed every last inch of her face. From the top of her hairline, to her ears and all of her neck. The stinging grew worse, and she hoped that she wouldn't break out in some sort of rash and have to explain herself to her mother.

When she was done, she snuffed out the candles with her thumb and finger (a ticklish trick that was not easy to do if one was afraid of the flame), rubbed away the sacred circle, and tossed away the remainder of the salt. She was about to toss away the ruby water, but then thought better of it. If this spell worked out well, she might be able to bottle the potion and use it another time. She had hidden a few empty perfume bottles by the stump, and filled one up to the brim. She then buried the Bohemian Ruby by the stump, along with the potion bottle, and crawled out of the bushes. Her face was now crusted with salt, but a quick rinse at the water pump cleaned it off quickly enough. In moments, she found herself snuggled safely in her bed, in wonder that she had just made her very first witch's potion and cast a witch's spell.

She awoke the very next morning to the sun streaming in through her and her sisters' bedroom. She leaped out of bed and ran to the mirror upon the dresser. When she saw her own familiar face staring hopefully back at her, her heart sank. The spell hadn't worked after all. Her eyes were still brown, as was her straight hair, and other than having a slightly rosier hue from last night's scrubbing, her skin still had freckles over the bridge of her nose.

She was not immortally beautiful. Her magick hadn't worked. She dressed sadly and went to the kitchen to help Mother with breakfast. Mother was pulling biscuits out of the oven. Without a word, Emily began setting the table.

"Here now. Go and fetch the milk." Her mother shooed her away. When Emily returned with the milk, her mother took the jug from her and paused.

"Come here, Em," she said. "You've got dirt on your chin." She took out her handkerchief from her apron, licked it and wiped Emily's chin. She cocked her head to one side and smirked.

"Oh honestly, Emily. You've such a pretty little face. Why must you always keep it so dirty? And don't you think you're old enough to start doing something else with that hair of yours other than those braids? Borrow some of Daniellia's ribbons, maybe the red ones. Red always looks well with brown hair and eyes. It's time you start presenting yourself as a lady."

She turned and continued putting out the breakfast things. Emily smiled. That was the kindest thing her mother had ever said to her. At breakfast, Papa kept staring at her with an odd look on his face.

"Little girl," he said thoughtfully, "I do believe you were having strawberry dreams last night. You've an angel glow about you, no doubt." Emily beamed, and Daniellia rolled her eyes.

"She's all red. What have you been doing to your face? It looks like a cherry," she said, tossing her blonde curls.

"Daniellia, hush." Mother gave her a sharp look.

Emily knew something had to be different. Later that day, she rode into the marketplace with her mother. Despite Emily's begging and protests, Mother sent her to the butchers to see if they were interested in trading firewood for a bit of meat. Emily hated going to the butcher's. The butcher's boy was a frightful bully, and she was always a bit afraid of him.

Emmet was an enormous, nasty sort of boy with yellow hair and always had a pinched look on his round face. He would make fun of the freckles on Emily's nose, which made no sense at all because he himself was covered in freckles from head to toe. Not to mention he often had a lovely crop of pimples across his forehead. But he wasn't a very clever boy. He nicknamed her "Spots".

His father was a kind man, and a friend of Emily's father. Every week or so, mother would try to get meat for the family, and when the butcher's greedy wife was not about, they would accept a trade. Lately, however, it seemed there was no room for charity, so Emmet and his mother would enjoy turning Emily away with her bundle of firewood.

Emily walked into the butcher's, a nice bundle in her arms. Emmet had been sweeping the floor. He glanced up from his work as Emily came in. All the color from his big red face deepened.

"Spots? I-Is that you?" he murmured, raking a hand through his unruly hair.

"Mother made me come," Emily said dryly. Emmet just stared at her, his eyes wide. She thought he looked as if he just swallowed a bug.
"What is it? What are you staring at?" She glared at him.
"H-Hello, Emily...What brings you here?" he stuttered.

Emily made a face. "You know why I'm here, stupid. Do you want this firewood or no?"

"Oh...Right. H-here, let me get that for you. It looks heavy." He dropped the broom with a loud clatter and came over to her, lifting the heavy wood out of her arms. He then stood there, holding the wood and grinning at her stupidly.

"Well?" she said impatiently. "Don't you have any meat to trade?"

"Oh, right, right. I'll go check with Papa..." he scampered away.

Shortly after, the butcher's wife came out. Her face was just as red and fat as Emmet's, only meaner and much more cunning. Emmet followed her, still carrying the firewood.

"We can't spare any extra meat today. Emmet, give her back the wood. We don't want it."

"But Mama...You sure we don't need any more? It's a cold autumn this year. And we've got all that extra beef stored away from-"

"Emmet, do as you're told." His mother glowered at Emily. "Now off with you."

"Yes, Mama..." Emmet sighed reluctantly, gazing at Emily. "I'm sorry...At least... Let me carry it back to the wagon for you?"

Emily raised her eyebrows. "Oh...Thank you."

Despite holding the cumbersome bundle in his arms, Emmet opened the door for Emily with awkward chivalry. He heaved the wood onto the wagon bed. She thanked him, and he smiled again at her in that strange, stupid way. Suddenly a thought came to him.

"I have an idea...Emily, bring your wagon to the back of the shop. I'll meet you there." He scuttled away, disappearing behind the swinging glass doors of the butcher shop. Confused, she climbed into the driver seat, and tugged the reigns of Papa's mule Daisy.

She rode the wagon around the corner of the shop, behind in a back alley. Emmet was standing there, holding four large parcels. He was grinning again. She climbed down.

He loaded them onto the back of the wagon, tucking them behind the wooden bundle and pulled a burlap over them.

Here. Don't worry, Papa had an extra side cut yesterday, and we don't really need most of it. Mama thinks we can sell it, but there's so much of it, it'll spoil before it's all sold. Papa said so, but she never listens. And it's not as if anybody has any extra money to buy this much lately anyway."

"Oh my goodness...Emmet..." Emily peered under the burlap at the large cuts of meat wrapped in paper, her heart beating happily. It would be enough to feed her family for a good while. Mama could salt it and perhaps make some stock.

"Thank you...Thank you ever so much!"

Emmet grinned at her again, shrugging.

"Ah...well...it weren't nothin' so much...You'd better go now. I'll catch it if Mama finds out."

Emily threw her arms around him and squeezed. He jumped, startled. His ruddy face had now become quite purple. Then she hopped into the driver's seat and urged Daisy out of the alley.

As she rode around the corner, she saw her mother standing in front of the butcher's, tapping her foot crossly. She had been trying to trade wood with some of the other grocers and it would seem none would accept her offer either. Her own bundle lay at her feet.

"Where on earth did you ride off to, young lady? You have no permission to..." She saw Emily's bundle of wood still in the wagon, and her face fell. She looked very tired.

"Never mind. We've wasted enough of the day. We're going home." Emily climbed out of the driver's seat and looked back toward the butcher shop. Through the glass window, Emmet was standing with his chin resting on the broomstick as he gazed out at them. He waved, and continued sweeping.

As the wagon rode farther down the street and onto the country rode, Emily tugged at her mother's sleeve. Her mother turned, eyes red rimmed. With a slight flourish, Emily lifted the burlap from the parcels. Mother immediately pulled Daisy to a halt.

"Oh my...Oh my goodness...Emily, where did all of this come from?"

"The butcher's boy gave it to me," Emily said truthfully enough. She was smart enough to know not to mention the manner of how he had done it.

"Oh. Oh those wonderful people. And they didn't even accept the firewood. I must light a blessing candle for them tonight. Oh what good, kind people!" Her mother actually dabbed her eyes.

As they rode home, they passed a young man by the side of the rode, tending to his horse's bridle. When he saw Emily, he paused and flushed. He removed his hat and smiled. A bit later, another wagon passed that was loaded with farm boys on their way homeward after a day's work. All their heads turned and stared at

Emily as they rode past. Mother caught the direction of their gaze. She tousled Emily's hair, smirking.

All the way home, Emily's heart hit an excited beat. She had never gotten this much attention before. Her beauty spell had worked. It had to have. She didn't really see that she looked all that different this morning, but somehow she *was* different. And everyone else saw it but her.

When they arrived home, she helped Mother carry the parcels into the house along with the remainder of the firewood. Mother set to preparing the meat for brine, and Emily excused herself for a moment in her bedroom. She sat in front of the mirror at the dresser. Tipping her chin to one side, she examined herself. Every day, she'd looked into the mirror and seen herself and known what to expect. But this time, it was different.

She never noticed before how her lips were so full and naturally red. Or how her large, brown eyes had a soft, velvety glow to them, thickly fringed by doe-like lashes. She smiled. She had a tiny mole just above the left side corner of her mouth that reminded her of a period at the end of a sentence, accentuating her smile in a declarative way. Her freckles, dusted merrily across the bridge of her nose, reminded her of pepper. She unbraided her long hair and began brushing it. It wasn't curly, but it did have rather a nice color. The sun streaming in from the window gave it a lovely reddish tint. She wondered if perhaps she wasn't still too young to wear her hair up. Daniellia had a pair of wooden combs on the dresser.

Emily swept up the hair from the back of her neck and piled it high upon her head. She pinned the combs in place, and a few soft brown wisps spilled down at her temples and behind her ear. She never realized how high her cheekbones were, or how she had such a long, graceful neck when she wasn't slouching. She leaned into the mirror, and a strange thought came to her. A thought so odd that she felt herself blushing under her own scrutiny. She watched her thin eyebrows arch downward as she frowned thoughtfully. Could it be?

No, never.

Not her.

She was almost too ashamed to even entertain the idea. You're not supposed to think things like this, not when you're the second to youngest and nobody ever notices you.

Could it be that she was actually...*pretty*?

At the idea, her cheeks burned even brighter. Could it be that all this time, she was actually pretty and never knew it? Even without the golden curls, the dimples, the smaller nose or blue eyes, or all the other things she admired in other girls that she thought were prettier than herself. Was it possible that she could actually had been beautiful all along?

She shut her eyes and opened them again. When she did she saw herself almost as if for the first time. A graceful, lovely young girl with the freshness of a blossoming rose. She put her thin hands on her hot cheeks as tears created bright melted star bursts in the darkness of her eyes, then spilled down her oval face. She was beautiful, and for the first time in her life she saw it.

"I...I *am* beauty..." she whispered. Spoken aloud, the words both frightened and thrilled her, feeling both right and wrong at the same time.

"I am beauty."

## AUTHOR'S NOTE

*She typed. And typed. Numbers. Letters. She didn't even know what they meant. It didn't matter. Just as long as she kept typing.*

He can't get into my head this time. I won't let him. I'll forget everything on purpose. Everything he thought he could have will be gone. And the nightmare man, the one who touches my face as I sleep is a big piece of nothing.

*She held her breath as the lights danced through the window. Moments later, everything was silent. She shut her eyes. Who was she kidding? No one ever sleeps here.*

Weird, random memories. Boring to read. *I'll just write something else then. Something angsty and poetic, no doubt. Mental flatulence.*

*My arms are a mile long,*
 *Ever stretching out before me*

*Like two dirt roads into the horizon.*
*If I pull, I can drag myself forward to the edge of the world*
*Burn up in the sun. It will hurt, but only for a few moments,*
*The glory of it will be worth every last bit of pain.*

A poem. Some collection of words that have intense meaning to me, but will probably come off as a pretentious attempt to appear "deep" to everyone else who reads it. I told you, I'm no writer.

## END NOTE

Outside of the fenced corral at the entrance of the Royal Stables, the only sounds that Lord Chauncey could hear were the distant hissing of the croe bugs and the creak of his leather saddle as he sat and waited for the guards to return. He mopped the back of his neck with his handkerchief as the sun blared down.

It was a hot day for this late in the month of Vendemiaire beneath his ceremonial hat, wig, and white robe. Despite the warmth, the spiritualist Nelios stood wrapped in his thick linsey-woolsey cape. The old man was even smoking a pipe. He stood in the humid, murky heat peacefully, a smile resting upon his lips. His eyes were half-closed underneath the white tangle of his eyebrows, and he looked almost as if he were half asleep. In combination with the morning heat, Lord Chauncey found the old man's calm unnerving.

After their brief discussion on of King Theodore's state, the old man claimed he desired to meet the stable boy. Lord Nelios claimed that he wanted to meet the boy in his most familiar surroundings.

*Nonsense is what this is, pure nonsense! If I had known this buffoon intended to lead us all about the palace proper, I never would have sent for him...*He held his throbbing forearm in silence. They waited for the guards to return with the boy.

Kulbit's eyes adjusted to the sun as he followed the guards to the entrance of the royal stables. They brought a message stating that his presence was requested outside.

*Now what have I done?*

He was surprised to see Lord Chauncey, perched atop his brown charger, and the one they had called Lord Nelios of Caramoox, waiting on foot beside him. The old man seemed far taller than he had remembered.

When the wizard spotted the colorful Kulbit, he began to choke on the smoke of his pipe, and fell into a wheezy coughing fit that sounded suspiciously like laughter. When the wizard finally composed himself, he waved the smoke away from his face and came forward solemnly, extending his hand.

"Hello, my boy. I am Lord Nelios of the Caramooxen Court. I have heard much of your adventures regarding the strange happenings in the city of Post as of late," he said. Kulbit took his hand and shook it. The old man's grip was firm and icy.

"I was wondering if we may discuss the matter with you, if you please. You see, we may need your help." Kulbit gazed into the old man's face. His eyes were steady, honest. And so though it was madness to do so, he agreed to go with him to the palace.

# Chapter 9

Deep in the dungeon of the palace for the first time in his life, Kulbit wondered how he had gotten himself into this bizarre mess. He never asked to be any Chosen Vessel, or Tool of God, or anything of that sort. He hadn't wished to be involved with strange, magickal affairs. All he had ever been guilty of was reading and daydreaming a trifle too much, and hearing his own voice in the center of his head. And there was his evident purpleness, of course. Who would have guessed that things as harmless as these would get him into such trouble?

They came to a great round chamber deep in the recesses of darkness that lay below. The Seigneurs Du Cordovan were assembling there, their faces only lit by the dull orange light of candlesticks held in their hands. Kulbit could see fear in those faces.

None had ever been this far in the torture chambers of the dungeon, though many of them had sentence a poor soul or two to be sent down here. Lord Chauncey shivered. To come down into this place, where he had others sent but never the courage to enter himself chilled his blood. Strange metal devices hung about the great round chamber. In the air hung the faint salt and metal scent of sweat and blood. Lord Nelios had required a dark, round room to perform his ritual. And this was the darkest round chamber in the palace.

When they descended, Nelios had followed the Seigneurs Du Cordovan down to the torture chamber with a stern look in his face. Short, angry little puffs of smoke floated up from his pipe as he muttered, "Palaces with torture chambers. No wonder evil has been drawn to curse this kingdom." Lord Chauncey held his tongue.

As they filed into the great echoing chamber, Kulbit bit his lip and shuddered. The old man Nelios had said they were here to do some sort of examination on him to find out what exactly why he was able to stand against the night hexes. He assured Kulbit that it wouldn't hurt, but as the boy eyed a spiked iron device behind a rack of whips, he wished he were back in the stables. He hoped he wouldn't do anything stupid like wetting his breeches. Suddenly the old man turned to him and took his hand.

"All is well my boy," he soothed. "These places are full of darkness, but today we hope to seek light." Kulbit relaxed a very little, though he could not fully understand what the old man meant.

They came to a large round oaken table with two stools. The Seigneurs Du Cordovan stood in a ring about it. They watched, keeping a safe distance as Nelios had instructed. The old man lowered the haversack that was riding on his shoulder onto the table and began rummaging through it.

"Now, boy. If you can, please lie upon the table. Place your head at the very center. Shut your eyes…"

Kulbit did as he was told. If he had ever been to a physician before, perhaps he would not feel quite as nervous, but he hadn't, and there are not many doctors who examine patients down in torture chambers. There seemed to be an inner chill deep within his belly that would not stop him shivering.

He felt the old man place a hand upon his chest, and the trembling ceased. Nelios began to whisper to himself.

*"Incurro, Archverphos. Teleo…Teleo…"*

`He placed white and black candles beside the boy's arms and shoulders as he spoke. He produced a braid of sweet smelling herbs and lit them in the candle's flame. Thin wisps passed over the boy's purple face.

Lord Rexmeyer bristled. "This is witch craft."

"Be still. It is too late now," said Lord Chauncey.

*"Teleo…Rector mini obvius universitas de phantasmatis…*
*Ut ego vires nin perdo vestri semita*
*Nin atrum locus…Teleo, Archverphos. Teleo…Teleo…"*

A warm and steady calm fell over the room like a soft blanket. Kulbit eased, though the tiny hairs on his forearm stood on end, he felt himself drifting away to sleep.

"I know you feel very tired, boy. You wish to float away. But you must not drift too far. You must remain with me for a bit longer yet. Do you understand?"

Kulbit nodded his head sleepily. He hadn't expected to feel so relaxed lying in the center of the palace torture chamber, let alone be able to fall asleep there. But he wished to all the same.

"That is a good lad..." He turned to the guard. "Bring him in."

Kulbit felt as if he were adrift in a sweet smelling haze of purple behind his closed eyes. Everything was purple. The table he rested on was purple, the stone walls of the chamber were purple, the stone floor was purple, the guards were purple, the Seigneurs Du Cordovan were purple, and yes he was purple, the color he hated most and yet plagued him all his life it was all so purple only this time it was good so sweet so sleepy that he wanted to float into the smoke of it the softness of it get lost in the purple of it because the purple was himself and the purple was also everything else and he was both himself and a part of everything else the room the guards the palace the sky all purple all a part of him in his mind in his heart everything in all places all together and one in purple clouds he was higher than everything the sky was endless and full of stars and he flew high in the sky he was the sky the sky was himself and he was going to flip it all and make it his own...

He knew his eyes hadn't opened, yet he could see the lovely lavender sky about him, and he was soaring free. Far below him, in the distance of his mind he felt his ears hear the faint echo of a scream. But why would anyone be screaming now? Everything was so lovely, so peaceful. He could actually see the scream as white curl of smoke dancing in the sky of purple that surrounded him.

*This is loveliness...*

\*     \*     \*     \*

The Seigneurs Du Cordovan were in an uproar. Two guards carried Theodore, the mad boy king of Thom into the chamber, tied in chains to a stretcher. They placed him upon the table, the top of his head nearly touching that of the peacefully still stable boy, who seemed lost in deep repose. Theodore thrashed and shrieked, foam spraying from his lips, his eyes darting back two and fro in his head.

"This is an outrage! It must be stopped!" Lord Gallis said.

"This is the Sorcery of Haddus! An abomination to the Blessed Virgin!" Lord Yeough blessed himself several times.

"SILENCE!" bellowed Lord Chauncey. All were silent. The fierce glow within his eyes made them obey.

The old wizard placed his hands on the mad boy's cheeks.
"Calm," he said.
Theodore eased, staring blankly into the old man's face.
"Sleep," said the wizard, and Theo's eyes shut. His head rested against the wood of the table, the top of his head nearly touching the top of Kulbit's.

*　　*　　*　　*

Before Kulbit, the little white scream evaporated as softly as it had come, and all was silent. He could get lost…if he could just get lost a little bit more… just a little bit farther…

"Kulbit," came the voice of the old man. The words appeared as a ribbon of bright electric blue that surrounded him gently, tickling him. "You're adrift too far. Stay near. Stay here."

But he did not wish to stay, he wanted to drift and drift and drift in this sky world where purple was allowed and welcomed…he wanted to *flip it* the way he usually flipped his own dreams. He almost felt certain he could if he thought hard enough.

"Please, Kulbit…Tell me you are still here. Speak."

*I cannot speak I cannot, I am naught but a mute a stupid little mute…*

"No. You can speak. You are speaking with me right now. Your voice speaks from the center of your mind."
*You can hear me?*

Kulbit opened himself wider in his mind, thought his eyes were shut tight. He could see only the purple sky and he loved it. But the old wizard had heard him speak through the voice of his mind. No one except his dear horse friends ever cared to hear him. Perhaps this wizard would be Kulbit's friend as well. He had so longed for friends for such a very long time. He so longed to be heard.

This was enough to make him tarry while longer. He allowed the blue wisp of the wizard's voice to touch him again and wrap around him like ribbons of silk and pull him earthbound. It was not so much fun to go back down, but the feel of the warm blue words of the Wizard felt comforting.

"Keep speaking to me, boy. Let me hear your mind within my own. Can you do this?"

*Why yes, of course I can. I think I can do it quite easily. But please...Why was someone screaming? I thought I heard a scream. Why would anyone want to scream? I've no desire to hear screaming. This is loveliness. It is all as purple as I am, and it feels so lovely here. So jolly fine. Is this heaven? Please say I may stay here forever...*

"Do not float away into the mists. This is your Darka."

*What is the Darka?*

"It is the Web of Consciousness that connects all minds. But as lovely as it seems, if you lose sight of your life and get lost in your own head, your Waking Mind will collapse in a Death Fall into the Darka. Then you will be lost to madness. Not all of the Darka will be as lovely as that which is your own. Please resist the temptation to lose yourself."

Kulbit's heart sank. He would not be allowed to stay. He was now surrounded by all kinds of light, all in shades of violet, lavender, fuchsia, peach, and gold. The light billowed and swirled within itself, and he marveled at the beauty of it. This was a place where there was no time. No beginnings, no endings. He could merely exist here, and never grow old, never grow bored or tired. He was floating among stars and galaxies; in the gentle rocking arms of the universe.

He knew without knowing that this place was his own secret space. And yet, the wizard's warning rang true in his heart. As lovely as this place might be, he was needed in the reality of his own life. He must be a Hero. He could not make this place his home. But he wished to enjoy it while he may. He wished to never forget it.

\*     \*     \*     \*

The old wizard took out black candles and placed them about the King, in opposition to Kulbit's. He brought two flat, oval bits of sliced of white crystal out of his sack and placed each one upon the boys' foreheads. Theo moaned.

"Theodore, I know you are also very tired. Your mind is ill, and you are trapped. Let me help you to discover the peace that you were meant to have."

The boy's voice came as a croaking whisper. Tears streamed back his temples from the corners of his eyes. "Yes. Please. Help me..."

"Theodore, you are not in this place with us. You have become lost in the Darka. Where are you?"
There came no answer.

"Where are you, Theodore? Show me an image of where your mind dwells."

All at once, a bright cone of light shone from the crystal atop the king's head to the ceiling of the chamber. The Lords backed far away from the table, murmuring, trembling. One even started toward the door. Within this cylinder of light an image began to form. An elegant white door, crowned with a gilded fanlight. The door opened and one could see the things inside of a room. A chair. Behind this, a fireplace mantel. The hearth was cold and barren. All that was within the room was a pale shade of dull white. Not a bit of color could be seen.
"Theodore, what is this door? Tell me where this place is."
The king's whisper was so faint that it was almost unheard. His face crumpled in anguish.
"Pale Room...."
"Where is this pale room? Can you show me?"
No answer. The old necromancer shook his head. "He does not know."

"Lords, I believe now is the time. Lord Chauncey, I beseech you to consider-" began Lord Marsen. He was silenced by a look from Lord Chauncey. The old Seigneur's eyes dropped.

Nelios' gaze passed between the two men, but they intended to say no more. He returned his attention to the purple boy.
"Kulbit, are you still present?"

*Yes.*

"Can you feel my finger touching the crown of your head?"
The old man's fingertip dug through the colorful mass of blue curls
until it was touching Kulbit's scalp.
*Yes, I think so.*

"There is an opening at the top of your head as the blossoming
of a rose. Free yourself of this rose, but stay near. You mustn't lose
yourself."

\*     \*     \*     \*

Kulbit felt his surroundings, seeing with the middle of his
mind. He felt himself sliding up and up, and suddenly the purple
haze was gone. He was spinning, spinning in a tunnel of darkness.
The feeling of loveliness had vanished.

\*     \*     \*     \*

"Kulbit...where are you?"
Silence.
"Show yourself in the outer Darka. Please."

Suddenly, a second cone of light shone from the crystal upon
Kulbit's head. An image formed. It was of Kulbit himself. He was
hovering footless above his own face within this cone of light, his
hands over his eyes.

"Kulbit, will you serve your king, and prove your honor as a true
hero?"
Silence.

The Seigneurs Du Cordovan cowered against the walls, many
of them whispering prayers as they gazed at the floating apparition
in the cone of light before them.

"His spirit...It has emerged from his body," whispered Lord
Marsen.

Nelios placed a hand on Kulbit's chest. "Attend to me, boy.
There is a door that lies behind you. Beyond this door lies the
secrets of the King. Call to him, and aid him in his secret world.
But within this world is much pain. You must face the pain, and

never turn your back on it. If you do, you will also be lost to madness."

The image of Kulbit slowly turned, lowering his hands from his eyes, facing the image of the door that hovered above the cone of light over Theodore's face. The apparition moved forward, out of its own cone of light and into that of the King's. Kulbit perched on the edge of the pale room's door.

The light that shone from Kulbit's forehead melted away like a snowdrop. His body sagged nearly lifeless on the table. In the cone of light, the image of him looked about the room. The silhouette of his back cut darkness into the cold light of the pale room. It raised its hands to its mouth and called.

*Your Majesty! Where are you?*

There was no answer.

Nelios ran his hands over his face. "The king is farther lost than I had supposed. He is lost from his own secret place in the Darka, and is now roaming the unknown."

Suddenly, the pale room dimmed. The elegant door vanished. Only the image of Kulbit was left hovering footless over the king's sleeping face. The image turned.

"Nah, boy! Do not turn your back on the pain,"- began Nelios. Suddenly, Kulbit's body arched his back on the table, gasping for air. His lips paled and began moving silently, his brow furrowing in thick grooves.

The image of Kulbit's eyes widened. He looked about the torture chamber. His lips parted, and he spoke.

"W-Whaa-huh?" said a thin voice.

Kulbit's straining body began to writhe, his boot heels thudding against the oaken table. His eyes opened and rolled back into his skull, as the crystal slice upon his head fell to the ground, shattering to pieces. Foam began to form at the corners of his mouth. Nelios struggled to hold his wrists. Kulbit's arms spasmed, his fingers flexing into two purple claws.

"He's seizing! Help me! Hold him!" Nelios shouted. The guards and the Seigneurs Du Cordovan just stood, blinking stupidly at each other.

Kulbit's apparition gave a start. His hands flew to his mouth. He began to rise slowly. His eyes began to spill over with tears.

*Please…Help… I'm slipping away…*

Kulbit's body kicked free of the old man's grasp.

The apparition of Kulbit began to fade as it rose footless into the air. It looked pleadingly at those around him.

*The darkness…It is making me drift. I'll be lost…Please!*

"No, lad! Hold tight to yourself!" shouted Nelios.

As if woken from a nightmare, Lord Chauncey rushed to Nelios' side. He grabbed the boy's kicking legs. He thundered at the guards. "FOOLS! HOLD HIM! HOLD HIM FAST!"

The guards finally began to move. They surrounded the boy, holding his arms and legs to the table while his head whipped back and forth. The old wizard fumbled in his haversack for a large red stone. He placed it over Kulbit's chest.
"Brace and ground yourself, boy! Hear my voice or all is lost! *GROUND!!!*"

The apparition threw back his head and howled silently as it became smaller and smaller, finally disappearing. Suddenly, Kulbit sat up gasping for air and sputtering, eyes wide with panic. The guards released him. Nelios came to him, holding him. Kulbit eased, though the tears would not stop falling from his face.

"It is over, boy. All over. You are safe, you brave, strong, wonderful, gifted child," he soothed. "But tell me. Did you see him in the darkness? Did you see the King?"
Kulbit shook his head slowly.

"Then it is true. The king's mind is truly lost."

\*     \*     \*     \*

Late that night the old wizard was once again in the statehood wing. The two boys were both sent to their beds; one into the safe warmth of the royal chamber, and the other to a hayloft above a stable. The court room was silent. The old wizard stood in the clearing of the great pillared room, before the Seigneurs Du Cordovan. He fingered the crystal bauble atop his cane. Finally, he spoke.

"The king's mind is lost in the void of the Darka. It will not be easily retrieved. His body remains present, but the spirit and mind are far gone. He has hidden himself for all these years so deep in his own head, so skillfully that he has now lost himself. This has driven him to madness."

"But what of this stable boy?" asked Lord Marsen. "Is he truly...the Tool of God? Can he not be made to find the king's mind, lost in this Darka realm?"

"This stable boy is a simple lad. In all my days of magick I've yet to see a Chosen One that is not simply one who has made The Choice for themselves. But he is gifted. His mind is a strange thing that I have never seen. It is unlike any other. The Waking Mind, that tells us our thoughts, our decisions, how to live our lives. And the Sleeping Mind, that hides the deepest of secrets even from ourselves are both a part of every beast, man, woman, and child. All have both of these. But this stable boy's Sleeping Mind is...to say the least...Awake.

"Where at times our minds play tricks upon us, his mind plays none. Where at times our minds hide thoughts from us, he can find them and change them to suit his fancy. This boy is incapable of full nightmares because when nightmares arise, his mind is Wakeful and can subdue them by his will. Even in his deepest sleep, he is still awake. And so the Darka magick spell of this Craddosche has no power over him. In fact, through all of the Darka Realms, between minds and universes and beyond, he is empowered."

The lords murmured softly. Lord Chauncey arose and turned his back to them, lost in deep thought.

"What shall we do then? What, pray, do you propose we do with these two children who hold our fate within their minds?" asked Lord Marsen.

"We are cursed," said Lord Rexmeyer.

"I must take both boys back to Caramoox with me. The purple one does not know of the power that he has while Craddocshe's spell remains over this part of the Waking World. We are fortunate that he is not of a more sinister nature. With his great power comes the chance of endless danger, if he is not taught to wield it. But he seems to be a good young man. Simple, gentle, and stout-hearted. His deepest wish is to be a hero. I shall train him in the skills of Darka magick, so that his mind can be strong enough to fight against the spell cast, and pure enough to resist the pathways of fear that could lead to destruction. The King shall come with me as well, for I may give him magickal remedies that will ease his mind. While the crown is upon his head, the fate of Thom is yet tied to its contents," said Nelios.

"What madness is this? To give our king to a foreigner," huffed Lord Gallis.

"And the Empress of Tirfan? What shall we do when war is in the horizon?"

"But we cannot be crownless! Think of the fear of the people!"

Suddenly Lord Chauncey spoke, silencing them all. "Silence. The church shall always be our figurehead. But even still...This stable boy may be key to all ends..." The strange light in the High Lord's eye returned.

The old necromancer caught his gaze. "We may ride to Srye, and make ready our ships for Caramoox."

"We shall decide this matter within our own council," Lord Chauncey said vaguely. His hand absentmindedly stroked his cloaked forearm.

"Here here! We'll not have outsiders decide affairs of state. These are Thomish matters."

Lord Nelios ignored this, his eyes never leaving Chauncey's face. "My friend, your eyes speak louder of your intentions than your voice. What is it that you wish to do here?"

"Lord Nelios, we thank you for your aid. You are free to retire," replied Lord Chauncey. The greed in his eyes shone like fire. The two older men stared at one another in silence. Finally, Nelios bowed gracefully.

"It is my honor, Seigneur," he said, and with another bow, he left.

\*  \*  \*  \*

Kulbit lay in the warmth of his bed in deep sleep, as his mind reveled at the happenings of the day. He was soaring in the great purple expanse again. It was not quite the same as it had been before. The warmth and loveliness had lessened. But he promised himself that he would never forget this place. He decided that this was to now be his favorite dream. It was here where he would build great towers of glass and gold. It was in this space where he planned to slay dragons and woo lovely princesses. It was this place where he *flipped*. But not today. Today he did not feel for telling stories and flipping dreams. He wished to think and think very hard.

He found himself sitting by a brook, his chin resting on his palms, and gazed calmly into the clear water. His own reflection gazed back at him, flecked with tiny glimmers of light off the silver backs of a school of fish swimming beneath. Today was a different thing. The purple mists that had so lovingly enveloped him, and lifted him high while deep within the torture chambers of the castle. It had chased away his fear of the present and delivered him into his own essence. This mist...this sky world... It was something he only experienced in the privacy of his mind. It was freedom.

And today, that strange man from across the Indigo showed him a thing he never could have imagined possible. Something was released deep within his mind, and instead of hiding inside this place of comfort, the comfort came spilling through him out to the real world. It surrounded him. And they could all see it. Just as they saw the great beast that attacked at the Post. It was all around him. He was powerful. He had never felt such a strength within him before.

But there was another thing. The strange white chamber; this Pale Room. So desolate. So thick with sadness. As Kulbit stepped into the room, he could feel the cold stone under his feet. The room had such heaviness. It stank of the sweet, sick smell of death. It was more than he could bear. He longed for the purple sky again.

And so he turned about, although he was told not to. He did as he had always done. He *flipped.* He wished to leave that painful place, and go back into the purple freedom he had come from. He did not realize that he might get lost in whatever lies beyond. Kulbit sank his cupped hands into the icy water, and drank. It was delicious, and calmed his mind.

What was happening all around him? What is this new, peaceful thing? Was it the same force that had driven the king mad? That had caused the night hexes? Kulbit lay back into the soft grass and gazed at the clouds through the soothing mists and knew that it most certainly was. It was only a shame that what felt so calming to him meant fear and pain to others.

*       *       *       *

Later that night, Lord Chauncey took another Drip for the Sandman's Ship as he scribbled across the parchment paper what he and so many of his councilmen decided to be the best course of action.

> *"The Seigneurs Du Cordovan, High Court of Thom, declare upon this day, the three and twentieth of Vendemiaire, the necessity for an Article of Impeachment, and Depositus upon the head of monarch King Theodore the First, son of Leonard the First, son of Eller and of Elmondierre and of Adrien..."*

*     *     *     *

Nelios sat in the high veranda of his richly furnished guest's chamber, the moon a great silver half in the sky. The room was dark save for a single candlestick upon the table, the moonlight, and the soft intermittent glow of his pipe. His dark eyes were troubled. The men of this country were so proud, so founded in tradition. But beneath this pride lay an ocean of fear.

The strange, hungry glow in the eyes of the High Lord of Cordovan...His plans would not result in the ways that he believed they would, just as poor Theodore's plans did not end accordingly. If only these men had the sense and courage to heal instead of hide. If only...

Nelios' brow furrowed into a white wiry mesh. His eye sharpened as something approached in the distance. A fluttering cloud in the horizon. All at once he was surrounded by a small cyclone of yellow butterflies. They landed all atop him, their wings swaying open and shut upon his shoulders, his beard and his nose. He stood, a mass of fluttering wings.

"What news?" he whispered, holding open his hand. As he moved, the butterflies on his arms fluttered momentarily, then returned to his sleeves. One particularly bright butterfly alighted in his palm. Its tiny legs folded beneath its body, and obediently spread its wings open and flat. Across each wing were letters written in blue ink; on the very left hand corner of one, a crest symbol was penned. Nelios' face fell as he read the message.

"Oh, *Ragazza.* Not again," he muttered to himself. He immediately turned into the room, the cloud of butterflies leaving him and disappearing into the night. He lit the candelabra and brought out a quill, parchment and an inkwell from his sack.

*To my most gracious hosts, the Crown and gentry of Thom,*

*It is with utmost regret that I and my party must depart ThoBromis at once. We must return to Caramoox immediately due to a most regrettable development. My adopted ward, the Silver Princess, Lady of the Looking Glass; who is as much as a daughter to me as well as my protégé and a valued seatholder to the Caramooxen Court, has gone missing. My apologies for this sudden departure in this time of your dilemma. Be assured that I will return and attempt to assist the court as soon as our own matter has been resolved.*
*Blessed Be,*
*Lord Nelios, High Seatholder of the Caramooxen Court, Wizard of the Moon*

He rang for the page and sent him off to Lord Chauncey's personal estate with a gold piece in his pocket and the letter addressed to the High Lord of Thom. As the Caramooxen flew covertly into the night, a single tear trailed down the cheek of Theodore as he lay strapped to the cot in the dank dungeon cell. His dark eyes were wide and stared absently through the slit of a window at the half gibbous moon.

The next morning was cold and wet as the townspeople gathered around the Post. A rider from the palace had come in the night and placed a notice on the pillar.

*By Sovereign Decree of the Seigneurs Du cordovan*
*It is hereby announced to the peoples of the kingdom ThoBromis that upon this day, the nine-and twentieth of Vendemiaire, that King Theodore, son of Leonard, son of Eller, Elmondierre and Adrien of the Trydus Line, through examination of the High Priest of Thom, and the Church of ThoBromis is declared unwell and unfit to rule. The Minister of Titles is to investigate the next bloodline anointed by Our Lady, Mother of God to be appointed to become bearer of the Crown of Thom.*
Theodore was deposed. ThoBromis was to have a new ruler.

# Chapter 10

Two days later, Kulbit had been mucking out the stables. He was covered in filth from head to toe, and stank of straw, sweat, and manure. When he heard the royal guard's horses approach the stables for the second time, his blood ran cold. He had no desire to have any more fooling about with magick. It was strange enough that all he wished to do since the first visit was dream of that purple sky world, or that there were still people following him about calling him all sorts of tools and vessels and things. He turned and bent over his work, hoping they might have other business than to bother with him.

*I daresay I never thought magickal adventures could be so tedious. Perhaps if I just mind my own business they'll go away...*

He had hardly any time to wonder what has happening to him before two armed guards stormed into the stables, grabbed him on either side, and were dragging him down East West Road. If he was not a mute, he would have asked many of the usual questions of why and what and when, as one does when one finds themselves in manacles, surrounded by guarded men on horseback and placed in a carriage with bars in the windows. As they slammed the doors closed on him, all he could do is gaze wide eyed and silent out through the small slit between them, his heart throbbing within his chest and roaring in his ears.

*What now? Good gracious!*

As he was now seen by many as the Chosen Vessel of God, it was not long before the handful of onlookers who had come to be near the Holy Stable Boy and watch him at his work began to protest and stand in the way of the horses.

"Here, what are you doing? Where are you taking him?" shouted Mrs. Templeton.

"Stand aside, woman." The guard atop the carriage said.

"No. You must let him go. He is the Tool of God!" cried Mrs. Bonnaire.

"Heigh, what's the lad done? He hadn't done nothin'. You let him be," said Bugger. Six or seven other men had come with him. One was carrying a shovel. A few women trailed behind them, crying.

"Stand aside!"

"Here then!" shouted Mrs. Templeton. Kulbit saw her stoop and grab a lump of dirt. It flew from her hand and hit the roof of the carriage. Soon after, all was chaos.

A large number of people came and surrounded the carriage. He heard the guardsmen shouting, and the sound of dirt and stones thudding off of the sides of the hansom. Very soon, he was being jostled and shaken as the crowds pressed inward, lifting and rocking the hansom.

*They're going to topple us!* He braced himself against the wall. He saw a brilliant flash of red coats from between the doors as the guardsmen began to fight back against the people. He thought he heard Mrs. Bonnaire scream, and through the crack between the doors he made out Mrs. Templeton sitting on the ground. Blood trickled from her forehead.

*No... No! Everyone, stop this!*

Suddenly, he was thrown off his feet as the jail carriage thrust forward across the cobblestone. The guardsmen were fleeing, and as Kulbit gazed between the bars behind them, he saw the crowd of townspeople following in hot pursuit. Some were still throwing stones.

*"Free him! Free the tool of God!"*
*"They'll crucify him!"*

"OPEN THE GATES!" came the voice of one of the guards. The carriage raced behind the great stone walls of the palace proper with a loud crash that Kulbit would never forget, as the gates closed them in.

The horses slowed as they approached the Statehood Wing. Kulbit's heart roared in his ears, terror silencing even the thoughts of his mind. What was all this? Was he to go to trial?

The doors of the jail carriage opened suddenly, white light shining in and blinding him. He froze. Outside there seemed to be a crowd. Kulbit slowly rose to his feet and climbed cautiously out of the carriage. A guard grabbed his hands and unlocked the manacles, then stood aside. Rubbing his wrists, Kulbit gazed about.

Assembled before him at the great doors of the Statehood Wing stood the entire company of Parliament. Kulbit gave a start as fanfare suddenly screamed at him from the top of the assembly. The Royal Herald stepped forth, dressed in a fine gold doublet with rows of ruffles all about the sleeves and throat, his hair powdered white. He walked stiffly down the aisle toward the hansom in silence.

The Herald approached Kulbit, his hand extended. He bowed. A dark object gleamed from within his gloved palm. Kulbit took it. A heavy sun made of red gold with a large garnet in the center of its circle of flames. It was the High Crest of Thom, Amulet of the King. He had only ever seen its image in the paintings of the kings of old within the halls of the library. And now here it was, resting in his filthy purple palm.

The herald spoke.

"By the Blessed Virgin, and by the Will of God, the King is dethroned. All hail Kulbit, King of Thom."

The entire assembly bowed on bended knee.

The party spoke in unison. "Hail, Hail. Hail to the King of Thom."

Cold prickles of gooseflesh spread up and across Kulbit's back. He was to be the next King of ThoBromis.

\*     \*     \*     \*

It was a difficult task to execute, to find reason to place the crown on a mute, discolored orphan from the stables. But the Seigneurs Du Cordovan were well practiced in the art of maintaining the law to their own means. Kulbit was by official record, a nameless orphan taken under possession of the Crown. According to the chronicles of titles, he had no namesake, no heritage. But like many things in ThoBromis, though unofficially recognized, there was still room to deviate.

Kulbit was of the line of Trellendale. And although this was not of a strict royal lineage, it was a very old lineage, and could be traced back thirteen generations to the blood of royalty. It was upon this feeble claim that the Minister of Titles declared him to be the next rightful heir to the throne. Theodore, the Former King, was unceremoniously stripped of all rights and titles, and had now become nameless, property of the Crown. It is very rare that the tables turn so drastically and so fast. But ask any who has lived more than a decade in this world, and they will tell you it is a possibility.

Kulbit did not know what to do as he stood before the entire Thomish Parliament on bended knee before him, and had to be led to the next order of things by the Herald himself. He was taken to a lavish blue carriage still covered from head to toe in stable filth. He rode in it with the guardsmen to the center of the palace proper, and there he came to a place he had never set foot before; the Royal Community in the heart of the palace reserve. He had never seen what lie beyond the gray wall that surrounded the great estates of the royal family and the high bloods, and now this was to be his home.

*This must be a dream...It simply must be.*

He stepped down from the royal carriage before the great stairs. Hundreds of nobility stood ready to receive him in utter silence. At the top of the great steps, six trumpeters arched their gleaming horns into the air. Fanfare pierced the solemn stillness of the morning. Silent lightening flashed overhead.

"His Royal Majesty, King Kulbit of Trellendale, High Sovereign of Thom!"

The yard fell silent again. The courtiers parted. Kulbit blinked, unknowing of what was expected of him, until a brief nudge from the armed guard behind him told him. He walked slowly through the great parting of noblemen and women. As he passed, they made no effort to hide their stares of disdain. For he wasn't true royalty, but a strange looking peasant. Yet he would now outrank them all. He came to the great steps, and they all bowed in silence. The heavy gates of the Royal Community closed behind the procession with a loud groaning thud that echoed across the courtyard.

The guardsmen took him down a great opulent hall, their boot heels clicking in loud echoes through many corridors and marble steps, and through the great oaken doors to the apartments of the King. This was to be his new home. The two guards that escorted him bowed and exited, leaving Kulbit alone in the enormous room. He stood, gazing about himself in disbelief. Only what seemed moments ago, he was minding his own matters. And now here he was, the Crest of Thom in his hands, in the very bedchamber of the royal monarchy. It had not quite yet dawned on him that he *was* the royal monarchy.

*This must be a dream. Why can I not flip the blasted thing?*

The room was roundish, and rich colored draperies hung high upon each wall. There were panels of deep crimson bordered with gold filigree and delicate scroll work. Great fans of peacock feathers hung amidst each panel. Gilt, crystal, mirrors, velvet and fine artistry filled the place, but what stood out to him was the strange smell. As if something had been burned.

In the sleeping area of the main room, there was a large empty space, the carpet on the ground before it was covered in patches of soot. There was no royal bed in that space, though there was meant to be. But in its place still hung the heavy velvet canopy that once hung over it, fringed with gold and stinking of fire and ash.

Kulbit came to the middle of this space. The drapes were blackened from flame. The ground there had been swept clean, and all that remained was the cold marble floor. This was the great space where hundreds of Thomish kings had been born to rule, rested during their reign, and died at their end. The look of it gave Kulbit's skin a cold prickle.

He closed his eyes and saw the room with the middle of his mind. And what he sensed there gave him no comfort. This ancient chamber had seen much pain, torment, and many deep secrets. Kulbit, who was quiet himself therefore normally didn't mind quietness, was unnerved by the silence. He tried to open the great oaken doors, and found to his dismay that they were locked. He was trapped.

*The least they could do is perhaps have someone come in here and talk to me. I'm still not certain as to what the meaning of all of this is...* After several more weak tugs at the brass handles, he gave up.

All about the walls were hung many paintings. In the paintings were the kings and queens of old. Kulbit did not like what he saw in some of their faces. The women were plump and lovely and pale, their cheeks, lips and fingertips rosy. But in their eyes was such sadness, such desperation. The men were hard-faced and dark-haired. A noble ancestry, to say the least. He stood for a long while, marveling at the strangeness of it all.

He went to the glass doors of the windowed wall that led out to the balcony and sat upon a lovely white bench, gazing over the great smooth lawns of the Palace. Extravagantly clad nobility dotted the green expanse, meandering here and there idly. The grayness of the sky reflected bleakly in the unwavering surface of the lake beyond the neat apple orchard. Everywhere he looked, there was such elegance, such grandeur. But it also seemed so very cold and unfriendly.

Hugging himself, he returned indoors. He sat on the bench of a beautiful white harpsichord and wished that he were back in the stables. He was no stranger to the strange whim of noble folk. But being King was not his business. He nearly jumped out of his skin that evening when the doors opened and an old woman came doddering in with a cart.

"Hello there, Little Mansie. Aren't you a pretty one! They said that you were all lovely colors. I've brought you a present." The old woman talked as she began to lay out nightclothes out for him.

"Don't you fret, Little One," she was saying, "We'll be getting you a nice new bed very soon. Lord Chauncey says you aren't to leave to royal bedchamber at all by yourself, so Maggie brought Poppet in some storybooks to read. I'll have the page come in with your tubby and hot water after supper so Poppet can have a bath before bedtime, and wash those lovely blue curls."

She pulled the cloth off of the cart, and to Kulbit's delight there were stacks and stacks of books underneath. He smiled at her gratefully. The old woman gave him a kiss and wished him good night. Shortly after, another cart arrived with a sumptuous feast.

The supper was delicious, of course. Roast venison, red cabbage, onion soup, and all assorted cheeses he'd never tasted before, and a bottle of the finest white bubbled wine. For dessert there was what seemed to be a mountain made of brightly colored macarons and petite fours. Much better than the bowl of stew and a hunk of bread he had usually gotten from Mrs. Templeton, save for the times when she could sneak him a pastry or two. He wondered if she was all right.

He poured himself a glass of bubbled wine and nibbled on a purple macaron while gazing again out the windowed wall. His breath taken away by the sight of the city lights of Post beyond the palace proper.

*I suppose I should be happy. This is the sort of thing that occurs in stories, is it not? A poor man suddenly becomes rich, a pauper finds himself to be the heir to the throne. But I do not wish to be king. I had always wished to be a warrior, to fight for honor and adventure. This isn't my dream...perhaps these are the fantasies of someone else. Why am I here?*

He recoiled as a rat skittered across the chamber floor. It stopped at the far corner, hiding behind a side table. It stared at Kulbit with glinting black eyes. He was used to rats in general, but never thought to see one here in the Royal Palace. Perhaps the Palace was not very much different from his stable loft, after all. Kulbit waved a hand at the rat. He tried to say *shoo*, but all that came out was:

"Shh! Shh!"

The rat stared up at Kulbit curiously. Kulbit laughed at himself. He was a fool. A pure fool. All his fantasies of being the wandering hero were pure drivel and he knew it. He couldn't even frighten a little rat.

The little rat sniffed the air and stepped closer cautiously. Kulbit broke off a crumb of cake and tossed it. It took the pastel piece of sweet and scampered away.

*There you go now. You'll probably come back while I'm sleeping and gnaw my ears off. What a big, fancy palace this is. Filled with rats, like anywhere else...*

He sipped the bubbled wine and wished there was a way he could ask for answers for all of this. Never in his wildest dreams would he imagine this, nor would he imagine anyone else would dare imagine it. No one had ever thought he'd amount to much, but then they all called him the Tool of God. And now, he was King? Strange indeed.

The taste of the sweets and bubbled wine and all the finery surrounding him brought the memory of the Contessa Elisabetta Di Marcheris to his mind, and with it came the smells and sounds of summer. Of the scent of lavender and the trumpeting of swans and the taste of salted cheese over berry cream tarts. He hadn't thought of her in a while. Not that he could fully forget, of course. How could he when the memory of her still stung? Though he was certain that she had forgotten him.

*I wonder what she'd say if she could see me now?* The thought made his heart skip a beat.

From the day she discovered his secret writing book to the end of that summer, he continued his duties to the Ladies of Copplea. He cared for their horses, rode them out to the country, served them and cleared up their picnic things. But the loveliness of it all had gone. She was still the most beautiful girl he had ever seen; still kind to him and invited him to enjoy their outings, but her beauty and kindness had seemed to take a certain unbearable coldness to him that only pained his heart.

And now, the silly Besotted Stable Boy sipped wine in the king's chambers. Would she presently consider his proposal of marriage? What noble lady would turn down a chance to become Queen of Thom? He suddenly felt quite dizzy.

*She was too good for me before, and she saw me as nothing. But now, with this strange magick, all sorts of things are possible. I shall no longer be a funny colored stable boy to be laughed at.*

He ate the last of the petite fours and found himself growing drowsy. The page had come and arranged his bath. As he sat in the warm water, his mind wandered in the strange silence of the chamber.

\*  \*  \*  \*

Lord Chauncey awoke to loud thudding at his study door. His head swam as he raised his head from the desk. The candle before him had only half melted, and the moon shone in through the ornately gilded window pane. His neck cracked as he sat up, the first thing his hand reaching for the empty bottle of corn whiskey in front of him.

"My Lord, My Lord! You must come quickly!" Louisa's voice came through the doors.

He rose and staggered to the door. "What is it, Louisa? It is not yet morning."

"Forgive me, My Lord. But please, you must come. A peasant has come to the estate. She claims that she is your daughter..."

"What...What foolery is this?" Lord Chauncey's skin grew cold. His head throbbed as he followed Louisa down the corridor, his eyes blurring with drunken anger. He was exhausted and hadn't slept through since the night of the Banshee's visit; the night he injured his arm. Whatever idiotic prank this might be, he would see that they paid dearly for disturbing him.

Lord Chauncey threw open the white doors to the great drawing room. Standing by the fire was the smallish form of a young lady dressed in a white laced gown. A golden braid hung down her back. Delicate strings of pearls were woven into her hair. The young lady turned, and when he saw her face, his heart suddenly stopped.

*What is this? What is this?*

"Papa..."

"Ana..."

"Oh, Papa!" The young girl cried out. She ran to him, throwing her arms about his neck. He collapsed to the ground, his eyes wide and staring.

"No... No. this is trickery...The night hexes..."

"No, Papa. It is me, Ana. I've come home to see you. Oh...Papa, you've grown so thin. How long have I been gone?"

Chauncey recoiled, pushing her away.

"Keep away! I'll have no more images appear to me in my sleep! Away!" He scrambled to his feet.

"Papa, *please.* Don't you know me? I am your daughter..." The girl reached for his face, but he batted her hand away.

"I see that you are afraid of me. And with good reason. Oh, Papa, I have been to the place of eternal Light and beauty...Oh, such wonderful things I have seen! If only I could describe them all... But I heard your voice crying, and I followed it to the dark valleys for what seemed to be forever. A door appeared. A Dark Door. I came to it, and found myself here at the door of my old home, as if I have never left. It is all so strange, and I am so frightened. Papa, please hold me." She reached out to him, but he pushed her away, blessing himself.

"You are a devil...You are Haddus..."

Ana straightened, gazing at the old man sorrowfully. "For so many years...what torture have you given to yourself that you should be so afraid of me?" The old man shut his eyes, refusing to look at her. He mouthed prayers to himself.

"I did not come alone. If you will not have me...Would you have your grandson? Look how he has grown. Come, Elliot. Meet your grandfather..."

Timidly behind the back of a great chair peered the small face of a fair-haired boy. He was also dressed in fine clothes of white. He stepped from behind the chair, smiling.

"Hello."

"He has grown with me in the Light. It was he who first spotted the Dark Door. And now, here we are. Please, Papa..." Ana reached out her hand to the old man, her face full of hope.

Lord Chauncey looked into the large brown eyes of the boy that stood before him. In that moment he noticed everything at once; the missing tooth in the boy's grin, the purple bruise upon his knee. The way his ears stuck out oddly from his head, just like Carolene's.

The old man approached the boy, slowly reaching his fingertips to his little pink cheek. The boy giggled, shying away and ran to hide behind his mother. Ana placed the back of her hand to her mouth as she fought her own tears. The gesture reminded him so much of the little girl that Chauncey had raised for twenty years that he could no longer restrain himself. It was her. It must be.

"Ana! My Ana!" He rushed to her, holding her tight.

"Oh Papa... What is happening?"

"Louisa, go and fetch Lady Carolene at once! Our daughter...she has come home." Lord Chauncey turned back to his bewildered daughter. This was no night hex. This was because of the crowning of the Purple King.

\*     \*     \*     \*

Kulbit watched the flames dance, sitting in the great crimson armchair by the fire, dressed in the finest silken nightclothes. Four page boys carried away his used bathwater. He thought he recognized one of them. Yes, the one with the curly black hair.

*His name is Mason, and he's always hanging about with Jared, smoking behind the kitchens.*

Kulbit smiled as Mason spared him a curious glance. The smile was not returned. He sat alone in the unnerving silence of the grand chamber. Thoughts of his mother drifted into his mind. It must have been that far too familiar carriage ride. A ride in a wagon with barred windows. That reminded him of her. How could it not? *My mother saw Father as below herself.*

Contessa Elisabetta Di Marcheris was the most beautiful girl he had ever before seen, he had believed at the time. But he hadn't always thought so. Before that, had anyone asked (and had he been able to speak back in return), he would have reserved such an esteemed title for his mother. He remembered a lovely young woman with beautiful skin and shining hair, such a bright shade of strawberry red it looked as if it were made of spun silk. Her eyes were gooseberry green, just like his own.

*Nay,* he remembered. *Not both of them. One of them blue. Yes, she had one blue eye and one green eye. Grandmum always said that it was her bewitching, strange colored eyes and titian hair that always won her plenty of suitors. But she chose Da because he was the most handsome. Mother always laughed and said that it was because Da was the only suitor who didn't want her only for her dowry. That he had not the sense to be interested in it.*

He was seven when he last saw his mother. He remembered seeing her sitting on the parlor floor, weeping. A crumpled piece of paper was in her hand, both of her fists pressing into her belly as if it ached. He sat next to her. The velvet carpet was gray with little pink roses on it. This was his Grandmum's great big estate. Granda left it to her when he died. They were living there because Da went away. Kulbit tried to wipe the tears away from his mother's beautiful face. She was too lovely to shed tears.

*Don't cry Mother,* he spoke to her with the center of his mind. (He hadn't yet learned that none could hear the things spoken in his head. Even if he wished it with all his heart.) She pushed him away roughly, and he fell back. He looked up at her, blinking.

"Don't you touch me, you ugly little beast!" she shouted. "Don't you understand? Your father is dead. *Dead,* do you hear? He is never coming back! Do you not see? You don't. You can't even speak. Oh why couldn't I have a *normal* child?"

She rushed at her little purple son, grabbing him by the shoulders, shaking him violently.

"It isn't fair! It isn't fair!" she screamed. He began to cry. Grandmum rushed into the parlor, ripping Kulbit away from his screaming mother.

*"Aileen, stop it! Stop it at once!"*
Kulbit buried his face in his grandmum's ample bosom, sobbing silently.

"Oh mother, I'm sorry," Aileen cried, crumbling to her knees again. "But it just isn't fair. It isn't!"

Grandmum huddled with her daughter on the velvet carpet, little Kulbit sandwiched between the gray lace that covered his grandmother's stomach and the soft pink linen of his mother's gown. All three of them wept in silence.

So his mother never wanted him. It was obvious enough. She said so in the way she looked at him. The way she never wanted to touch him, as if he were covered in muck that might dirty her pretty little fingers. Even as a toddler, he sensed this. She was repulsed by him.

His Da had loved him, though Kulbit also had a sense that he was also ashamed of his strange looking son. He wouldn't let Kulbit play outside with the other children, sometimes acting as if he had no son. He remembered his father telling him to hide in his room when the naval recruiter came. He heard him tell the man that they hadn't time to have any children. Yes, Da was ashamed of him. But Mummy was *more* than just ashamed. She hated Kulbit. It was all because of his color.

Kulbit lay down by the warm fire in his royal cot, wrapped in blankets.

*I suppose I would've once said that I'm the most unlucky boy who has ever lived to be born such a funny color. But here I am, King of Thom, still as purple as can be. Perhaps there truly is no such a thing as luck.*
He remembered hearing his parents quarreling before Da departed to join the Royal Guard at Sea. He woke up in the night to use the lavatory. Down the great hallway, he heard raised voices. Kulbit winced as he heard his mother's shrill, angry laughter. She always seemed to laugh when she argued with Da.

"You require a bit of cultivation, my dear sir! And I see fit to do the task!"

"I require no such thing!" his father was shouting. "We live in this house upon your insistence! I had a home, a good home. I had my farm, my own land!"

"A dirt farm with a worthless little cottage!" she laughed.

"My father and I built that cottage with our own hands. I worked the land, and the land repaid me! But it was not enough for you. You treat me as if I'm beholden to you, Aileen, when I desire none of this foppish life. You do not respect me as your husband. You do not respect me as a man."

"Man! I see no man! What man houses his bride in a shack cabin? What man needs his mother in law to provide a decent home for him?"

"Enough!"

"You are no man. You are some disfigured thing! An ill-bred mongrel that only produces *spoiled pups!*"

Suddenly his father burst into the lavish hallway. He grabbed a large vase from a little table and sent it crashing against the wainscoting. Mum's shrill laughter came from the room.

"Bark, little mongrel, bark!" she screamed.

Da seized the double bedroom doors and slammed them shut with a roar. Mum was still laughing at him from within. Kulbit froze, his heart pounding in his chest and ears as his father walked briskly down the hall toward him. He stopped when he spotted the frightened child, and his anger seemed to melt away into something far worse. Shame.

He tried to smile at the boy, but couldn't. Kulbit just stared at him, wide-eyed. Finally, Da came to him. He tousled the small boy's hair.

"What are you doing out of bed, little one? Go back to sleep. Go." Kulbit immediately scampered away to his room.

Kulbit's thoughts were interrupted when he heard a scratching sound behind the royal bookshelves. The little rat he had fed had friends. He shut his eyes and shivered. The grand fireplace was indeed warm enough, but deep inside of his belly he could not melt an inner chill.

Mother blamed him for Da's death. For if her son hadn't been born mute and purple, she and her husband wouldn't have quarreled so much. And if she and her husband hadn't quarreled so often, perhaps he wouldn't have run off to fight the pirates from Tirfan and gotten himself killed.

Days after the letter came telling of Da's death, a man came in a big black carriage with bars on the windows. He came for Kulbit, but would not take the little carpet bag Aileen had packed for him with some clothing and a few toys.

"There is no need for personal effects," the tall, somber-looking man in gray had said. He opened a black book filled with papers. "The child will be properly provided for at the asylum. Now, Mrs. Trellendale-,

*(Trellendale...That was my father's name, not my mother's. The name that now lays claim to royalty. And she looked down on him, she thought he was nothing...)*

"-I'll need you to sign these royally sanctioned statements renouncing all family claims to the child. He will lose his namesake, his claims of inheritance, and will now become the property of the crown."

Kulbit buried his face in his grandmum's apron. Her, knobby fingers were hidden in the blue fuzz of his hair. She was crying bitterly.

*Please, Grandmum. Don't let her do it. Please do something to stop Mother from sending me away!*

Grandmum said nothing. She stood there weeping.

*Won't you take me then? Won't you keep me as your little boy, and Mother can be happy again without me and you and I can be happy together. I could stay with you and look to the heaviest chores around the estate so you don't have to work too hard. I'll be very good and never make you angry. Please, Grandmum!*

He gazed up at her pleading. She only looked at him, shaking her head sorrowfully, as if she heard his thoughts. Her answer was no.

Kulbit's breath was swept away as he suddenly felt the gray suited man lift him from his grandmother and place him in the chamber of the carriage that had bars upon the windows. Before he could even realize what he was about, the man closed the door, locking him in.

He stood on the tips of his fine, polished leather booties to peek out of the barred window. He saw the man tip his hat to his mother and grandmother. He remembered the sounds of the carriage rumbling down the drive of Grandmum's big estate, and watching his mother and grandmother grow smaller and smaller in the gray cold of the morning. He never saw either of them again.

The children's asylum was a cold, sterile place in the bustling city of Post. Kulbit didn't much like Post; he was born in Ende. He was used to the countryside. Lady of Post Children's Asylum was not a bad place all together. It was very quiet and everything was white. The halls were white, the beds in the sleeping barracks were white, even the lavatories were white, and everything smelled like lye. All the boys in the asylum had to go about with shaved heads, and Kulbit wept bitterly as he watched his blue curls fall to the ground. When he saw himself in the mirror, the thought he looked like a purple summer melon.

It was bad enough to have blue hair, but no hair at all was far worse. One of the boys began to laugh when he returned to the boys' barracks bald-headed, but after getting his ears boxed by Sister Merril, was sure to never laugh again.

The abbey nuns, hovering silently about the halls of the asylum in their white robes like flocks of ghosts, were very kind, but quite strict. They would whip your legs with hickory sticks if you misbehaved. Kulbit always managed to keep out of trouble, and the sacred sisters appreciated his inability to speak and make the tiresome sounds that most children make. His time at Lady of Post seemed to blur past quickly.

A few years later, one night he was told that he was old enough to earn his own wages. The next morning, he would be starting his new position serving the crown. He was sent to work for Bugger. He had been living at the Royal Stable Houses ever since.

He hadn't thought about any of these things in years. Kulbit's heart ached as he gazed at the fire, surrounded by the best finery of

Thom. He didn't know why he was there, or what would become of him. He thought of the poems in the book that Bugger threw down the river. He read them so often, he had them memorized in his head, and began reciting them to himself, his silent lips moving, his eyes shut. Soon after, his heart eased.

If he were a hero in a book, then he would make do despite all odds. That was how it usually seemed to work in all the stories. Things got quite strange for the hero, but it wasn't of consequence because he would always save the day. And everyone would be happy.

There would be a great parade tomorrow, and pretty damsels would curtsey at the sight of him. They would all see that they were wrong about him. His mother especially.

As usual, that night he had pleasant dreams. He willed it to be, for it was to be his only escape from the questions that still needed answering.

\*     \*     \*     \*

The next morning was again cold and dour, and an icy autumn wind lay over the crowd that had gathered at the Post. This coronation was quite different from that of King Theodore. The townspeople cheered and cried and threw flowers and waved flags. Throughout the entire city of Post could be heard the roaring chant:

*"Hail to the Tool of God! Hail to the Tool of God!"*

The loudness of it all made Kulbit's ears throb. He was carried in as Theodore was a few years earlier, dressed in splendid finery, and riding underneath a silver arch of blades saluting his majesty. It was not very hard to imagine the cold steel coming down upon him if he were to make any false moves.

The people of Post went wild at the sight of this strange, purple king. At his arrival, an army of armed guards were made to draw into the pressing crowd, forcing the people back. The frenzy of it all was terribly frightening, and Roger balked as a particularly loud woman screamed, reaching her arms between the heads of the Royal Guard, eyes wild. She wished to touch the Tool of God.

*Fear not. All shall be well, Roger...At least I hope so...*

When the ceremony was finished, Kulbit was led amid maddening screams and cheering back into the royal carriage and returned to the royal bedchamber. The great doors were once again locked behind him.

And that was that.

Heavy was the crown placed upon his head, and heavy were his thoughts as he removed it and put it in its glass case on a pedestal. He sat in his cot with a sigh. Upon the great shelves were many odd toys and games, and Kulbit tried to amuse himself by looking at these. The ominous silence after all the commotion was frightening. Kulbit whistled to keep himself from becoming quite spooked.

On his first formal night as king, an old farmer discovered gold coins in his fireplace. A young girl received a letter that the richest baron in the kingdom wished to make her his bride, and shower her with jewels. An old woman looked into the mirror to find that the beauty of her youth had been suddenly restored. There were no more horrors of the night. No evil spirits lurking across the marshlands. No sad memories haunted the doorways of the distressed at heart. For their king had slept well, and so all was well in the land for the time that followed.

## Chapter 11

Being beautiful is a fine enough thing for a young girl of thirteen years. But Emily's whole world had changed. For one thing, boys no longer taunted and teased her. Some stared, and some would fall all over themselves to help her. Grownups were a good deal more kindly to a girl of rare beauty, and even mother was a lot less stodgy. But there was a downside to becoming beautiful, as Emily soon learned fast. Other girls had become quite a bit meaner. Daniellia had become downright horrid, as if she wasn't tiresome enough before Emily became officially beautiful. She would taunt and tease, making underhanded insults about Emily's hair and figure.

"Oh, Em. You don't need another slice of bread. Your middle is getting thick enough as it is."

"Emily, you might want to borrow my blue ribbon today. It might spruce up your hair and make it less dull."

"Em, you do know that little girls like you shouldn't be staying up so late. You'll need your beauty rest."

It was terrible. She would say these things low enough so that Mother wouldn't hear. Had Emily not known why her sister treated her so unkindly, she might've begun to feel that she must be the most beastly creature in the kingdom. But Emily had a witch's knowing that was slowly growing keener. She knew that Daniellia said these things out of spite and jealousy. She just never imagined that her own sister could behave like this.

*I suppose it's what comes of always being thought of as the beauty in the family, only to wake up one day and find someone else is getting a little bit of attention for a change. Poor Daniellia. That being the most beautiful of all is so important to her that she could grow to be so mean to her own sister. Why can't she just be happy for me? Why should she take my being beautiful to mean that she isn't? She's every bit as lovely as she used to be, and she didn't need any magick spells. My becoming lovely doesn't change anything about her. Why can't we both be thought of as beautiful? Why can't we both enjoy sharing the attention?*

The two sisters never were the best of friends, and with Emily's new found beauty it would seem that they never would be. This saddened her greatly. She wondered if there was a spell...

But the trouble was, she didn't want to cast those sort of spells. The kind where you make other people feel something other than what they would normally wish to. That type of spell struck her as cheating. Giving them a slight push in one direction in trivial matters was one thing. But changing someone's heart all together was quite different. If she and her sister were to ever truly become friends, it would have to mean that they both chose to do so.

Despite her sister's taunting, Emily decided her spell was a success. Now it was time to try another. She hadn't known it at the very top of her head, nor had she any sense of it deep in the bottom of her belly. But somewhere inside of her, she had decided that she wished to learn how to become the most powerful witch she could possibly be.

Very soon apple season had come to the people of Keppington Valley. This was a great time indeed. The Lord Mayor of Ende came to the valley, and they would hold the traditional Thomish Apple Tournament. Everyone in the valley would harvest wild apples, and they would make a myriad of delicacies. Apple pudding, apple fritters, apple cider, and all other sorts of other tasty things you can bake and fry and stew with apples. On the day of the Tournament, everyone would decorate the village with red and green ribbons, flags and banners.

The ladies would dress in lovely crimson cloaks and frocks, and the men in vibrant green capes and doublets. Everything in the normally dull village became elegant and refined. Musicians would play, and the youngsters would do court dances in the streets. Storytellers would sit and weave tales of winter faeries so beautiful that when they kiss the pixies of the green apple trees, the fruit would turn bright red with bashfulness.

The Lord Mayor and his party of wealthy gentry would then sample every apple treat, and the best of these would be awarded two year's wages in gold, providing they also share their secret recipe with the Lords and Ladies of Thom. Some recipes had done so well at the tournament that it was said that they were used by the Royal Chef himself. There was a rumor that in the days of the widower King Adrien, one young woman named Juliana made an apple cider so scrumptious that she was summoned to the city of Post by the king himself after she had won the Tournament. According to the story, the King fell in love with Dame Juliana, and he would pay her a year's worth of wages every year until the last days of his reign, just so he could have her prepare cider for his Christumas Feast.

It became a custom for the Lord Mayor to make a toast before the tasting would start: "By the health of Dame Juliana, may the Apple Tournament begin!"

Mother made the thickest, richest apple cake that anyone could ever eat. She had a very secret recipe that was passed down from her mother, and her mother's mother. One day, when Emily got married, Mother would share the recipe with her, too. It wasn't very often that their family could afford the ingredients to make it. But once in a while, they would have enough saved to enjoy it at their own little Christumas Feast. When they did, Papa would hold up his stein of warm beer and toast in a most foppish impression of the genteel, to Dame Juliana, just as if he were the Lord Mayor, and everyone would giggle and laugh. Even Daniellia would find it funny.

Emily didn't expect that they would be having any apple cake this year. Papa had made some lovely, delicately carved apple wood furniture to sell at the Tournament. These were going to be hard items to sell. When King Leo was still alive, the family would sell lots of furniture to the nobility that came to Keppington. Not this year though, to be sure. It just seemed to be their luck as of late. However, perhaps with a little bit of magick...

Emily awoke in the middle of the night to peruse her witch's book. There had to be something she could do to help out Mama and Papa. Perhaps something to make Papa's furniture seem so fine to the rich nobles that all of it could all be sold. Or...

Emily's thumb stopped on a particular page that caught her eye. It was beautiful. Images of flowers were sketched along the border of it. Emily shivered with cold and drew her cloak closer around herself. She spread the book atop her tree stump and huddled over it, careful not to spill candle wax on any of its pages.

*A Spell to Win*
*This is a spell to win at most things that one might*
aspire. *To win at games, to win arguments, or to win at*
*competitions. This spell is not to be taken lightly, for no matter*
*what you do to win, your heart will always reveal what you feel*
*you truly deserve in the end. One must take care to see that what*
*they wish to win harms none, especially oneself. Be sure that*
*winning does not affect your fate disagreeably in the end.*

Emily sat back for a moment. This must be a powerful spell to warrant such a warning. A silly beauty spell was one thing, but to cast a spell that might affect one's fate disagreeably is another more serious thing. Mother had always said it was unwise to tamper with the Sisters of Fate. They can be cruel teachers.

But Emily was thinking of the Thomish Apple Tournament. Mother's cake was so delicious that it would most certainly win. Papa had often tried to get Mother to enter it into the contest, but Mother refused. She said that contests were for fools who dared trifle with the Fates, and it will always get them in the end. But Emily noticed how Mother's cheeks would turn pink with pleasure any time Papa suggested this. Perhaps she secretly wanted to enter it into the contest, but felt silly in admitting it. Just like Emily felt silly in admitting out loud that she was beautiful.

Emily twirled her hair thoughtfully. Sometimes, if one is to ever do anything wonderful, one must take risks. Mother was not one to be brave enough to ever try winning on her own. Perhaps this would be a good time for someone to give her a little push in the right direction. What's the worst thing that could happen?

Her heart would be broken if she lost. That would definitely be bad enough of a thing to suggest not trying it at all. But suddenly a lovely thought came to Emily. Perhaps she didn't need to know her cake would be entered into the contest at all?

"That's it!" Emily said aloud to herself. "That's exactly what I'll do! I'll enter the contest in secret. Mother will be so busy with helping Papa try to sell his furniture, she won't notice I've gone missing. If she wins, then that would be simply wonderful! But if not, no one will ever need know it. Emily Marie, you are becoming quite a clever-o*h, oh dear!*"

She recoiled, the hair on the back of her neck standing on end. Spread across the page of the book like a great hand, was an enormous spider. She would have immediately squashed the spider flat with her shoe if in an instant she hadn't recognized it. It was the same glittering black spider with the purple star from the very first night she had ventured out to the old witch's cabin.

It regarded her with all eight of its black, unwinking eyes. It cocked its head to one side inquisitively. Two furry, mustache-like mandibles fluttered under its downy face. She bit her lip anxiously. What was it doing here?

*Well. I suppose if I were just a silly, ordinary girl I should be scared, perhaps think that this was a bad omen of some kind. Or just simply because spiders are rather creeping sorts of things. But I am a witch now. And witches aren't supposed to scare easily.*

"Hello again, Spider." Emily cleared her throat. "Lovely evening we're having, isn't it?"

The spider simply looked up at her, mandibles never still, the light of the candle reflecting in its eight liquid eyes.

"Is...Is there anything I can help you with? I was just about ready to get on with reading about a spell on the page that you're sitting on, so if you would be so kind..."

The spider crawled from the page of the spell book to the edge of the tree stump. It lifted its abdomen in the air, and a silvery thread of silk shot out from the bottom of it. The silk landed upon a low hanging sprig of broom bush. The spider suddenly took to the air and reeled itself onto the bush. It folded its long legs underneath itself and once again, those large, black eyes settled on Emily, waiting.

"Hmm...I supposed it can't hurt if you watch me read. Just please stay where you are and don't climb on me or...or anything..." Emily swallowed. She didn't much care for spiders, nor did she care for anyone or anything else to be present while she was thinking about magick. She suddenly felt self-conscious. But the creature didn't seem like it intended to go away any time soon. She sighed and continued reading the spell aloud to the spider.

*"The items you will need for this spell:*

*Thirteen chamomile flowers*
*Thirteen sarsaparilla seeds*
*Oil (no scent, cooking)*
*White candlestick (unused)*
*Mortar and pestle*
*One Pin*
*Bottle (to keep solution)*
*One witch's attuned broomstick, or the branch of a tree that has fallen naturally and still bears leaves of green*
*Muddy water...*Muddy water? How strange...

  *"On the Night of Thunraz; fifth night of the week, under the light of the waxing moon, cast your magickal circle just before midnight."*

Emily paused, glancing at the spider. It watched her.

"The Night of Thunraz? When on earth is that? I suppose it's symbolism for something, and on that night the magick in the air would be just right for this kind of spell. But who is Thunraz? For goodness sake, this is going to be more complicated than I thought. There is so much that I don't know. Is Thunraz some sort of spirit? I do hope it isn't a devil or anything horrible like that. If only I could go visit the library at Post..."

She didn't wish to invoke some demon or something she knew nothing about. Also there was all that business about a witch's broomstick. She thought she could find a naturally fallen tree branch easily enough. That would have to do for now, but all that business of witches using brooms was the stuff of fairy stories. Did this mean she had to go and find a broom, and go flying through the night? This was getting stranger and stranger. She read on.

  *"The casting of the circle in this spell is very particular, as there are those creatures of the shadows who might wish to seek a chance to wreak havoc with your luck. A simple circle casting will not suffice for the protection necessary."*

Emily winced. "Oh dear. This is very serious indeed. I may be in over my head with this one, Spider. What creatures can she be speaking of?

  *'With a pin, carve the words 'I shall have victory' upon the unused white candle. Walk widdershins around the circle,*

*declaring that you shall not allow evil to enter. Place the candle in the center of the circle. Then with witch's broomstick, sweep outward around the circle walking deosil, whisking away any evil spirits or shadowfolk that might be watching. Declare that you banish them from this place. Walking widdershins, sprinkle the muddy water around the exterior of the circle so that the power of Earth and Water shall be contained within. These are the powers you will harness to make your spell come into fruition. Facing the east, declare aloud while saluting your broomstick:*

*"Hail to the East, Powers of Wind. Blow my victory soon within."*

*Facing the north:*

*"Hail to the North, Powers of Earth. Bring with victory blessed mirth."*

*Facing the south:*

*"Hail to the South, Powers of Fire. Light the path to my desire."*

*Facing the west:*

*"Hail to the West, Powers of the Sea. Flowing spell, so mote it be."*

*Sit in the center of your circle next to the burning candle. By that light, take thirteen chamomile flowers and grind them into a fine powder with the mortar and pestle. Imagine yourself winning in the greatest of detail. Then add the thirteen sarsaparilla seeds. Continue to grind until the mixture is as fine as dust. Mix the herbal dust in with the oil in the bottle.*

*You now have the potion for your winning spell. Rub this potion on your hands before beginning anything that you wish to win at. With your anointed hand, touch the hand of those whom you wish to sway in your favor. Add the solution to drink or food.*

*NOTE: It is very important that you do no snuff your victory candle. You must allow it to burn all the way down until there is no candle left, no matter how long that may take.*

*NOTE: You must close the circle and thank the elements for assisting you in your magick. Walk deosil with the finished candle wax in your left palm, and thank the North, South, East and West. If you do not take the time to close the circle properly, your next magickal attempt will be tainted by bad fortune.*

Emily Marie closed the book with a sigh. This seemed like a harder spell than the last. Would she be able to find the items she would need? She knew how to identify chamomile flowers in the wood, as well as sarsaparilla plant. But it would they be too late in the season? She did not know. Mother might notice if a new candle went missing. Or if someone had used her mortar and pestle. And in all of this, she just realized that she hadn't given much thought to exactly how she would get mother to make the cake in the first place. They were barely making enough money to live. Mother would never agree to spend any extra money on getting the ingredients she would need to make it. Emily would have to do some serious lying, a thing she hated to do for the most part. She had a very talkative conscience at times.

"Never mind," Emily said to the spider, who hadn't moved from its spot on the broom sprig. "I'll do it, no matter how difficult it might be. This is two year's wages we are speaking about. It's worth all the trouble, even if I get caught being a frightful sneak. I mean...even if one is to go doing sneaky things like lying and such, it's all right if it's meant for good, isn't it?" The spider said nothing. It simply watched, its mandibles twitching. This annoyed Emily greatly.

"Oh listen to me, asking advice from a spider like some sort of ninny. As if you understood anything I was saying! And where *did* you come from, anyway? Crawling all over my book, watching everything I'm doing. I suppose you expect me to believe that you're the very same spider that I saw at the witch's cabin. Well do you know what? I don't believe it. I refuse to. You and the other one were probably just some strange breed that I hadn't noticed crawling about until now, that's all. You shan't scare me. So shoo! Off with you, now. I'm going to bed." Suddenly, the spider scurried away in the bushes. Emily stuck out her chin after it.
"Pooh."

She gathered her book and snuffed out her candle, then sneaked back to bed. She had a long day tomorrow. A day of sneaking and conniving and wheedling and lying. And she didn't like it one single bit.

The next day, she spent the entire morning thinking. She helped Mother with the chores, practiced her arithmetic, reading and writing. The whole time her mind was rolling about in her head, trying to figure out different ideas to trick her mother into thinking the way she wished her to think. Finally, as she and Carrigan helped mother prepare for lunch, it struck her.

"My goodness, Mother. Wasn't it just wonderfully lucky for us that the butcher and his wife had given us this much meat? I shouldn't be surprised if we had enough for Christumas Feast," she remarked as she kneaded a slab of dough. Carrigan was peeling potatoes. She had sneaked a book about insects into the kitchen, and was reading it secretly in her lap as she peeled. Her spectacles were slipping off the edge of her nose, but she didn't seem to notice.

"I thank the heavens for that blessed man and his wife. I don't know what we would've done otherwise," said Mother as she minced beef for a pie.

"It's really a shame," Emily murmured. She stole a glance over her shoulder and saw that her mother had paused, her knife frozen in the air.

"What is a shame?"

"Hmm? Oh, nothing, Mother. I was just thinking...after all this time, it's a shame that we can't do anything for them in return. It sort of makes us seem...ungrateful."

"Emily, you should be ashamed. We *are* very grateful, and one should never insult charity by measuring its worth in back pay, young lady," Mother said crossly.

"I'm sorry, Mother," said Emily humbly. Mother's knife began knocking on the wood board again.

After a moment Mother spoke.

"Yes, well...I was thinking of having Papa make the butcher a lovely new rocking chair. That is, if we can get enough lumber for one."

"Oh yes," said Emily absentmindedly. "A rocking chair would be very nice...even if they do take such a long time to make. And even though Papa said that every bit of lumber is so scarce lately."

Mother's carving knife began chopping in faster, angry little beats. Emily decided to tread lightly. She wanted to push her mother, but not make her angry.

"You know," Emily said carefully, "Just the other day Emmet was telling me how much he simply adored apple cake. He hoped that they would be able to buy some at the Apple Tournament. Do you remember that year when you and Papa brought some over for their Christumas Feast, and we all sang songs out in the snow? Emmet's father said he had never tasted an apple cake so fine."

"Young lady, what are you driving at?" Mother raised a suspicious eyebrow at Emily.

"Oh, nothing at all Mother. I just found it funny that he should bring it up, that's all. It was so long ago...Do you think...Do you think Emmet was trying to ask me if you might make them an apple cake this year? But maybe he wasn't allowed to..."

"Well. The butcher's wife is a stubborn one. Heaven forbid she should ask me herself," Mother said wryly. "But I'd be happy to. You go and tell that little boy that if his mother wanted me to make them a cake, all she need do is ask. After all, with so much meat we have now, we had saved such a pretty. It would be more than a fair trade."

"Well I do think that's a lovely idea, Mother," said Emily nonchalantly. Inside she was dancing with excitement.

And the next day mother took two gold pieces from the money jar, and went to the market place. She bought everything she would need to make the cake, even expensive vanilla whiskey. Carrigan and Emily Marie went out into the apple forests with a large basket to gather wild apples. It was great fun to pick the apples, and the other townspeople had done the same as well. Some were having picnics out in the sunshine, bundled up from the chilly air with blankets and furs, munching apples and laughing.

After this job was done, Emily stole away from her sister into the woods to secretly gather the things she would need for her spell. She needed to have the potion finished before Mother made the cake. If her thoughts were correct, the night that the spell should be cast would be as the witch's book had said; on the fifth night of the week. The moon was waxing, and if all her plans worked out as she had hoped, the potion would be ready the morning Mother had planned to take the cake to the butcher's family. She hated what she would have to do after that...

"But never mind that," she told herself aloud as she hunted for the tiny green buds of wild chamomile flowers. "A witch must do what a witch must." She had remembered reading that somewhere in Grenna's book. High in the branches of a nearby apple tree, a large spider hung from her web, her eight gleaming eyes watching the young girl hunch over a clusters of wild herb.

# Chapter 12

As a stable boy, Kulbit felt he had many troubles. There was much work to be finished, and there was always the threat that Bugger would be in a foul mood. But as King of ThoBromis he had other worries. Foremost, Kulbit was naturally a very shy lad. Despite his strange looks, he would always manage not to draw attention to himself, but as king he would have to nearly always be the center of it. He was required to be present for any and every little thing. Most of these he barely understood. But such was his royal duty.

So when the High Chieftain of the Royal Treasury came to present budget concerns to the Seigneurs Du Cordovan, poor Kulbit was made to sit very still in a rather tall, uncomfortable chair in the Statehood Wing, with a heavy formal Statehood crown upon his head. When the Seigneurs Du Cordovan decided to hold a meeting discussing said finances of the chieftain, Kulbit was forced to attend as well, still wearing that tiresome crown. He had accidentally dozed by the second hour of this meeting, and the ugly thing toppled off of his aching head with a loud clatter. No one chided him for this, but he did receive stern looks from all of the lords attending, and could only smile sheepishly as he scrambled to pick it up, place it back on his head and resume his seat.

Every moment of King Kulbit's days were planned, from the very moment that he rose in the morning, to each meal, to the last moment when he was finally allowed to rest his head on the royal pillow.

It wasn't all bad, being king. There was plenty to eat, no one to box his ears, and they had reconstructed an opulent new bed for their king, far more comfortable than his own bed of hay. What's more, he now had the power to send a letter to his mother in Ende, and perhaps see what had become of her. But all the same, Kulbit did not wish to be a king at all.

In all his fondest dreams and wishes, he was a wandering knight, a hero who fought for the honor of a fair maiden, glory and adventure. He didn't wish to be a king; trapped in the pomp and stodgy air of court and state matters. No more than he wished to be a poor nameless stable boy. He wanted so much of everything all at once, and things never seemed to go as he would like them to.

*　　　*　　　*　　　*

Mother's cake was wrapped in oiled gauze and left on the table. Delicious smells filled the entire Osterling cottage. Papa had said it was a shame they wouldn't be eating the cake themselves, but Mother hushed him, chasing him away from stealing a pinch of the large, dense pastry. In the morning, mother would ride out to the butcher's.

While everyone was asleep that night, Emily Marie lay in her bed. Her eyes were shut and her mind was quiet. She knew that she had gone too far with this plan to turn back now. Mother had taken all the time and effort to make a cake for the butcher's family. A cake that they didn't truly ask for. A cake that they would never get. If Mother were to show up at the butcher's, his greedy old wife would take the cake, no questions asked. But if Mother were to mention that Emily had said that they had wished to ask her for the cake? The butcher's wife would call her mad. And everything would be ruined. No, Emily had to see this to the end.

When she felt for sure that everyone had been quiet long enough so that they couldn't help but be asleep, Emily rose from her bed silently. She took the large cake under her arm and glided from the house without a sound. Everything was ready and waiting for her at the stump. Goose pimples began to prickle her arms and neck as they seemed to now each time she was about to begin a spell. Only this time, she was afraid as well. She was thinking of those Shadowfolk she had read about in the witch's book. She lit the candles and cast the circle, whispering to the corners of each direction. Among the broom bushes, eight eyes glistened by the candlelight.

She followed each step of the spell to the letter. As she did so, she kept her mind on the end prize. No more wondering over that careworn look in Papa's face that made crow's feet at the corners of his eyes and wrinkles around his mouth. No more hearing Mother's constant reminder of how poor they are. All of these worries would be gone once this spell takes effect. And she believed it would. She *had* to, or else it wouldn't have a chance.

She ground the herbs with the mortar and pestle, her arms beginning to ache, a wayward forelock of hair falling over her eyes. She worked hard into the night. A while later, she was sprinkling the oily potion onto the cake. Not too much; she didn't want to spoil the taste. But just enough. She poured the rest of the potion into a little bottle. The candle was low, but not quite burned out. For the rest of the night, she sat still, watching the flame flickering and shivering with cold, her mother's cake in her lap. The night sky was growing purple with the oncoming morning when she hid the cake in an empty wine barrel in the barn. And as she finally lay down in her bed, it was only a few moments later when she heard her father stirring from his. Her sisters were up shortly after. Though she was terribly tired, her eyes burning for sleep, she arose with them, yawning and stretching and pretending to be refreshed and ready for the day. As she dressed, she was not the least bit surprised when she heard her mother gasp. She strolled into the kitchen.

"Now what are you going on about, woman?" Papa was saying.

"You did it, you did it, you greedy *pig* of a man! Gone and eaten the butcher's cake, have you?" Mother was very cross, pacing to and fro in the kitchen, opening cupboards and hunting about in the pantry.

"I've done no such thing."

"Then where has it gone? Vanished into thin air?"

"I dunno, you must have misplaced it."

"Misplaced-Why, you tiresome oaf! I haven't done anything of the sort. I took it from the oven and left it here on the table. Children! Come into the kitchen at once!"

Carrigan and Daniellia came into the kitchen, puzzled looks on their faces. Emily Marie did her best to match their expressions.

"What's wrong, Mother?" asked Carrigan.

"One of you has taken the butcher's apple cake. Now I want to know which one of you has done it."

"We didn't take it, Mother," said Daniellia. Emily remained silent.

"Honest, we didn't," chimed in Carrigan.

"Well then I suppose it must have grown legs and walked out of the house on its own then!"

"Ach, don't be daft, woman. You must have put it back in the oven for safe keeping."

"I've checked the oven. And whom are you calling daft?"

"Only a loud mouthed woman who calls her husband a pig and an oaf," Papa retorted.

Papa and Mother began to quarrel, and the three girls glanced at each other in confusion. Emily's heart thudded in her chest, but she simply shrugged her shoulders and said not a word. All that day was horrid. Mother and Papa weren't speaking to one another, and Emily's sisters seemed frightened and confused. Emily felt awful.

"But...a witch must do as a witch must," she reminded herself throughout the day. The next morning was the day of the Apple Tournament. She tried her dearest to believe that the end justified the means. She thought of the lovely new house they would be able to buy, new clothes for everyone. Maybe Mother could even have a garden. But none of this made her feel any better about it.

At supper, no one said a word. And in the morning, though Mother and Papa and the girls worked to load the furniture Papa would try to sell at the festival together, the chill between Mother and Papa was clearly evident. The girls all carried lunch sacks with them, and unknown to any but Emily Marie, one of them contained Mother's apple cake. When they arrived at the village commons, Emily hid the sack in a briar patch near the woods. Among the leaves, glittering with orbs of morning dew sat a spider's web, its creator nowhere in sight. Emily half wondered and half knew that the web was spun by a large black spider with a purple star burst on its abdomen.

The festivities began shortly after, and before noon Emily and her sisters were dismissed by Mother to go wander and see the sights of the celebrations. Daniellia ran off immediately, and Emily knew she would be looking for Jon Hannigan in hopes of being asked by him for a dance. Boring old Carrigan had brought a book about the growth of fungi, and had sat down in the shade to read. Now was Emily's only chance. She stole away into the woods and crouched under the briar patch. Atop the sack the large shining spider stood, its long legs spread wide in all directions.

"Thank you for watching over it, Spider. I'm sorry I was cross with you before," whispered Emily. The spider crawled up into the briars and disappeared.

Emily cautiously picked her way to through the crowd, eyes watchful for anyone who might recognize her. No one seemed interested in the least by a young girl holding a sack, and she had preferred it that way. She made her way toward the big red tent where the Lord Mayor would be sitting. It would be here where she would have to enter the cake for judging. A long line of people stood at the entrance of the tent, where a woman sat at a small table with a large book and quill. Nerves suddenly shot through Emily. That was the book she had intended to do a bit of magick on. She reached in the pocket of her apron and felt the little bottle of potion inside. She would just take a drop of it and put it on her name, if she could only unscrew the cap...

Suddenly, she felt oily liquid running down her thigh. The bottle had opened, and all the potion had spilled in her pocket.

"Bother, bother, bother," she muttered to herself. Her left hand was an oily mess. That was the last of the potion. She stood staring, wondering what she was to do.

Suddenly, an idea came to her mind like a flash of lightening. Holding her hand out cautiously, Emily took her place in line and waited. Women chitchatted about recipes, each holding a parcel wrapped as secretly as her own, each eyeing each other's bundle suspiciously. When it came to be Emily's turn to sign her name in the book, she used her right hand instead of her left, and the letters of her mother's name sprawled childishly across the line.

"Thank you, my dear. Please place your submission on the table to your right." The woman did not bother to look up.

"Um, if you please, Miss... I do have one request..."

The woman looked up, surprised. She wasn't accustomed to having requests. Emily continued.

"Would it be possible that I might be able to perchance meet His Honor the Lord Mayor Percival Descartes? I'm just a simple carpenter's daughter, and it would mean so much to me if I would be able to see the Great Lord Mayor of Ende." It was a feeble attempt, but she knew she would have to try.

"I'm sorry, little girl. But the Lord Mayor is not available for-" began the woman, but just as she spoke an older gentleman with a merry face and a white beard came out of the pavilion. He was richly dressed in a fine, thick cloak of bright green. He was sipping a steamy flagon of spiced wine and smiling as he chatted with two other lords, as splendidly dressed in green robes as himself.

Brilliant green and red feathers bobbed from his bejeweled hat. Without waiting for the woman to finish, Emily pushed past the little kiosk. The lords were flanked by two armed guardsmen.

"Lord Mayor! Lord Mayor!" This was madness, but a witch must do as a witch must. The two guards closed in on the nobles protectively, but she was too small and quick for them.

"My dear Lord Mayor," said Emily breathlessly. "Please. It's simply such an honor to meet you! To have someone such as you come to our humble village. Please, good sir, might I shake your hand?"

The nobleman turned, surprised. One of the guards intercepted her, but the Lord Mayor laughed, waving them off. "Stand down, fellow. It's merely a little girl. I should be happy to shake your hand." He laughed again as she extended her left hand awkwardly. He shook it, shaking his head.

"It is the right hand you are to offer, my dear. And even still, it is more becoming of a lady to curtsey and not shake hands at all. Handshakes are meant for boys and men."

"Oh my," tittered Emily with a half curtsey. "My apologies, Sir. Thank you very much! Goodbye!" She gathered her skirts and scampered off. The other noblemen laughed.

"These simple country folk," chortled one, sipping his wine. "They never teach their young ones proper manners."

The Lord Mayor looked down at the palm of his hand with mild chagrin. Some sort of oily grime smeared his palm. "Nor do they teach them proper cleanliness," he said dryly, wiping his handkerchief over the mess.

Emily Marie ran and ran, her heart thumping wildly in her chest. She found herself running into the woods by the briar patch. She sat down with her back leaning against a tree, her cheeks ablaze, her hand pressed over her heart, and the wisps of her breath curling through her lips, rosy from the crisp autumn air. She laughed to herself in disbelief. She had actually done it. She didn't think she could, but she did. Her head reeled with swimmy exhilaration.

"I did it...I did it..." She had never felt so alive. Even if the spell didn't work out as she hoped, she was very proud of herself.

She actually followed through with it. The idea was frightening and wonderful.

Suddenly, just before her face hung the giant black spider from a shining string of silk. She laughed aloud again, and blew at it softly. It swayed.

"Hello, Spider. You're the only one who knows of my secret magick. I think that now we should be friends. I've never had a friend that I could share any *real* secrets with."

She held out her hand hesitantly. The spider reached out its long, graceful legs and landed lightly on Emily's palm. Emily gritted her teeth and waited for the initial chill to pass. She wasn't going to be afraid of spiders any longer. That was just babyish silliness. The spider looked up at her with its shining black eyes. Emily smiled.

"You like to weave and sew, just like Mama used to, before she had to sell Grandmama's fine loom and spinning wheel. Though I bet you can weave a great deal better than any person would, no matter how nice a loom they may be using...I think I'll call you... Spindle. Do you like that?"

Of course the spider didn't reply, only looked up at her, its mandibles never still.

"I don't know if spiders get very cold, but you're welcome to warm yourself in my apron pocket if you like. I'll do my best not to squish you." She held open the pocket of her red apron. The spider's ticklish little feet stretched for the edge of the pocket and in a moment it disappeared.

Emily slowly came out of the woods and made her way towards her mother and father's display. Nothing had sold since they arrived, and Mother and Papa were still not speaking to each other. Emily could tell that the day had made them both very cross. She decided it might be best to simply wander about by herself. She wondered if she might be able to win herself an apple fritter by throwing a stone at a set of bottles at a booth. She hadn't any money, but they always let you have the first try for free.

"What do you think, Spindle? Do you think I should have a go?" She waited behind a group of young boys. The one who was throwing had long sandy hair and green eyes. He glanced over and spotted her. He smiled and squared his shoulders. He threw with a flourish and missed. Frowning to himself, he tried again and missed a second time. He again glanced at her, setting his jaw.

*He wants me to watch him win,* she thought to herself. She had forgotten that she was still immortally beautiful. This would take some getting used to. Well, she hoped he hadn't gotten it into his head that he would keep trying until he's able to show off. She wanted to have a turn, as well.

But at the third try, the boy hit all three bottles so hard that they shattered to bits. His friends all clapped him on the back and tousled his head. He grinned at Emily triumphantly. She smiled. The old man who was running the booth came to the boy with a piping hot apple fritter. The boy turned to Emily, his grin smug.

"Hello there. My name is Adwin."

"Hello." She felt her cheeks growing warm. "I'm Emily."

"Did you see my throw? I broke all the bottles to bits."

"I know. I saw." And because he seemed to be waiting for more, "Well done," she added.

"You can have this," he said handing her the fritter carelessly. "I'll probably just win another one when I feel like it."

"Oh...Thank you. Thank you very much," she said, surprised. The boy just shrugged and turned back to his friends. One of them snickered at Emily, and Adwin punched his shoulder hard. They wandered off. Emily took a big bite of the steaming apple pastry as she strolled down the lanes of the fair.

"Did you see that, Spindle? *I love being a witch!"*

She sat on a bench nibbling the warm fritter. Spindle peered up at her from the inside of her apron pocket. "Would you like some? I've always heard that spiders only like to eat nasty things like flies and beetles."

"Talking to ourselves, are we?"

Emily spun around. Smiling behind her was her sister, Daniellia.

"Oh. Hello, Sister."

"Where did you get that apple fritter? Don't tell me you've won it. You shouldn't be throwing stones like a boy. People might find out that you're not very ladylike." Her pretty blue eyes narrowed at Emily nastily. Emily scowled at her.

"Oh, no. Someone gave it to me. A boy. He won it *for* me."

"Why, you little liar."

"It's quite true. He just walked up to me and said I could have it." She sniffed primly.

"Look at Little Em, playing at make believe again. She sits all alone during the Apple Tournament on benches, talking to herself, like mad Old Lady Grenna."

"Excuse me, but I wasn't talking to myself." Emily stood at her full height, looking up at her sister defiantly. "I was merely talking to my new pet spider. Ellie, meet Spindle!"

She suddenly held out her hand nearly and inch away from Daniellia's nose. Spindle's long springy legs skittered quickly up Emily's arm, and stood at the end of her fingertips, hissing. The spider's sharp fangs glistened black against the wet pinkness of the inside of her maw. She held her front legs up at Daniellia menacingly.

Daniellia screamed and backed away, just as an old woman was walking behind her with an edgy basket of apples. The apples tumbled out and into the dirt, and the old woman howled with anger.

"You clumsy ox! You young hoodlums!" the old woman shrieked. Emily, darted away. As she did, she couldn't help throwing her head back and laughing at the sky. Had she been able to hear herself she would've recognized it right away as the cackle of a witch from a fairy story.

Emily stopped running and leaned against a tree, still chuckling to herself. She felt sorry about frightening her sister, but Daniellia was becoming so horribly beastly it was nice to get the better of her for a change. Spindle climbed swiftly down the front of Emily's dress and back into her pocket. She strolled aimlessly, nibbling the now cooling apple fritter and wondering about her parents. She knew their quarrel had been her own fault.

But it wasn't simply about the cake. Mother was always accusing someone of something lately, especially Papa. She had a sharp tongue, and it had only been growing sharper and meaner. And Papa was tired of it. He would spend hours in his shop, but Emily knew he wasn't working. His furniture was not selling, and he hadn't gotten any requests to go to anyone's house to fix anything. But still, he would come back from his workshop later and later and later every day. He was hiding from Mother and her sharp tongue.

Emily knew it was because they were so poor. The family had always been poor, but never this much. They were lately having none but soup for dinner, and Mother would thin it down so that you could hardly taste anything but water. Emily thought about how she had frightened Ellie, how she had stolen Mother's apple cake and lied about the butcher's family wanting it made for the Christumas Feast.

She knew Mother had spent the last of her savings on buying the ingredients for it. Mother felt obliged to because of all the meat Emmet had given them. She had no idea that the butcher's wife would've probably had him beaten with a switch for it if she found out what he had done, or that she would have demanded payment for every last morsel that they had eaten.

So Emily was now a liar and a thief on top of being a witch. Did this mean that she was now wicked? She didn't wish to be. But perhaps wickedness and witch craft came hand in hand? She didn't *ask* Emmet to give her the beef. She just wanted to be beautiful for once.

Emily sat upon a log and watched a team of jugglers as they tossed apples into the air effortlessly. "Spindle," she whispered. "If one does do *some* things against the rules time and again, that doesn't mean that they are wicked all around...Are they?"

A while later she heard fanfare, and the crowd began to move back toward the commons. It was time for the Apple Tournament, and the announcement of the Lord Mayor's grand prize. Her heart leaped into her throat as she stood slowly. "Here it is, Spindle. It's out of my hands now..."

The crowds gathered around a dais festooned with red and green ribbons, flags and banners. Emily could see Papa and Mother's booth to the far right of the commons. They watched, surrounded by Papa's lovely apple wood tables and chairs. Mother was standing with her arms akimbo, and Papa was sitting on one of his stools. He looked very tired. They must have just had another quarrel. They hadn't sold a single piece of furniture. Emily wondered if she should watch the tournament with them and decided against it. She hung about nearby. Lord Mayor Percival Descartes stepped out in front of the townspeople, and everyone cheered. His nose and cheeks had become very red. Perhaps he had a bit too much cider.

"My good people, I thank you, I thank you. Welcome to this year's Thomish Apple Tournament! I must say that this year had been quite a fruitful one," the Mayor chortled. The townspeople chuckled along with him.

"I am very happy to announce that the winner of this year's honorable prize was not an easy decision to make. My belly is full and my heart is warm; for no hamlet of Thom might honor the Crown more than the delicious delicacies of Keppington Valley Orchards!" The crowd cheered, and Emily bit her lip. She wished he would hurry up and get on with announcing the winners. She was so nervous she felt her stomach might very well give over that apple fritter.

"And now, let us get on with the event that we've all been waiting for. Seven Lords and Ladies of Thom have come from the Royal City of Post to decide this year's Apple Tournament Winner, and we have all finally come to a unanimous decision. May I have the contest results please?"

Unconsciously Emily's hand slipped into her pocket, her index finger lightly stroking Spindle's soft, furry back. She never thought a spider could bring her so much comfort. The woman who was sitting at the kiosk handed the Lord Mayor a piece of paper rolled up and bound in a red ribbon. The Lord Mayor untied the ribbon and unrolled the parchment.

"Good people of Keppington Valley, I am pleased to announce that this year's winner is none other than... Mrs. Amelia Osterling, the carpenter's wife! Will the Osterlings please come forward?"

Emily looked at her parents' startled faces as the crowds cheered around them. Slowly they stood with bewildered glances at one another. The crowd parted before them, and the Lord Mayor clapped along with everyone else as they began to make their way toward the dais. Emily swallowed hard, hoping Mother wouldn't say anything to ruin things. She stepped through the cheering people and came to the front of the crowd as Papa and Mother ascended the steps hesitantly.

"Ah, there they are. My friends, well met! I congratulate you. And I daresay this honor is well earned; the apple cake that you have presented was by far the best that I have ever tasted."

The townspeople cheered once more, and Emily's eyes met those of her mother. Mother looked at her questioningly. Emily nodded slowly, color mounting on her cheeks. Mother frowned darkly, her lips pursing into a tight little line.

*Now I'm in for it.*

"Please you, dear woman. I do believe that the royal Houses of Thom might be a duller place henceforth unless you may agree to share with the royal cook your recipe for Apple Cake. Pray tell, what is it that makes it so delicious?"

Emily bit her lip. *Please don't say anything ridiculous, Mother...*

"Well...It *is* a family secret." Mother smiled pleasantly at the Lord Mayor, and Emily breathed a sigh of relief.

The crowd laughed, and Papa beamed at his wife. From the front row of the crowd, Emily heard him lean closer to her and whisper, "You've plotted this all along from the very start, didn't you? You made all that story up about the butcher's wife in case you lost the Tournament. You cussed, clever woman of a wife! Why not just tell me?"

Mother only smiled. But her eyes again caught Emily's, and Emily knew by the stinging gleam in them that she was very angry indeed. Her heart sank down to her stomach when she realized that she also saw pain in her mother's eyes. She was hoping feebly that Mother would be pleased. She knew instead her mother felt betrayed.

Very much happened after all of that, but it all passed over Emily Marie like a distant blur. It was all out of the barrel now. She had lied to her mother, and her mother now knew it. And it had broken her heart. The Lord Mayor had awarded Emily's parents with two bags of gold, large enough to be potato sacks. According to the rules of the Apple Tournament, they were supposed to receive two year's wages. But compared to Papa's actual earnings, the contents of the sacks were more equivalent to four years.

The attention their family received in winning the tournament did well for Papa that day. He had sold nearly all of the furniture he had brought, save only for two stools and a side table that had a crack in it from traveling from the shop. There was also a rich family from abroad that had wished to order custom made bedroom set for their villa in Nageebah. Daniellia, Carrigan, and Emily Marie had to help Papa by writing sales lists and keeping a record of what the Nageebs wished to order.

At the end of the day Papa went missing, and when he returned he had pulled Mother aside. Emily stole away to where they were speaking to each other in private. The setting sun made their two bodies look like black silhouettes in the gold washed light. Papa kissed her deeply, bent down on one knee and presented her with a little velvet box.

"I was never able to give you a proper ring when I asked you to be my wife. Now, I didn't buy it with your winnings, but with some of the money we made with today's sales. So this ring is yours and yours alone, earned and given to you by the one who loves you most of all..."

Inside the little velvet box winked a glittering purple diamond set in a gold so pure it was rose colored. Surrounding the stone in intricate filigree were deep golden colored diamonds, the kind that can only be found across the Amillo Sea. It looked like something that should be resting on the finger of a queen. Mother's eyes filled with tears. Emily Marie smiled, and knew that no matter how cross her mother was, no matter how shameful it had been to connive and lie as she had done, it was worth it. That night their family rode home in a nearly empty wagon, singing winter ballads in time with the clippety-clop of Daisy's hooves. Even Mother sang along.

\*       \*       \*       \*

The next morning Emily awoke early before sunrise to the sound of Mother making breakfast in the kitchen. She was singing softly to herself. Emily rose and dressed, nervousness growing in her throat. When she finally entered the kitchen, Mother stopped singing. She gazed at Emily balefully, then turned to finish beating the batter. Emily stood in the kitchen doorway, not knowing what to do with herself.

"I expect you'd like to give me some sort of an explanation." Mother didn't turn around.

"Yes." Emily sat down at the kitchen table. "Mother, I'm sorry I lied to you about the butcher's wife and the cake. You see, I... I knew that if I had asked you to make one for the Tournament, you would have said no."

"You made a fool of me, you realize. Me carrying on about the cake, shouting at Papa as I had done."

"Yes, I know. I'm...I'm very sorry, Mother. But if I had told you..."

Mother set the bowl of batter down and turned sharply. "You have no right to try and meddle with the things I decide to do!"

"I know. I'm sorry-"

"And imagine if I had said something to the butcher's wife? That woman has wagged her tongue about me enough without you adding to the mix!"

Emily said nothing. Tears stung her eyes and prickled her nose.

"Em, I'm not as cross with you about your plans as much as I am cross about you lying to me."

"But Mother, if I had asked you, you wouldn't have-"

"No! I *wouldn't* have!" Mother hissed. She turned and picked up the bowl, whisking furiously. Emily swallowed hard, forcing back her tears.

"Em, I am a prideful woman. When a woman's got not a bit to spend nor a bit to live by, her pride is all she has left. But...pride often does lead one to foolishness."

Emily looked up.

"I do wish you hadn't lied to me, but I am glad you helped our family. And I am grateful. But please promise me that you will not lie to me again. I've no wish to have a daughter so cunning that I ought not to trust her. I wouldn't want that for all the sacks of gold in the kingdom."

"Yes, Mother."

"Now off with you. Go and fetch the milk."

Things had changed between Emily and her mother after the Apple Tournament. Mother didn't seem to be cross at Emily any longer, and how could she be? After all the good that had come to their family. But there were times when Emily caught her mother looking at her strangely. As if she didn't know quite what to make of her own daughter. Sometimes, the look in her eyes even seemed to be suspicious. Emily didn't like this very much at all.

# Chapter 13

Madame Carolene and Ana sat in the estate's grand veranda, wrapped in fine furs and sipping hot melted chocolate with milk. They watched Lord Chauncey playing with his grandson in the great lawn. There were piles of autumn leaves dotted here and there, but the Lord of the house had told the gardeners to cease cleaning them up. Little Elliot did so enjoy thrashing about within them that they could not deny him. The little boy had buried his grandfather in a pile of bright yellow, red and orange so that not a trace of the old man could be seen. Suddenly, he burst forward in a flurry of leaves, and the boy ran away squealing. The ladies laughed.

"Do have them come in and have some chocolate," said Carolene. "It's so cold; Elliot will be sure to catch a chill."

Ana's smile grew wistful. "No, Mother. I will have them play as they wish. Elliot can never catch a chill as other ordinary children might, you understand."

"I see," Madame Carolene's smile also faded slightly.

"Mother...I see it as a blessing that we have this time to be with you and Father. But it is still so strange. Neither of us know why we are here. Tell me, do you know? Is it some spell or magick?" Ana's eyes searched her mother's face, but Carolene would not meet her gaze.

"Well...I see it as a gift from God and the Virgin. God is pleased with the crowning of our new king. The line of Trellendale must be the truer line of the throne," said Carolene. "As long as the Purple King sits upon the throne, God has defeated death on our behalf as a reward. And you can remain here with us."

"You and I both know that is not true."

Madame Carolene sipped her chocolate defiantly.

"Mother please listen to reason. You know that our presence here is...unnatural. Think of my son. He can never grow as other children do, and I will never age and become as you are now. We are in a strange in-between sort of way in time; neither living nor dead. This morning, Elliot asked me if we ever were to return back home to the Light. What am I to tell him?"

Ana placed her hand upon her mother's. Madame Carolene finally met her daughter's eyes and felt an odd pang of guilt at the confusion she saw there. She forced a warm smile despite. "Tell Elliot that he *is* home now."

"You cannot keep us here forever, Mother. We belong to the Light. Our time in this world has already been spent."

Madame Carolene did not reply.

*　　*　　*　　*

Kulbit sat by the fire late one night, a letter from Ende in his hand. It had been brought to him the previous morning by a page. The Trellendale Estate had been repossessed by the Crown; the property abandoned. Grandmum died two years prior. There was no report of the Widow Trellendale in the brief inscription, save that some had rumored that she remarried a wealthy foreigner and left Thom.

*Mum had always done well to look after herself...Of course she would find someone wealthy soon after Grandmum passed. Perhaps she now has the handsome son she'd always wished for, and can forget about Da and I. It was what she'd wanted all along, wasn't it? But if she had only waited...how proud she would've been to call herself the mother of the King, pretending she had loved me all along and claiming her residence here at the Palace as Queen Mother. At least I could've finally made her happy. If only she had waited two more years...*

"Your Majesty seems disappointed in the result of his correspondence."

Kulbit gave a start. The letter fluttered to the ground. Lord Chauncey was standing in the great doorway of the royal apartments. Kulbit was so lost in his own thoughts he hadn't even heard the doors open. He quickly stood and bowed to the High Lord.

"Oh, no, Your Majesty. The king does not bow to his inferiors. It is I who must genuflect to you," said Lord Chauncey, lowering himself gracefully. "It is also custom that none shall speak to the King unless His Royal Majesty addresses them first, but given your condition I believe we may make an exception. Would you not agree, Sire?"

Kulbit blinked. Lord Chauncey closed the oaken door behind him. There was a chill in the air that coursed up and down Kulbit's back. The High Lord wandered to the silver gilded case of glass under which the Crown of Thom rested. He gingerly stroked the glittering filigree. The sleeve of his grand robes fell back enough to reveal a brief glimpse of a set of white scars across his forearm.

"The Diadem of ThoBromis. It has been said that this crown is older than the nation of Thom itself. Do you know why it is that the head of the king is adorned with gold? No. I did not expect you would. Wise men do not question matters of monarchy, but accept them as truth. It is the obedience of the people that grants power to the high bloods.

"Before the heathen Moonsmen were defeated, the ancestors of Thom had dwelled across the sea, in a land of fierce conquerors. It was from these lands that the tradition of a crown was brought to ThoBromis. With them, they had also brought the wisdom of the One True God, and His Holy Mother. It is God who decides whom should wear the crown, and it was believed that God speaks to Kings in rays of sunlight through the tops of their heads. This is why a crown of gold and jewels is worn by he that sits upon the Throne. To honor the voice of God..." Lord Chauncey smiled at the boy in the flickering light of the fire.

There was a look in the High Lord's eyes that sent coldness through Kulbit's blood. Kulbit hugged his robes closer to himself. Lord Chauncey opened the elegant glass case and held the crown high. It glimmered and made tiny rainbow lights dance across his face. He stood before the boy, the ancient treasure still in his hands.

"The Line of Trydus has always been the chosen line of the Kingdom of Heaven...but now it would seem the common bloodline of Trellendale shall wear the crown instead." He placed the heavy diadem upon the boy's blue hair.

"You shall wear this in honor and dignity. But His Majesty must always remember his humble origins. The Trellendale line is beneath even that of the State, and by Thom must be of service to the State. Remember, Your Majesty...A King who abandons his crown is little more than a man with no honor. And a man with no honor is little more than an animal, and shall always be hunted and slaughtered as such."

Kulbit swallowed hard, his heart beating fast.

"You shall not have a need to send anymore correspondences, Sire. I shall humbly serve as your mouthpiece hereafter. I do not expect that Your Majesty would deny me my servitude again in an attempt to contact any outside of my protection. Remember how God has placed you upon the throne. And just a quickly, He may remove His Grace...if tested. Good night, Your Majesty." The High Lord of Cordovan bowed and left.

Kulbit stood alone before the fire, the glittering crown of Thom on his head. He tossed the letter from Ende into the flames. As he watched the paper burn, he realized how much of a prisoner he had truly become, chained to a throne and at the mercy of the State.

### *The End*

# AUTHOR'S NOTE

It's all lies. This isn't the end. This isn't even remotely the end. But I had to stop here because this is where things really start to shift. For me, for Kulbit, for Em, for everyone. I know, you may be thinking, "What are you talking about? Becoming rich or becoming king isn't enough of a shift for someone?"

Nope. It's not. See, when things start to change on the outside, that doesn't always mean a person is ready to change in the inside. You can get a new job, a new girlfriend, a new apartment. But nothing changes until *you* make the shift on the inside.

Also I was just running out of page space. They say when you publish a book, it's better not to go over 200 pages or your reader will get bored. I'm pretty sure if you were going to get bored you would've already done that by now, but either way, this is where I'm stopping. Call it abrupt, call it awkward, call it whatever you want, but like I said before: I'm no writer. See you in the next book.

## END NOTE